The Fisherman's Daughter

by

I.J. Workman

To Lynne & the Sequel Book Club

Hope you all love the life of Emily

I.J. Workman

PublishNation
www.publishnation.co.uk

A huge thank you to Clare for your support, encouragement and boots-up-the-backside to keep me going. Also Charlotte for her extraordinary artistic expertise and, of course, to David and Gwen helping to meet my goal.

Prologue

"Afternoon' Frank, I don't like the look o' them clouds and them winds are gettin' up."

Frank Mulligan stepped down in to his coble 'The Henry and James' followed by his sons Pat and Brendon. He turned to look at Old Tom on the quayside and smiled. The old sailor dressed in his grubby waterproofs was in his normal pose: clay pipe stuck in the corner of his mouth, his eyes looking skywards and frowning.

"Ye said the same yesterday an' it was a millpond all evening."

"Aye, but this is different like. Ah can feel it, wind's different. It's bringing in a storm mark me words."

Frank shook his head but still smiling. Old Tom was a character. A sailor all his life and many a story to tell and he had heard them all many times over. Too old for the sea himself it didn't stop him seeing the fleet off each day without fail. He would offer his advice and warnings requested or not. Most times he was off the mark but no-one was offended or rude. It was just Old Tom.

"Aye an' ye said that yesterday an' all." Frank was still smiling but he felt a nagging unease. On the way down to the harbour he knew the wind had changed, now gusty, chilled. Clouds were gathering on the horizon before being driven quickly overhead rolling over each other as if being chased. Stepping down the ginnel to the harbour he saw the water in the harbour was calm, tranquil even but through the throat he could see white water.

"Come on Da, let's get gannin."

"Mmm..." Frank studied the sky. "What do ye think o' this lot?"

Brendon his eldest son copied his father. "Ach same as yesterday and it turned out to be a duckpond. Take no notice of him." He nodded to Tom now talking to the crew of the next coble along the quay.

"Alright but I canna swim, ye two will have to save me." He chuckled to himself and made his way to the bow, dumped his bag and prepared for the night's fishing.

The six cobles followed each other through the harbour throat and set sail for the herring grounds. It was a good catch last night and they knew the fish would still be in the area maybe now just a little further out. As each boat passed the point the wind caught their sail twisting the hull sideways. Frank could see the crews quickly making adjustments to keep on track. 'The Henry' veered the same way and once in to the open sea all the cobles headed to separate areas to fish. Frank made for an area to the South of the others hoping for a better catch. He knew it was a gamble but if he was right they would have a celebration in the 'Fishers'.

Two hours passed, the nets were cast but there was no duckpond. The increasing, howling winds swirled the mountainous banks of clouds above them turning the last daylight hours to night. Repeated flashes of lightning could be seen to the East. The sea was alive, the cobles tossed among the heaving spray crested waves. This was no time or place for fishing. The other cobles were already making their way home. Frank and his sons pulled up the netting and set off some way behind them. Frank felt a hand on his shoulder. Pat was pointing at a starburst further East then another – distress signals. He had seen a collier earlier making its way South to Tilbury. Could it be in trouble? Without a second thought he turned 'The Henry' towards the flares and towards the approaching storm. He knew it was a gamble, a risky manoeuvre in the conditions but how could he ignore it. The collier could be sinking, men jumping into the sea to their certain deaths. He had to try.

After an age of battling against the increasingly belligerent waves 'The Henry' was alongside the collier. Frank noticed a man illuminated by the lights hanging on by one hand to the cabin rail and bellowing into a loud hailer then waving it as if to send them away. He couldn't understand: Did he need help or not?

Then, above everything, an almighty crash roared from the opposite side of the collier. Frank saw the man dive back into his cabin just as a huge wall of water rose into the dark sky clearing the collier completely and dropping vertically onto the...........

Chapter 1

2 years earlier

"Enough of ye moanin', get yorself an' ye brotha doon to the beach an' don't hang about."

"Aw Da, ah did it yesterday, haven't we got enough coal for now ahm worn out." I see his face turning red and I don't wait for an answer. I grab Con and push him towards the door before we get cuffed. The side of my head is still sore and swollen from the last time.

"Leave off her, she'll gan, she always does. Don't ye dare hit her again, ye hear?" Despite her own red, swollen eye and the dark bruising round about, Ma was looking fiercely at Da, head thrust forward daring him to argue.

"Ach keep ye hair on missus, ahm off to the boat. An' tell them lazy buggor sons of yours to get doon there quick." He grabs his coat and cap pushes past me and Con and, still muttering, slams the kitchen door on his way out.

I look back at Ma now leaning over the sink dabbing a cloth on her swollen face.

"Ye alright Ma?

She puts the cloth away and turns to me. "Ay, I'll live. Ye best get down to the beach with Con before your Da gets back. I'd bettor shout at your big brothas again."

I leave, grab the wheelbarrow and a protesting Con and make for the beach. We trudge down the track our bodies almost bent double battling against the wind, but I'm not bothered about the weather. I'm wondering how Ma puts up with him. I heard him come in late last night with my older brothers. They must have woken the whole street with their raucous singing and laughter. I knew the jollity wouldn't last, it never does. Every time they get back from their trips away it's always the same. They don't come home first; it's straight down to the Fishers Arms until closing spending their catch money. Then back for their dinner and a fight if Ma gets in the way or doesn't give him what he wants. Screams, shouts, thuds as fists hit flesh and crunches as bones hit walls and floor. Lying in bed I can hear everything, Con starts crying and I put my arm around him, the twins sleep through it, lucky them.

Ma's bruises and black eyes are the talk of the village. "Ye should tell him to buggor off. Leave him before he kills ye." But she won't. "He's alright when he's not had a skinful. Anyway where would ah gan like, who would tend te my lot? Talk about me, your face didn't look too canny the other day."

I remember these overheard conversations, I put extra effort in to pushing the barrow, Con now running to keep up. My silent resolution is driving me relentlessly forward. This violence seems to be a way of life. I made a vow there and then: no way is this going to happen to me.

My mind is racing. I'll run away, borrow a bike and get to Newcastle. There's bound to be a job I can do. I can clean, run errands, anything. We reach the beach where we were yesterday but there are too many other kids doing the same thing so I go on. Con complains and sits down, arms crossed looking determined. I want to shout at him but stop myself in time. I sense his frustration and in that instant I realise running away would just heap more problems on Ma. How would she cope without me to help with the young-uns, who would get the coal in? I feel trapped, frustrated and flop down beside Con and cover my face with my hands.

We stay in this position for a long time probably looking like we're set in stone. Con stirs and I feel his arm around me, my tensions release and tears start flowing.

"Sorry Em I'll come. Sorry ah made ye greet."

I lower my hands and look at him and smile through my tears. I know he's not a bad lad in fact he's got a good brain. He should be at school but there's no chance of that. There's little doubt he'll end up on the boats like his brothers or maybe down the pit. I put my own arm around his shoulders and we stay there in a cameo of companionship until I pull myself up and mutter to myself but too loudly.

"Ah don't even know which way is Newcastle."

"Are we ganin to Newcastle?" Con wide eyed looks at me hoping for a revelation.

I laugh. "One day we will, ye just wait."

"That'll be class, ah canna wait."

We continue our battle along the top of the beach looking for a suitable place. We chatter about what we might do in the big city, two kids in dreamland. We walk for another half an hour to an area we haven't been before. There is a bit of land which sweeps out in to the sea and on the far side is a near vertical rock face. There was no-one on the beach.

"This looks bonny, we'll try here."

It is a good place. Plenty of good coal lying about or as Da calls it, 'sea-coal', because it comes out of the sea. I can't really understand this. Herring and squid come out of the sea, and seaweed but coal comes out of the pit. Perhaps the colliers drop some on their way to Newcastle and beyond. Whatever it is and where ever it comes from it burns in the fire, cooks our food and keeps us warm.

We leave the barrow at the top and follow the cliff face down on to the beach and start collecting the coal into our aprons and then stagger back to the top to fill the barrow. It's a slow process and we don't exactly rush. We have plenty of time to stop and talk. We spot a deep shadow in the cliff face at beach level and go and investigate.

It is a large hole in the rock. I know this is a cave and tell Con showing off my knowledge.

"Yas too young to remember our Granda but he used to tell us stories about a magic cave. Ma says he was never the same after. She says it drove him to the drink an' he never recovered."

Con eyes are like big round saucers. "Really?" He pauses thinking and then looking very worried. "Oh no, no, if this is the magic cave maybe we'll be driven to the drink?"

I laugh. "Ah think Ma was jokin', she also says it was Grandma who did that."

We peer inside eyes wide and with a hand held up in front of our faces we bravely step into the blackness. There was a sudden rustling followed by almost silent swishes from flying objects making us drop to the floor. We turn and see them splaying out in to the daylight.

"What are birds doin' in here?"

"They're bats." I'm showing off again. I'm nearly twelve and I've been to school for almost two years and among other things I've learnt to read. "They live in caves an' come out at night to feed. Ah think we've just woken them up like."

"Well ahm leavin' an all, we might wake somethin' else, come on Em." Con grabs my hand and pulls me back out.

"Alright, we're nearly done we can get back fo' our tea."

"Ah that's canny." Con stops, he's thinking back. "Ah hope it's not squid again ah canna keep it doon, even the look of it makes me reach."

Da brings back all sorts from his fishing trips, stuff he can't sell and squid is one of them. I have to chop it up into small pieces then close my eyes and swallow quickly but poor Con can't manage even a mouthful. Yesterday he had to rush to the nettie. He made a horrible noise and looked white when he got back. Da always says that he can't have anything else unless he eats it but I know Ma gives him something else on the quiet.

The barrow is fully loaded and very heavy but we've got the wind to our back now and it's still not raining which is a blessing. We join in with other kids wheeling their own barrows. We talk about what we're going to do tonight and what's for dinner but don't mention our beach and the cave we've found. We keep it to ourselves. Not until we get

4

home, tip the coal in to the bunker and get into the kitchen do we tell Ma.

"Yor Granda always went on about strange folk who live at the far end of some tunnel. Yor Granny always said it was this that drove him to the ale." She laughs. "More like it was herself that did that."

Con pipes up. "Brendan told me he was always steamin'."

"Well he shouldn't have." She puts down the spoon she was stirring the dinner with and came over wiping her hands on a cloth and sat down with us. "Your Granda, my Da, was a good man, ye remember that. He worked hard all his time an' ah might add he never laid a finger on anyone." She went quiet but her silence couldn't hide what she was thinking.

One of the twins still in their drawers by the stove starts to whimper.

"Someone needs feedin'. They've got built in clocks them two, just when our tea's ready."

I can see Ma's tired and suggest they can wait until after we've had ours. She smiles over to me.

"Thanks Emily love but it's best if ah feed her now before she wakes her sister." She quickly dishes out our dinners and joins us with her own in one hand and with the other holding the now contented baby latched on to her breast. I wonder if the food ever provides anything for Ma before being sucked out again.

Chapter 2

1907

We're late for our tea. I've forgotten the time, it is such a horrible day, rain sheeting down and the wind, unbelievable. It keeps whipping my hair into my eyes no matter how I try to tie it back. The track is running with rain water turning it into a sea of mud making pushing the barrow much harder. On the beach we sheltered in our cave making up stories. I told Con that if we stand outside in the wind, hold our arms up and then flap them up and down like a bird the wind will carry us off over the cliff and drop us in Newcastle. He tried of course but only succeeded in staggering backwards, falling over a rock and banging his head.

We often speak about Newcastle and sometimes even London where the King lives. Our big brotha Brendan has actually been to Newcastle. He went with his sweetheart and when he came back he told us all about it. He spoke of thousands of people running around like ants in a nest, the men wearing suits and the ladies in fancy dresses. "Ye canna move for horses, street lights everywhere an' huge buildings with muckle, great doors big enough for a railway locomotive." Then, I remember, he went quiet. When he got all our attention he whispered that he'd seen horseless carriages called automobiles. They move without anything pulling them because they have an engine, not a steam engine burning coal but using something called petrol, like oil. And they were fast almost as fast as a galloping horse. He said he was going to get one and show it off to everyone in the village. It was so exciting, our Ma and Da didn't believe him of course but me and Con did, we wanted to be the first to ride in one.

No-one I know has ever been to London.

We turn through our back gate and immediately hear and see lots of people about. I recognise them as villagers but don't understand what they are doing here. It isn't anyone's birthday and it's not a special occasion as far as I know. We both stand motionless still holding the barrow of coal when old Mrs McConachie comes out of the nettie and sees us. She normally doesn't have much to say or even notice us much but she comes over and puts her arm around my shoulders. "Don't worry about yor Da, he'll be back."

I look at her confused and worried. I think Da must have run away somewhere. I want to find Ma, now. I grab hold of Con and squeeze through the open but partially blocked door and into our kitchen. Eyes turn down to us, half smiling faces, no not smiling, pitying faces. More hands on shoulders and low mutterings."Still hope lass." "Another harbour." "Don't ye worry so."

Ma is by the stove rocking in her chair gripping both Gertie and Flo close. I struggle to reach her through the crowd "Ma what's happened?" She hears me and turns quickly. I notice her eyes are red her cheeks wet with tears. She sees me and Con and somehow manages to grab us both and hold us squashing our lasses. Her eyes are closed but they can't stop the flow of tears. "Ma, what's happened? Why are all these people here?"

She can't seem to speak but the nearest person, our next door neighbour Mrs Stephenson, bends down to us and holds her head so close to us that I can smell tea on her breath. She answers for Ma. "The Henry didn't come back with the others pet. Don't ye worry. Your Da will have taken her in somewhere else ah 'spect."

Ma has stopped crying and can now speak. "There's been a bad storm, they all turned back but they lost sight of yor Da's boat." Her voice peters out and Mrs Stephenson continues. "Yor Da answered a mayday call from a collier in trouble on the rocks somewhere, so he was a bit awa from the other boats."

At last I understand, I throw my arms around Ma and hold her tight. She's sobbing again, her shoulders heave in my grip. "Don't greet Ma, please don't."

Another hand lands on my shoulder, heavier, larger. It's a man's hand. Somehow I know who it is even before I can smell his breath. The low voice of Uncle Joseph, Da's brother, resonates close to my ears, his closeness and his distinctive cigarette smoke and stale beer breath making me feel both nervous and sick. "Don't worry our lass I'll see your right 'til ya Da gets back." I feel Ma stiffen in my grip. I release her and she stands up, gently standing the girls by her feet then turns to him. "Thank ye Joseph but ah can see to me bairns myself." She gives him an unblinking stare that lasts for ages after she's finished speaking. He throws his hands up as an apology. "Sorry Ruby just tryin' to help like." She continues her silent stare until he walks away and starts talking to another group.

Soon our neighbours start to drift away back to their homes. They give Ma a kiss and a hug and reasons for hope. The house is now quiet. I can't take it all in. My Da and brothers in danger, maybe safe somewhere, maybe floating lifeless in the sea amongst wreckage of 'The Henry and James.' Surely they're alright, they're good swimmers, well, my brothers are. I have this nagging memory that Ma had said that my Da had never learned.

I pray as best I can for their safe return but I don't really know how and I don't really believe in God. I know Ma does and over the next few days I see her praying, holding her crucifix tightly and speaking quietly her eyes closed. But as the long days go by one by one our hopes grow less. I try to be positive but I can see Ma is losing hope. I help as much as I can even cleaning the nettie and playing with our lasses and taking them for walks down the street. But I keep meeting neighbours, I know they are all well meaning asking if there's any news, but I can see what they're thinking, all hope is lost.

Over a week later Uncle Joseph returns. I have never really noticed before how much Ma hates him. I assume Da kept him away. But he's back with news that wreckage has been found washed up on a beach further North, It is our fishing boat. Hope has finally gone. My Da and my two older brothers are dead, all drowned in the North Sea.

Chapter 3

Over the next few months Uncle Joseph visits us more and more often. Ma seems to have changed towards him. I can see she has no love for him but she seems resigned, lost the will to fight back. Often he stays the night, he sleeps in Ma's bedroom, I hear noises, his groaning, the bed bumping but nothing ever from Ma. In the morning she looks drawn, haggard and sad but she keeps going, feeding the bairns and me and Con and keeping the house as clean as possible. She never talks about him and she never answers my questions. She just passes them off by saying. "Sometimes in life ye have to put up." Whatever that means.

She's teaching me to cook so I can help her. I do some odd jobs for our neighbours when I can and Ma takes in clothes to wash and mend all for some extra pennies. Con has even run errands for people for a farthing. People have been so supportive even though they can't have much themselves. Without the income from Da and my brothas life is much more difficult. There are no treats, on Sunday or any other day and there is Uncle Joseph.

It's our tea time and our usual stew is simmering on the stove, mainly vegetables with some meagre bones given to us by the butcher. I know what Ma and Con are thinking. It'll be the same as I'm thinking, I hope he doesn't come today. But he does.

I hear the gate swing open noisily on its hinges and then our back door opens with a crash. He stumbles in and leers at us.

He never seems to work at any time I don't know how he lives. Today he is completely drunk. Great waves of stale beer and cigarette smoke hit me in the face and I want to be sick. He must drink at the Fishers every day only today he is worse than normal, he can hardly stand. He staggers over to the table and grabs Ma's chin, pulls her towards him and squeezes it. "Let's have some dinner before fun eh?"

His face contorts, suddenly reddens and passes wind. "Ah that's better." He slumps down on a chair and demands food. We can only watch, our appetites gone, even the girls grip each other in fear. He finishes his bowl in seconds. He shouts "Is that it?" Ma nods. "That's all your gettin' ye pig."

He looks over to our bowls still full. Ma can see what he wants. She picks up the metal ladle and holds it within an inch of his nose. Her face contorts with rage.

Touch their dinner an' I'll break your neck.

He laughs contemptuously, gets up and waves away the threat.

"Keep your hair on lass. I'll need ye later."

He gets up unsteadily and looks at me his eyes sweeping my body. "Mmm yas ganin to be bonny like your Ma." He turns to Ma. "How old is she fourteen, fifteen?"

This was more than Ma can take. She hurtles in to him, arms thrust out pushing him towards the door. "Get out an' stay out ye foul faggit."

He misses the door and bangs in to the frame, cursing loudly. He recovers his bearing but turns before leaving. "Ahm ganin but I'll be back tonight, ye better be ready pet."

We hear him use the nettie. He doesn't come back in, we hear the yard gate hinges creak and we all breath sighs of relief.

Gertie and Flo are the first to speak although only to themselves. They seem to understand each other when no-one else does. They chatter away playing on the floor with some coloured pebbles and a bowl.

"I'll warm your tea up. Sit yourselves doon it won't take long." Mum reaches for the bowls and pours their contents back in to the large saucepan on the stove. No-one mentions Uncle Joseph's visit although I'm sure each of us can think of nothing else. I can only hope he doesn't return tonight. I don't want to see him tonight, or ever again. I wished it was him that died in 'The Henry' and not my Da. I know these are bad thoughts and God wouldn't like them but I can't help it. I

11

even try to pray but I still can't. I mean, if he's so good why does he allow people to die so tragically and why does he let people live who shouldn't?

We eat our tea quietly and I get down to my chores. I've also got to run an errand for Mrs Stephenson next door. I give Ma an extra special big hug, say goodbye to Con and the girls who are now all playing with the stones, and leave the house. We are a very special family. The deaths of Da and my brothers have brought us closer together. We look after each other, hold hands and cuddle when someone gets hurt and laugh together, and we still can. There is no fighting or arguing, it's strange but it's nice.

Mrs Stephenson was scrubbing her kitchen floor. She's always on her knees scrubbing something, she must love it. Her floors are always sparkling, never any dirt or bugs crawling about.

"Alright pet how ye doin'? I'll be with ye in a minute, just cleanin up. Oooh me poor ol' knees." She stops and sits down to rub them, one hand to each knee. She beckons me to sit down with her. "How's ye Ma doin?"

"Alright, thanks Mrs Stephenson."

"Ye can call me Ettie if ye want, everyone else does."

"Alright Mrs Stephenson, umm ah mean Ettie."

She laughs out loud and I smile no doubt blushing red.

She loses her smile and leans over to me. "Ah saw your uncle again just now looking the worst fo' the drink. He didn't upset anyone did he?"

I answer quickly, probably too quickly. "No." I drop my head and looked at the scrubbed floor.

She reaches over with her bony hand and holds mine. "I'll gan an' see yor ma when a've finished here."

I look up in to her kind but worried face. I'm so pleased, Ma will enjoy the company. "Thank ye Mrs, er, Ettie.

12

She smiles broadly showing off her two remaining teeth. "Now ah want ye to skip doon to ol' Ma Maxwells an' get some cheese, about thrupence worth an' a packet of those new marshmallows. They're easy on me teeth." She leans forward. "An' get some of them jelly beans for yourself." She gives me some money and her shopping bag.

"Alright ah won't be long." I do skip. I love going to the shop. I always look in through the window whenever I pass but when I have something to get I can go in and have a good look around. She sells all sorts, not only food and sweets but clothes, mostly second hand I think but nice and even some toys.

I burst through the half open door eagerly looking around. I see Mrs Maxwell but I stop, rigid, Uncle Joseph is here buying something. I can smell him. He's trying to sort some coins in his hand to buy some cigarettes. But he's swaying and has to hold on to the counter with his other hand. He looks up when I come in and a slow leer forms on his face. He puts the coins back in his pocket, staggers towards me and reaches out to touch my cheek with the back of his hand. He gives me the same look as before.

"Ye are gettin' big aren't ye, you'll be a bonny catch fo' any man."

"Whisht yourself Joe an' pay me fo' those ciggies." A stern faced Mrs Maxwell comes from behind the counter and demands payment.

He reaches back in to his pocket without taking his eyes off me. He offers his change. "There, help yourself."

"Thank ye now off with ye an' behave."

At last he makes for the door but turns back before he leaves. I look away but hear him. "I'll be seein' more of ye later, pet." He laughs as he leaves. Mrs Maxwell follows him tutt-tutting and shuts the door. "Don't ye mind him, he's all talk an' he pongs the place out." She waves her hand around trying to waft away the smell but then looks over to me and sees me crying. "Hawa pet, forget him, don't let him upset ye. Ah know." She disappears in to her back room and soon comes out holding a glass of her home-made lemonade. "This'll cheer ye up pet."

The lemonade is delicious and does help cheer me. Sometime later, having bought the cheese and sweets and after having a tour of the shop I leave much improved. She waves at the shop door as I walk back. I look up and down the street, she does the same but there is no Uncle Joseph. I run with the shopping swinging and banging against my leg.

Mrs Stephenson is not at home and I guess she's with Ma. I'm right. Passing Con, Gertie and Flo now in the yard I find her supping tea in our kitchen. They were actually laughing together. It was the first time I've seen Ma really laugh since the day of the storm. I run over and give her a hug probably tighter than normal. She asks. "Ye alright pet?"

I nod and hand over the bag of shopping to Ettie and give her the change. She finds the bag of marshmallows and hands it round. The children playing in the yard with obviously a sixth sense come in and look eagerly at the bag. So there we are all six of us quietly chewing. Con makes a face exaggerating his mouth movements that makes me smile and then laugh. Mum and Ettie catch the mood and follow suit and then Gertie and Flo, hands to their mouths, start to giggle looking wide-eyed at everyone else but not really understanding the joke.

Chapter 4

I walk back with Mrs Stephenson to her front door carrying her small bag of shopping. She presses two pennies in to my hand and smiles.

"Thanks pet, you're a canny lass an' your brotha too. Ye both help your Mam champion. If ye need any help come an' get me, any time, alright."

I nod. "Bye Ettie." I smile pleased that I remembered to call her by her christian name, I feel grown up somehow and that pleases me.

I return home and find Ma clearing away the dinner things.

"I'll do that Ma."

"It's alright pet. Why don't you two take your sisters doon to the beach, the tide'll be out an' ye can show them your cave?

I'm surprised she's never allowed us to take Gertie and Flo to the beach before. "Alright, we'll take the pram."

She laughs. "Ye call that wreck a pram? It'll fall apart before ye get there. No, take Bennie an' the cart. He could do wi' the exercise. Ah know ye can handle him well. And,"she added pleased with herself, " I got someone to fix the wheel."

My eyes spring open. I haven't actually ridden him since the storm, only led him to the local field and back again each day. The cart hasn't moved for months. I hope I can handle him with all the bairns in the back. I run and tell the others and we all help to get Bennie hitched up. He can tell there's something new on offer, he's excited, ears pricked, shaking his head and blowing.

Ma's at the back gate watching us as we leave the stable and head towards the main track and to the beach.

"Do ye want to come Ma?"

"No, ye gan an' enjoy yourselves, yas a canny rider an' he's a bonny cuddy."

"Come on sis, let's get ganin."

"You just sit tight there an' make sure your sisters do an' all."

I take the reins and Bennie walks carefully out on to the main track. I wave back at Ma walking behind us. I know she must be nervous leaving me in charge of her whole family, I feel very grown up. We plod past the houses and start to trot when we get out of the village and on to the softer track alongside the beach. I can feel Bennie enjoying himself and we wave at other kids picking coal. Con shouts.

"Hawa get him to canter."

It would be a smoother ride but I'm still not sure of the wheels. The other one may drop off. "No, this'll do." I sit with my back straight and do my rising trot just as Brendan taught me. I have to grip really hard with my legs, trotting with no saddle is not easy. But I feel important, responsible and although by the time we reach our cave beach I have collapsed in to a sitting trot, I feel really grown up and I love it.

The tide is right out and we make for the stretch of sand only visible at this time. There's no holding back the girls they're so excited. They patter over the stones, taking the occasional tumble and onto the softer sand and stand at the water's edge. They look down at their feet as the water spreads over them and their heels sink as it retreats back. They stamp and giggle and splash. I take Gertie's hand, she's the braver of the two and the one who gets in to trouble first. Con takes Flo's. I hitch up their dresses and my own and we wade further in. The water is cold. I tell them that they'll get used to it but I don't even believe it myself. Con splashes our legs and the girls shriek and try to do the same.

I take Flo's other hand and we stand there watching the waves and the far horizon, the four of us joined together. We notice a fishing boat on its way back to the harbour. I can suddenly sense something, someone is looking at us, not from behind or from the cliff but from the boat out at sea. I realise it's Da and my brothas Brendan and Pat, they're waving at us, they're smiling, they're happy. I release my hands and wave, unbidden Con does the same and the girls seeing what we're doing copy us.

The vision soon fades away but I'm not sad. I know they're dead but I'm so pleased to have seen them. They looked so happy. Con looks at me and smiles, we don't say anything, we kneel down in the water next to the girls and have one big cuddle. The water ebbs and flows soaking our clothes up to our thighs but none of us care or even notice, not one little bit.

Chapter 5

We all peer in to the cave. At this time of day the sun's rays miss the entrance only illuminating the cliff face above so nothing can be seen inside. Me and Con both know the layout, at least for the first few yards. We grab the girls' hands and make for our stone seat just inside. The girl's eyes are stretched wide.

"Come on you two, you're safe with us."

We find the big lump of stone and help them climb on top and we sit beside them. I know we shouldn't but we tell them scary stories and make ghostly noises to make them jump. They hold on to our hands tightly and look further in. Our eyes are all getting used to the darkness and we can make out some of the rock formations but the dark abyss is still there leading to who knows where. Although I've been here with Con lots of times I've hardly been any further in myself. Our stories, despite being totally made up, are even scaring us, just a little, and when some bats suddenly leave with whooshing of their wings we all jump and scream.

The girls want to stay on the beach all night, so they say, but we have to go home. I need to do my chores I can't leave Ma to do them.

With a last wave at the sea we get on board our cart and I turn Bennie and set off for home. We slow down to a walk at the houses and I see the tail end of a dress disappearing down the snicket leading to the back of our house. I smile to myself, I know it was Ma, she's been waiting for our return. Con and the girls jump down and he unhitches the cart. I tie up Bennie and he starts on his well-earned feed already prepared. I look around, I was going to clean out the stable but it's been done, it's spick and span. Our Ma has been busy.

Before we go in we use the nettie except for the girls who giggle at each other.

Gertie looks embarrassed with her hand over her mouth. "We did it in the sea." I smile. "Come on then you two."

Ma sits at the table mending some clothes. "Oh there ye are, did ye have a canny time."

I smile, as if she hadn't noticed we'd arrived. I don't get a chance to say anything before the girls jump up on to her lap and start to tell their story about what we've all done.

Ma took it all in, alternating between smiling and looking shocked. Then she looks over to me with a feigned cross expression. "So girls your brotha an' sister told ye scary stories did they?" They were bouncing, eyes wide enjoying re-telling our tales of monsters and ghosts. Ma shakes her head. "Well your big brotha an' sister should know better, ghosts indeed. Well you two gan an' play while ah get some bread an' jam ready fo' your tea."

They jump down and run out to the yard still chattering at the tops of their voices.

Ma watches them leave and turns to us. "Ahm so pleased ye had a canny time, it's canny to see you all happy. Ye should do it again some time an' ah might just come wi' ye to make sure ye behave." But she smiles at me. "But maybe ah don't have to, you're gettin' to be a bonny grown up lass." Her smile disappears in an instant and she turns back to her sewing. I don't have to ask why, I know what she's thinking.

That night we all go to bed earlier than usual, even Ma follows soon after making sure we are all settled down. It seems and I hope more than anything and keep my fingers crossed tightly under the covers that Uncle Joseph stays away.

I was nearly asleep in that half way place between thinking and dreaming, when I hear the back door bang open. My heart sinks, I turn over and crush my face in to the pillow. I don't want to hear any more, but I can; heavy footsteps crossing the kitchen flags, Ma's door opening, a low voice, demanding, creaking, banging, then, after a while, silence. Eventually I drift off to sleep disappointed and very sad for Ma.

There is someone in my room. I sense it but I'm still mostly asleep. I feel Con stirring next to me but he's breathing heavily, still fast asleep. The cover is sliding off my bed, I try to grab it but something is in the way, someone. Then I feel it, heavy weights, it's two hands grabbing me, they move up and down my body, I sit up terrified. Then I smell him, I know who it is, I'm now wide awake terrified.

There's a swinging light at the door. I can just see Ma's face behind but I've never seen it so angry. The shadows accentuate every crease contorted with rage. She screams louder than I've ever heard.

"Get out of me house an' never come back."

Uncle Joseph twists round then jumps off the bed. I want, hope he just leaves but he grabs Ma's neck with both hands pushing her face up and she starts to gasp. I must do something he is going to kill her. I scream, jump out of bed and push and hit him with my fists. It has no effect. He's now shaking Ma's head like a rag doll her hands feebly trying to pull him off. The light has dropped to the floor but I can still see the torture in her face and hear her gurgling. I've got to do something. I need something hard. I grab our pottie with both hands and in one movement I swing it round aiming at his head. It hits him side on and jolts him into the door frame. I hear a crack. His grip on Ma releases and he slumps to the floor.

He doesn't move. I think, I hope, he's dead.

Chapter 6

PC Gladwin stands next to the body his face pale, eyes staring. He looks at Ma still speechless, he removes his helmet, kneels and examines the motionless figure of Uncle Joseph. He sees the head wound, the blood covered hair, the dark streaks tracing down his cheek and neck in to his collar. He carefully turns him over. I cover my mouth as I see his eyes wide open, staring sightlessly. I always thought eyes close in death. Ma just stares hardly a flicker of reaction maybe just a movement of her mouth, her eyes steely, focused on his face.

PC Gladwin struggles up straightening his back slowly and replaces his helmet. He looks over to Ma and finds his voice.

"Do ye mind if we sit down Ruby. Ah need to ask ye some questions?"

Ma's still staring down. She now has a definite gleam of victory in her eyes, her lips are compressed tightly. She realises she is being asked a question.

"Wey aye Jack. I'll get some tea." PC Jack Gladwin is a regular visitor to our house as he is to just about everyone in the village.

"Er no Ruby, don't worry about that. Just tell me what happened to Joe."

"Ah killed him."

"Why?"

"He was attackin' me daughter, ah hit him wi' this." She grabs the pottie from the floor and shows him the obvious damage.

"Ma!"

She looks at me her eyes half closed. "He came in drunk, he had his way wi' me but that wasn't enough."

"Did he threaten ye?"

"He called me a fat coo an' then he said he wanted someone younger, someone wi' a bit of life."

There was a whimpering behind me. I'd completely forgotten about Flo and Gertie, the two girls have slept through everything.

"Ye two gan to me bedroom. Let me see to your sisters an' I'll sort it wi' Jack. Go on with ye."

"But Ma." I stretch out my hands out in front of me. She stares back unblinking.

"Me bedroom, both of ye."

I take Con by the hand and lead him away closing the door behind us. We sit on Ma's bed and try to listen.

"But it was.."

"Shh, ahm tryin' to listen." There is no shouting. I can hear faint whispers of the two voices mostly low policeman tones. We wait silently until I hear the back door close and Ma comes in.

"He's ganin back to the station to call an ambulance. They'll take awa the body. Ah know it's hard but forget this. Get in to me bed an' get some sleep."

All three of us are in her bed, me on one side and Con on the other. She has her arms around us and squeezes us tightly. She's staring up at the ceiling, there are no tears. I can't sleep, no chance. I form and reform the picture of what happened in my bedroom, the dead body of Uncle Joseph lying on the floor. I hardly believe it. I don't know what's going to happen to us and start to sob. Mum squeezes me tighter and kisses me. "We'll be alright pet, don't fret."

It's nearly mid-day and the corpse is still here but is covered with an old sheet. PC Gladwin has returned and is now with a detective, a man not in a policeman's uniform but wearing a long coat. He's examined the body and has been asking Ma some questions, many more than PC Gladwin asked last night. He looks very serious. I've never seen him before. He asks me a question he had just asked Ma.

"Did this man attack you last night?"

I can only nod.

"Is that a yes, did he really attack you? Did he hurt you?

"Yes, he did." I look over to Ma in desperation she nods quickly and gives me a small smile. Gertie chooses this moment to start a fight with her sister. Con wades in and tries to pull them apart and now Ma picks her up to stop the argument but the noise continues unabated. The detective looks at everyone in turn, nods to PC Gladwin and looks at Ma.

"We'll leave you for now but will be back later. The body will be removed shortly." They leave without saying goodbye still looking very serious.

The rest of the day is difficult especially for Ma. We do our chores quietly trying to ignore the presence of the body in my bedroom. We all wanted it to be removed as soon as possible. I keep imagining Uncle Joseph would suddenly come back to life and just walk out the door and everything would be back to normal. It would be easier for us in a way but I can't help thinking, despite not knowing what was going to happen to us, that it was a relief. No more dreading his visits, his leering face and the terrible way he treated Ma.

At last a horse and open trailer pulls up outside. Two men come in and wordlessly carry the body away in a casket, back out the house, on to the trailer and slowly away down the street. Everyone in the village watches the events unfold. Most of them, certainly all the women, come to see us. It was only then I realise how many disliked, no, hated him. He had a reputation for being lazy, rude, drunken and lecherous. They congratulate Ma saying, it was about time, he had it coming, don't you worry they won't take you away, self defence. It was only then I feel a horrible desperate feeling spreading through me like hearing sudden bad news. I'm scared, suppose they do. What will they do with her? They hang murderers and wasn't this murder. I shut my eyes, I can't let me Ma do this, I've got to tell someone.

"What we've said is what happened. Don't say nothin' else." Mum is staring at me straight in the eyes, her arms on my shoulders. "Remember that, they won't be hangin' me."

Chapter 7

1907

I walk through the huge double door entrance holding on to Mrs Stephenson with one hand and my bag of clothes and things in my other. Con is on her other side clutching his own bag. The door is being held open by a boy in a very raggy shirt and short trousers. He doesn't say anything, just points to a door at the far side of the vast hallway. Mrs Stephenson, Ettie, is doing all the talking. In fact she's hardly stopped since we left her house nearly two hours ago. My mind is blank, I've no idea what she is saying, I stopped listening after the first five minutes. Con is also quiet but I hear him sniffing, I look over and see his eyes wide open looking around. He's frightened, I want to hold his hand and comfort him but I can't.

I know this is my all fault. It's been over six months since Uncle Joe died, since I killed him. No-one knows I did it except of course Ma and Con and they've never mentioned it since. I felt guilty when Ma was sentenced and sent to prison for four years for 'voluntary manslaughter'. They didn't believe it was in self defence, it was obvious but they still didn't believe it. When I say 'they' I mean the judge and the jury, all men of course. It seems that all men have a right to molest and punch women and children according to their desires. They are the master race, women are just chattels, do as they're told, lie down and take it. I felt so guilty when she was sentenced but no more. I know Ma is in prison and I know she's there for me but now I'm pleased I did what I did. He deserved it in every way, everyone agreed he had it coming and anyway he would have killed us all. Chattels.

Ettie, I call her that now, was speaking to me directly, looking in to my eyes as we walked across the room.

24

"Don't forget pet, you'll only be here for a short time 'til ah can get settled." She's smiling but her eyes are wet with tears.

I nod. She's told me and Con this several times. I understand what's happened, Mr Stephenson has died. I heard that he had fallen in to the harbour one evening and drowned. He was found washed up on to the beach the following morning. He had spent his money, hard earned, in the Fishers and lost his way home, some said. I wondered why men had to drink. They get paid for a job well done and instead of sharing it with their family they can't pass the pub on their way back. They're weak or as Brendan used to say 'they got no balls'. I don't understand why having balls make people strong. Brendan was a man but he always brought back some money, perhaps he had balls.

Balls or no balls Mr Stephenson still managed to provide something and together with little bits of money from Ettie, myself and Con we survived. Even some of the neighbours would help us with food and clothes they didn't need. We still lived in our house even with Ma in prison. Ettie would come in and cook for us and help us wash and clean, but now.

She still has Gertie and Flo to look after. She's taken them in with her saving the rent for our house. But there is no room in her tiny home for me and Con.

"Wait there will ye." The raggy clothed boy waves his hand at a single chair by the door then knocks and goes through in to the room closing the door behind him. Ettie takes the seat and we stand beside her, we still hold her hands. Ettie starts talking again, not really to us more like thinking out loud. I hear words; exciting, meeting lots of different children, good food. I look around and try to take in a hallway that could fit our entire house inside. There are more big wooden dark brown doors, a tall brown wooden case on legs with a clock on top. We used to have a clock over the stove, Da used to wind it every day. I think this clock needs winding as it's stopped and it's tilting over as if two of the legs are shorter than the other two. There are gas lamps sitting on shelves and tables some are lit now in the middle of the day. I realise the only window is half way up the wide staircase on the back wall but the small squares of glass are dirty reducing the amount of light that comes through. Ma would never have our windows looking like that. She would be up there with a cloth and bucket in no time, mind she would need a ladder, the ceiling is as high as the top of our house.

A door creaks open and slams shut and we hear echoing footsteps from the floor above. The owner of the footsteps appears on the landing in front of the window. A thick set woman her body like a barrel descends into the hallway. Her hair is swept back to a bun. She has a round face wearing a severe expression. She has on a dark full length dress and clomping boots. She only sees us when she reaches our level but there's no smile, no sign of any recognition, she has a moustache.

"Hello, me name is Ettie Stephenson an' this is Con an' ..."

"Wait." The large woman interrupts Ettie and marches straight in to the room without knocking. I hear a muffled. "Get out boy." The door opens immediately and the boy comes out, he looks scared. He looks over to us, I think he's going to say something but he turns away and runs up the stairs. I hear a door close upstairs.

There is more muffled noise from the room. It is only one voice, the woman's and there is no laughter.

It is five minutes before the door opens and the woman stands at the doorway her expression unchanged. She speaks, her moustache bristles like a caterpillar on her top lip. "You can come in now." Ettie struggles up off the chair with our help and we follow her in. It is another large room with large windows, the lower squares cleaner than the rest. The walls are covered with shelves full of books of all sizes. Sitting at a desk is a man with long side whiskers. He gets up immediately, walks around and approaches Ettie with a welcoming smile and his hand out. Ettie raises her arm limply and places her hand in his. He grabs it and shakes it up and down like he's working a water pump.

"Please take a seat, Mrs Stephenson isn't it?" Ettie nods. "Good, good, good we've been expecting you." He turns to me and Con. "You two can sit over there." He points to a long bench alongside. "Did you have a pleasant journey here?"

"Yes thank ye Sir. A friend brought us in his cart, um carriage ah mean. It's a long way."

"Quite so, quite so." He returned to his seat behind the desk. "Let me introduce you." My name is Charles Proctor. I'm the manager of this establishment." He then turns to the woman. "And this is Miss Sprote, she is the Matron here. You two will be in her charge."

We all look over and she gives a barely perceptible nod arms folded across her chest.

"All we need you to do Mrs Stephenson is to sign this form and leave the rest to us." He flips over a piece of paper in front of Ettie and points out where she should sign. I know Ettie can't read but she picks up the offered pen and pretends. After a while she makes a squiggle on the line and gives it back but I don't think she's fooled either of them. He picks up the piece of paper and coughs. Miss Sprote gives a small twist to her mouth changing it from the usual frown to a definite smirk.

"Thank you Mrs Stephenson you can leave any time you like, Con and er...Emily will be in safe hands now." He gives me and Con a small smile. I see the Matron's expression turn back to a frown.

Ettie doesn't just leave. I can feel she wants to say something but can't put the words together.

"Is there anything else?"

Eventually she grabs one of our hands each and speaks. "Ah errr.. I'll be back for them when ah get on me feet agyen...it won't be long now. They're a canny pair, hard workin' an' everythin'."

"Quite so, quite so."

There is a silence eventually broken by Matron. "Come on you two, I'll show you where you'll be sleeping." Everyone gets up leaving the manager behind his desk now studying some papers.

Outside in the hallway we say goodbye to Ettie in cuddles, squeezes and tears and a last wave while she falters by the front door. We climb the stairs following the bulky figure of Matron to see more of our new home.

Chapter 8

1909

I've been here for two years, I didn't know this until Teddy has just told me. I'm in her office waiting for her to return she's getting something from the kitchens. I'm allowed to sit on her armchair or rather in her armchair, it's so big and soft and I just love it. I lean my head back on to the cushion and feel the comfort. Teddy's nice despite her moustache. I smile at her nick-name, everyone knows it but no-one dares use it in earshot. She's fully aware of it but I think she's proud to be called after the king even if it is only because of his hairy face.

Two whole years, it sounds so long but it's gone quickly. It was painful at first, learning the routine. You quickly realise you do as you're told or suffer the punishment. Isolation in the 'Thinking Room' was bad enough but being sent to Mr Proctor was the worst by far. His very name makes me shudder and my stomach heave and I've only been there the once. The cane hurt but the stale breath, his red sweaty face too close to mine, his creepy hands all over me, reminding me. I make sure there was no repeat visit. He's known as Beetroot, it's happened for most of the girls and some tell me that it was far worse for the boys and I believe it. I picture Con, his skinny body under the rags, his ashen face. I close my eyes holding back the tears. Boys and girls only see each other at meal times and I always sit with him but he won't talk about it. He just sits there head bowed. I hear from his friends that he's sent to Beetroot regularly without doing anything wrong. I talk to Teddy about it, she gets very serious and angry and her face colours up. She knows what's going on but she can't stop it. I ask why do men do this but she has no answer.

The door opens and Teddy comes in holding a tray with mugs and a plate with biscuits. She sits down beside me and lays the tray between us. She smiles and says that this is a treat now I've been here for two years. I say thank you and grab my orange juice and biscuit, delicious.

"Tell me how's Mrs Stephenson? She comes to see you doesn't she?"

Ettie tries to come every week but it's more like every month. She brings some sweets for both of us and once even brought me sisters Gertie and Flo. It was lovely, they had grown so much but it was horrible when they left, they cried and cried. They haven't been back since.

"Yes thank ye, ah think she's fine."

"And your sisters?"

"Yes thank ye they're fine as well."

"Good." She sips her tea. "I wanted to have a talk with you. You've been a very good girl, really a young lady. You do as you're told, you're responsible, helpful and I think quite clever."

I'm shocked but very pleased; no-one has told me that for a long time. "Thank ye Miss."

"You now know everyone here and I need some help with the children so," She pauses for a deep breath. "I would like you to be my assistant. They all look up to you and I think you can deal with any problems that arise. What do you think?"

She takes another sip and looks at me over her cup. I don't really know what to say except thank you.

"Good, I'll still be around of course but I need some time to make other arrangements. I'll tell the other girls about you helping but of course," Her voice lowers and her eyes narrow. "I'll also let them know who's still in charge and remind them that the 'Thinking Room' is still there." Her smile returns and her voice lifts. "Let's start tomorrow."

I nod eagerly. "Yes miss."

She leans over and gently touches my hand. "You can call me Charlotte when we're by ourselves." Then adds, "And drop Teddy." I must have looked surprised but she just laughed. "You finish the biscuits and orange juice before you leave, 'I'll get on with some paperwork."

I leave Teddy's room and I'm swinging my arms high and then start skipping and doing pirouettes. I think I'm walking on air I feel so pleased with life. I know I should act my age but I can't help it. Some of the other girls stare at me as if I've gone loopy but I don't care. It's gardening day and I join my friends in the garden, they look at me quizzically but I just get on with some weeding smiling all the while.

"What's got in to ye Emy?"

I want to tell them all about my new job but I think no not yet, let Teddy or rather Charlotte do it. What a bonny name that is. I realise I have a secret no-one else knows but I know it has to be kept a secret or I might lose my new job. "Oh it's just a bonny day." I think what a daft thing to say.

"No it's not, it's cold an' ah can feel it's ganin to rain on us."

I smile weakly and try to change the subject. "The flowers look bonny don't they?" I pretend to examine some of the daisy like flowers."

Millie's my best friend and I know I can't fool her. We're both sixteen, well she is I will be in a couple of months. But she's been here all her life, abandoned as a baby and left at the workhouse door wrapped in newspaper. She's so thin, always has been, looks as though she needs a good meal but she's very strong and can lift me up with one arm. I look over and watch her weeding. As usual she's singing to herself. Surprisingly she has a lovely, tuneful voice but with her short hair and stick like figure she's often mistaken for a boy.

It suddenly strikes me that this could be the reason she's picked on by Beetroot more than the other girls. She swears she's going to get him when she leaves the Home. I hope she does. But mostly she's great fun and we dream about what we'll do when we do leave. Of course she has no idea what life is like outside the workhouse, this is her home, all she knows. I tell her all about my life and where we lived and what we

31

did. We are taken out the Home sometimes and there was one very special trip when four of us went to visit the local hospital. We were shown around a ward and a nurse told us what she did. I remember the trip very well, all of us do. We keep talking about it. We were dressed in new clothes kept for such occasions and we walked there holding hands all the way trying to take in all the surroundings. The hospital was bigger even than our Home. The nurse looked so smart in her uniform, the long blue dress, white apron and her hair swept back in to a bun below a little white hat with tails, I thought she was beautiful, everyone did. Of course we all want to be nurses now.

Millie talks while she's working on her knees. "They're just about done, it's Autumn an' we're ganin to have to cut them doon soon." She looks up at me and sees me looking at her." "What's up, am I doin' it wrong like?"

I laugh. "You're the gardener, ye should know." I pause I know I shouldn't but I must. "Millie ah got a secret an' ah mustn't tell ye."

She stands up, eyes wide. "Ye must, ye must, we're best friends, ye canna keep secrets fro' me."

I dither and look down.

"Come over to the shed so the other's canna hear us." She grabs my hands and leads me over to the lean-to at the corner of the yard. I don't resist and when we're there and I'm certain no-one else can hear I tell her the news, smiling all along.

"Good for ye Emy, ye deserve it." She pauses. "Ummm can ah be your assistant?"

"Wey aye, ah think I'll need all the help ah can get wi' this lot." We grin stupidly at each other and hug each other tightly.

"Come on you silly pair, you've not finished the weeding."

It was our Day Warden standing hands on hips trying to look stern. We release each other and walk quickly past her, hands over our mouths trying to stop giggling. As we pass I notice her face completely failing to maintain her ferocity and she breaks in to a smile. I just know this is a good day.

Chapter 9

1910

I'm helping the Meals Warden with the first dinner sitting. These are the youngest children and are usually very good. Some are frightened of me and look down when I approach with the water jugs. I don't know why I rarely shout at them, I don't need to. Some even call me Miss which I rather like but I don't think I should, I used to do the same when I first came.

They sit quietly at their long tables while dishes of food are placed in front of each child. Today they have a little bit of fish, potatoes with a very special extra, some peas grown in our garden. They start only when everyone has been served, the Warden has said grace and given permission. The noise increases tenfold, clattering of utensils on metal dishes, chattering and scraping of chairs. I walk around the tables for discipline but also to convince the fussy eaters to eat what they have in front of them because there is no chance of getting anything different. If they don't eat they go hungry.

I look up and see Millie at the door. She beckons me over, she looks very upset. The Warden nods and I join her.

"What's up Mills?" Her eyes are large, her cheeks are pink from running. She grabs my hand and pulls me through the doors in to the quieter corridor.

"Millie you've been runnin', you in trouble?"

She looks at me and then looks at her feet. I think she wants to tell me something but doesn't know how. "Hawa, tell me."

She looks up at me now determined to speak. "Oh Emy. Ah had to deliver a letter to Beetroot. He didn't here me knock but when ah knocked louder ah thought ah heard him say 'come in'. So ah did." She stops.

"Yes, well, oh Millie tell me."

"Ah went in, he was standin' at his desk with his back to me an' seemed to be pushin' it, bumpin' it. He heard me an' turned an' saw me. His face was red an' sweatin' an' then ah saw the boy. He was bent over his desk, holdin' the other side wi' his hands. His trousers were doon by his ankles." She stops.

I'm speechless I know this goes on. I know what he does and I know Millie has had a rough time with him herself but it still really upsets me and chills me all inside. "I hold her hands in mine. "Oh Millie. Look we've got te do somethin' we have te tell Teddy." Millie was still looking straight in to my eyes. She hadn't finished.

"Em, before ah left, the boy let go of the desk an' went to tug up his trousers. Ah could see his face. It was yor Con."

I close my eyes and grit my teeth. I picture my poor skinny pale faced brother. My fists clench. "Right we're ganin to see Teddy now, stay here." I run back in to the dining room and explain to the Warden that I have to see The Matron immediately. I don't explain why or wait for a response and I'm quickly back with Millie. "Hawa, this canna wait."

We run all the way. I know I should compose myself, be grown up but I can't slow down, through the huge entrance hall up the grand staircase and along the corridor to her room. I knock loudly and briefly and foolishly don't wait for an answer and rush in. We come face to face with Teddy and Beetroot. I realise they've been arguing. They both turn and see us and they both look as mad as anything.

"Get out of my office this minute."

I could only feel ridiculous and apologise and we both leave, closing the door behind us. I feel embarrassed at my stupidity but still determined. We try to eavesdrop but the door is thick and we can only hear the odd word: "no discipline, not good enough, change." I hear footsteps and a louder goodbye, we step back just before the doors swings open and Beetroot strides out. He glares at us, he's very red in

35

the face. Nothing stirs from within the room until the approach of footsteps, Teddy looks out the open doorway. "You'd better come in."

I apologise, "Sorry Miss we should have knocked. Ah didn't know Mr Proctor was with ye." I thought she would rant at us but she just sat in her seat, leant back and gazed unseeing at the ceiling.

"Sit down girls I have something to tell you."

Surprised we sit on the wooden chairs by her desk.

"No let's sit over there." She points to the comfy chairs gathered around the fire. I look at Millie who's gaping, star struck, I shoo her over. "And bring that plate of biscuits."

We sit straight backed nibbling at our biscuit waiting for Teddy to speak.

"I think I know why you've come. It's no surprise to me. I'm afraid Mr Proctor is a very sick man. I mean he is sick up here." She points to her own head. "Over the last two years at least I've tried everything to show him the evil in his brain but he denies it, pretends it's not there. I've seen the boys leave his room in pain, crying, for goodness sake I've even caught him at it." She paused as she gazes in to the flickering flames. "I've reported him to the Governing Body of the School. They replied that they have questioned him and have decided between themselves that it's a 'fabrication'. They think I have imagined it all and they have given him their full support."

I blurt out unthinking. "But it's all true he's done it to us, poor Millie here has had to put up wi' him loads of times an' she's caught him at it just now – wi' me brotha Con."

Teddy's hand flies to her mouth in shock and then holds her head in both hands. She recovers and looks at us both.

"I'm so sorry. I can do no more, the Governors have 'relieved me of my position in the School' or in other words I've been sacked. I have to leave as soon as possible. But I won't leave until a replacement is found."

We can't think of anything to say we're so shocked.

Teddy suddenly smiled. "There is some good news for you two. You remember that hospital visit?" We nod. "I saw how impressed you were and how much you wanted to be a nurse." We nod again. "Well you've both got interviews for a place on the nursing training course. I'm to take you there next week so that gives us time to prepare. We'll get some suitable clothes together and we can talk about interviews and what you should say and what not to say." She looks at us for a reaction. "Well what do you think?"

Beetroot vanishes from our brains replaced by the thought of working in hospital wards. I look at Millie, she's looking at me, we're both grinning ear to ear. I can't hold myself back I get up and give Teddy a big hug. "Thank ye, thank ye Charlotte." Millie follows more tentatively and gives us both a hug. "Yes, thanks very much."

"Now get back to your dinner duties and we'll talk later."

We leave for the door when I realise Teddy will have to find somewhere else to live and work. "But what will ye do?"

"Oh don't worry about me. I'll find some other school where I can box some ears. Oh and another thing." She suddenly looked very serious. "Don't barge in to a room like that, wait for an answer, alright?"

"Yes Miss."

Chapter 10

"Hawa Em, we'll look after ye. Get yor glad rags on an' we'll have some fun."

It's early evening on Saturday, I'm sitting cross legged on my bed in our bedroom watching them get dressed. All four of us are student nurses and share the digs. I love looking at all their clothes. They have so many to choose from and they always take ages to decide and their make up! I watch in great delight, the new straight dresses showing their ankles, the powders and rouge for their faces. I smile and laugh as they cavort about, showing off.

But I'm horrified when they ask me to go with them. "You've got to be jokin' ah haven't any glad rags, anywa, ahm too young."

"Millie's comin' an' she's the same age as ye, anywa ye look older than seventeen an' by the time we've done you'll look like us."

"Wey aye, class idea Rose, you're about my size. Em stand up an' let me look at ye."

To my horror Trudie grabs me and pulls me up and then stands back. All three of my flatmates examine me.

"Hawa shoulders back, chest out, let's see what you've got."

I'm wearing my only dress and I know it's too small for me. Matron gave it to me when I left the workhouse last year, it fitted then, but not now.

"Wot d'ya think Rose? Ah think she's more yor size, ma stuff's probably too small. Her bust an' bum are too big."

They tug me this way and that as if I'm a rag doll and without warning they take off my clothes and slip on one of Rose's dresses. It feels so smooth, so comfortable, I can't believe how different it is and I feel real posh. They all stand back again and look. Rose has her hand to her mouth. Trudie even gasps. "It looks better on her than it does on ye."

Rose looks hurt but then laughs. "Bloody marvellous, wears me dress an' she'll get all the attention." She walks all around me like I'm a model in a shop. "Mind the colour is amazin' on ye, it brings out the colour of those sexy dark brown eyes an' it does fit everywhere."

"Right that settles it, hand me some powder an' rouge." Trudie pushes me back on to the bed and starts adding the make-up. I groan but it is exciting. "Don't ye worry about the lads we'll look after ye."

For the next half hour I'm strapped in to some dancing shoes, my hair is clipped in to place, my face is pale and blushed and I feel amazing.

"Emy, ye look class."Millie understands my problem we've been through the workhouse school together and both have been interviewed and gained entry to the Nursing School. There's nothing she doesn't know about me. She understands I need encouragement for this sort of thing.

"Thanks Millie, so do ye."

So with a coat thrown over my shoulders I carefully step down the stairs and arm in arm we make for the bus stop. It's only when we queue at the dance hall do I get nervous. We join a crowd jostling to get in, large separate groups of women and men eyeing each other, not many couples. I look down at my shoes I don't want to make eye contact. It's a tight squeeze through the doorway, two men leer at me inches away, I smell their breath, see their spots. I turn my head, I remember, I don't like it. I ask myself why am I here, I don't trust men. It's ok in the hospital, everyone's doing their job or are too ill to flirt, but here. That's why they are here.

Trudie grabs my arm and pulls me in. "A've got your ticket now take your coat off an' leave it in the cloakroom, I'll show ye."

I do as she says and immediately feel exposed to all the stares. I follow my friends quickly through the doors in to the ballroom. The noise hits me like a wall. I hold on to Trudie's hand and follow her through the throng. Dodging this way and that we make our way to the far side. Amazingly we find an empty table, sit down and I can relax a bit. Rose disappears and re-appears armed with four full glasses of liquid. She shouts.

"There ye gan Em have a taste of that pet."

"What is it?"

"Vimto." She winks at the others. "It'll do ye good, make ye relax like."

I've heard of it. It's fizzy and tastes sweet. After the first few sips I get to like it and feeling more confident I look around me. The band has finished warming up and now is in full swing, couples are dancing. Some are expert gliding effortlessly around the dance floor while others are stuttering, laughing at their mistakes. I tense as a man approaches our table and asks Rose to dance. She gets up immediately and I watch her. She looks so in command, smiling looking in to his eyes, then laughing with him. She disappears into the crowd. Millie follows soon after. Trudie stands and tugs my arm. "Hawa pet I'll show ye. You'll soon get the hang of it."

"This is a waltz, it goes 1 2 3, 1 2 3 like this." She twirls me round and round. I soon pick up the rhythm, she leads me acting as the man. It's so much fun. I feel a tap on the shoulder it's Millie, she leans over close to me ear. "Ye look real class, havin' fun?" I nod smiling and we dance on by.

"I'm not dancin' wi' ye all night. You've picked it up real quick." We return to the table, she can see I was enjoying it.

"Thanks Trudie."

I finish my first drink and start on my next lined up behind. I feel relaxed and sit back watching the action on the dance floor. My friends have taken the floor with different partners. Rose is wearing dark red lipstick and looks stunning. Millie seems to have met someone she likes and is all smiles. When she gets back she's eager to talk about him.

I close my eyes and listen to the music and feel the throbbing of the beat. I look down at the dress I'm wearing. How different from my own and I only got that through the kindness of Teddy. I cannot forget how kind she was, so different from my first impression when I arrived with Mrs Stephenson and Con. Oh Con, my poor brother. I know he was upset when I told him I was leaving. He tried not to show it, he had smiled and said that I'd do well but I saw the tears forming, his embarrassment, his excuse that he had to go. I said I would be back for him and I will, of that I'm certain no matter what happens.

I feel a wave of intense determination. I grip my drink tight trying to crush it to powder. I hate that man so much, he never leaves my life. I have sworn I will get him somehow, somewhere. He's evil and doesn't deserve to live. The re-occurring picture of his gruesome death is in my mind's eye when I'm gripped by the shoulder, I jump.

"Come on Em, yas thinkin' about him again aren't ye? Yas here to enjoy yourself."

I release my stranglehold on the glass and look in to Millie's compassionate face and try to smile. I wonder how she manages to put him to one side, I know she has the same feelings, the same grudge.

"Sorry Mil."

"Look we're ganin to sit down together an' work out a plan to get the bastard. But for now this young lad wants to dance with ye." She nods towards someone who has joined our table and I haven't even noticed.

The man is talking to Trudie, I can see he's very handsome with lots of brown wavy hair. He notices me and stands up immediately and gives me a slight bow. He looks very casual and confident, when he speaks I realise he's Scottish with a lovely soft lilting borders accent.

"May I have this next dance please?" He holds a hand out to me assuming that I'd accept. I do and he pulls me gently but elegantly around the table and on to the dance floor. I glimpse a wink and thumbs up from Trudie behind him. I thought I would feel nervous when and if someone asks me to dance but I'm not. He's a good dancer not really at the Waltz but when a Charleston starts he's in his element.

41

"This is one of those new dances from America I'll show you."

I nod and he takes hold of my hands and we start swinging with the music, this way and that. We're soon in time with the beat and immediately it feels right. I can't help myself smiling, I feel like I'm on air, we smile and laugh at each other. This is fun. We continue through the first and then the next dance, I don't want to stop but the tempo changes. He nods towards the table and we leave the floor still holding hands.

The table is empty. My friends have disappeared into the dancing crush. I sit down leaving him standing beside me, he asks if I would like a drink. He's very relaxed and keeps smiling, his eyes twinkle as if they're wet with tears. He seems to like me and I'm certainly attracted.

"No thanks ah still have two here."

"May I sit with you?"

"Yes please." I feel embarrassed thinking that was too forward. I have an inner voice shouting a warning. He's a man, beware, they're violent, lustful, crude. I look down uncertain. He sits down beside me. He's not too close and we've dropped our hand holding, he takes a gulp of his own drink – a clear liquid.

"I'm Thomas by the way. I've not seen you here before."

"I look up. No this is me first time. Umm... Ahm Emily by the way."

"Hi Emily, you dance very well and you look really nice in that dress..."

He was cut short by a sudden commotion, the music has stopped and all three of my friends return with their partners. Laughter, chairs scrapping back, glasses clinking.

"Hi Em pet, how ye doin'?"

"Good, this is Thomas, oh." I turn to introduce him but his chair is empty. I stand up and search the floor but there is no sign. I slump down, my eyes fill with tears he must have been frightened off. Perhaps it was me.

Trudie sits down on the next chair leans over and puts her hand on my leg. "He'll be back if he likes ye enough. Ah saw how he looked at ye, yes, he'll be back."

Chapter 11

I'm sitting on the top deck of the bus with my three friends returning from the dance. Well I'm with Trudie and Millie. Rose is behind us in the arms of her new found beau. They're kissing and cuddling or as Trudie says they're canoodling. What a lovely word, it somehow fits.

I've enjoyed the evening. I've danced and danced and drunk and drunk and I feel tired and a bit woozy. Trudie has admitted that my first drinks were laced with gin – to make me relax. They certainly worked, my eyes are closed, I'm sinking in to the seat, the chattering on the bus including the giggling from behind me is growing distant and faint. The vibration of the bus is sending me to a half way house between waking and sleeping. A vision of Thomas appears, my first and by far the best dance partner. He's smiling, he is handsome and I so wished we could have danced together again. I did see him sitting at a table with other boys and girls. He kept glancing over, our eyes met briefly before I had to look away to concentrate on the dance. By the time the dance had brought me full circle he had gone, the table was empty and my heart sank.

My vision is changing, Thomas's smiling face is distorting gradually into the nightmare profile of Charles Proctor. I force myself awake, my eyes wide, now sitting upright and I stare unseeingly in to Trudie's face opposite.

She knows about him, they all do now. I've told them about him, his disgusting love of small boys. They know how he changed my lovely brother Con from an innocent fun loving boy to a morose, pale shadow. He wasn't the only one but no-one gave any credence to complaints, the committee, mostly men, always backed the owner. Teddy knew. She caught him at it often enough, she shouted, raved and tried to protect the boys as much as she could. He just laughed at her threats, told her she could leave any time. The grey men behind eventually lost patience and told her to pack her bags. She was staying on, loyal to the children in her care, until her replacement arrives. She found positions outside for as many kids as possible, including Millie and me. I remember vividly the day I left: the bus ride to the hospital, the interview, what she said about me – best girl at the home, bright, obedient, helpful. I'll always remember those words, no-one besides me Mam has ever said those things. Our parting at the gates, we both cried, yes, even Teddy, I love her.

I'm sitting up in my bed, I'm in my nightdress holding a cup of tea I don't really want. I'm very tired and my eyes are drooping but my three flat mates are perched one on each side and one on the end of the bed. They are wide awake, they are making plans.

Trudie started it, she's an organiser, I rarely see her relaxed.

"We have to get this Proctor man. He's buggering wee lads' lives just for his sordid satisfaction." She looks over to me. "An' probably not just wee lads." I look down in to my tea cup. "No, ah thought not. We've got to catch him at it."

Millie answers. "But no-one will believe us. He has a hold on the governors."

"They've got their heads in the sand. They don't want te believe it. Ah bet they do know somethin's not right but they're too comfy. Better to ignore it, let it run its course they don't want te rock the boat." Trudie pauses and leans forward making everyone else lean towards her and then in a stage whisper. "But if they catch him at it they would have to believe it an' they would have te do somethin'." She looks wide eyed at each of us in turn.

Rose understands the plan. "Wey aye... but how on earth do we do that?"

Trudie has obviously been thinking about it before. "Look at me, ahm skinny, got short hair. If ah dress up a bit or rather doon a bit." She gives me a quick look. "Ah would look like a wee lad. What d'ya think like?"

I am suddenly wide awake and stare at her. "No Tru don't even think about it. He might appear to be a friendly ol' man but he's completely evil inside an' he'll be stronger than ye, an' he's got canes an' he uses them. No ye mustn't even think about it." I pause lost for words, I grab her hand. "You're very kind, ye all are, an' ah really love ye for it but ye mustn't put yourselves in such danger."

"She has a point Tru an' why should the Committee believe ye. Ye may put yourself in danger for nothing."

Trudie hasn't finished. "But this is the canny bit. We time it for when these governors are due to visit. They must gan on a regular basis to make sure it's runnin' all right. That's right isn't it Em, Millie?"

"Ah suppose so, ah don't see them very often but ah know Teddy has to run rund before they come, cleanin' up like."

"There we are then, we just find out when they're due an' I'll gan in just before, wiggle me backside at him an' job's done." She smiles triumphantly.

I'm horrified and try to put her off, Rose does the same and all three of us are lost in frantic discussions when Millie starts to speak.

"Ye know, ahm sure this man'll be on his best behaviour before a Committee visit, so, however inviting your backside is Tru he'll want to save ye for later." She pauses and then continues in a lower tone. "But if we can arrange for them to visit unexpectantly like it'll be a different matter. For that we need Teddy's help."

"But Millie ye know she's been sacked, she was only staying on waitin' for her replacement. She may have left already."

Trudie as ever was the first to answer. "Class idea Millie, so the quicker we act the better. Em ye must get down there first thing temorra, it's Sunday an' you're off, so ye can." She stopped to think. "But ye need someone with ye. It canna be me, although, yes, it could be me, I'll wear your workhouse dress an' get me hair cut shorter, maybe wear a cap."

Trudie was cut short by Millie. "Tru, stop an' breath, you're like an express train. Anyway ye canna go, you're workin'. Ahm not an' it's much bettor if me an' Emy go, we know the place an' we know Teddy. It's really our problem."

The three girls are excited, they're chattering, making plans, determined to show to the world what Proctor is really like. But I'm filled with dread. I only ever go back to see Con and Teddy. If they weren't there I'd never want to see the place again. Just the thought of walking through the entrance makes me feel sick. I slump back on to the pillow and clamp shut my eyes. Con appears out of the darkness, a pale, forlorn figure. He's lost, he needs me. I know I have to try for his sake and for all the others. I must go through with it. I feel my own determination welling up inside. I sit up, the girls stop talking and all look my way. I grab their hands and speak very softly but clearly.

"Let's get the bastard."

Chapter 12

I have laid out our plan and we're waiting for a reaction from Charlotte. She's looking in to her fire, I don't know what she's thinking but she is thinking, she hasn't turned it down. We sip our tea waiting, the clock ticks the fire crackles we shuffle our feet. Sunday is an easier day in the workhouse school, religious services all through the morning giving everyone a break from the chores. I knew if Charlotte hadn't left her job then she would be reading in her room. She always protected this time fiercely and woe-betide anyone who interrupted her. But this was different. We were met at the front door by one of the Wardens, a woman we didn't recognise. But once inside the familiar sounds and smells washed over us in waves, our nursing training was forgotten and we were back at school. We were led past Beetroot's office, up the once grand now decrepit staircase with its cathedral like window still un-cleaned, Oh Ma. Then along the dark wood panelled corridor we clipped our way to Matron's office but she left us to knock and almost ran away to hide from responsibility.

All morning we had to urge and encourage ourselves to make the journey back to the place where we have so many bitter memories. The thought keeps rolling over in our minds; we're not doing this just for ourselves but for everyone, the girls and boys interned and for Charlotte herself. We have to do it.

The reply to our knock was a bellowed 'go away' the second knock started a crash of books, marching feet and a ripped open door. The stare she gave us could have frozen the sea, automatically our eyes widened in fear. Had she forgotten us? Within seconds the face relaxed in to a welcoming smile, thank goodness and our hearts regained their normal rhythm.

Without looking away from the fire Charlotte starts talking, slowly, but gaining momentum as she brings her thoughts and ideas to play.

"You know this could work. The Committee are very keen on using photography to record the latest improvements at the school." She turns away from the fire to concentrate on us her face lit with excitement. "I could send a note inviting them to see the latest camera from America."

"But have ye got one?"

"No, but my brother has. He only lives in North Shields. If we could catch Proctor in action, on film, we'll have him."

Her enthusiasm is contagious. "We could send the photo to the newspaper complete with his red sweaty face" "an' his trousers doon." Adds Millie smiling broadly.

"But wait." Charlotte's face shows concern. "The timing is crucial we have to know when they arriveS before you even go in to his room. There mustn't be any hold ups or you'll be in trouble."

We talk it through trying to see what could go wrong and how to make sure it won't.

"The big question is who's going to go in to his office to tempt him?"

I don't hesitate. "Me of course, it's me brotha, ah have to do it."

Millie's reaches out and holds my hand. "No, you're too shapely, too much like a grown woman. Look at me, cut me hair, dirty me face an' I'll look like a lad of fourteen, just what he likes. Don't forget a've suffered him for years, it's payback time for me as well."

Charlotte nods. "I agree with Millie, but the Committee, myself and my brother have to be right outside the door when you go in waiting for the signal. My brother can be showing off the camera while we wait."

I add. "Don't forget me I'll be there as well an' what's the signal?"

"Don't ye worry I'll shout at the top of me voice. Mind ah suppose he'll still fancy what a've got to offer."

"Millie, some things never change, but, in that unlikely event, just come out and we'll have to think again."

A thought crosses my mind. "Suppose he locks the door an' we canna get in?"

"I've thought of that. He doesn't normally bother, his grubby little mind's on his sick pleasures but to be certain I'll make sure his key goes missing." She smiles and pats her dress pocket and winks.

We're walking back to the hospital, it's been left that Charlotte will send a message confirming the date of the visit. I feel so nervous and It's not me that's going to be with Proctor but we've set the wheels in motion, there's no turning back. Millie is so brave I pray that nothing goes wrong.

The road back is busy, delivery drays plod by, jaunty gigs and pairs of horses pulling omnibuses overtake. Noise and activity everywhere but we walk quietly. I'm going through what we've just arranged, I realise Millie's doing the same when she pulls me into a much quieter side road and we sidestep in to a doorway, she looks worried.

"Emy supposin' he doesn't want te de anythin', ah mean he canna molest every lad or lass that goes in like. He may be too tired or he may not even like me an' it'll be all a complete waste of time, the committee will be there an' Charlotte's brotha an' everythin'."

Charlotte had suggested that Millie should go in with his morning tea. "Maybe ye should gan in before ye tek the tea to see if he wants anything with it an' smile at him."

"Hawa. It'll give him time to think about me." She laughs. "Perhaps ah should wiggle an' bend over to pick somethin' up right in front of him."

"Oh Millie how can you laugh about it?"

"Don't ye worry about me ahm only going to look fourteen, ahm eighteen an' strong. Ah can handle him if he gets out of hand."

She's sounds so confident, if I was in her position I'd be scared. I know what men are like; demanding, aggressive and very strong.

"Wey aye, don't worry I'll be fine. Ah want to tell Trudie an' Rose what's happened." Her excitement is contagious and we run back to the main road and then sidestep pedestrians, dogs and hand carts shouting and laughing like kids all the way back to the hospital.

In our room we collapse on to our beds red faced still chatting. "Look Emy you've got a note on your table."

"Ah bet they've changed me shifts or somethin'." It's a letter, I open it and read the note paper inside. I smile and re-read it.

"Well who's it from?"

"It's private."

"Not from your very best friend."

"It's from Thomas or as he signs it, Tam. He wants to see me again."

"Ooooh, anywa ah thought ye were off men."

I lay back on to the bed, arms supporting the back of my head facing the ceiling. "Yes ah am but, he seems different."

"Mmmm."

Chapter 13

It's the early hours of the morning and I'm creeping in to my bedroom as quietly as I can but there's sudden movement from Millie's bed she sits up. "Is that ye Emy?"

"Who do ye think it is, the bogeyman?"

"But what time is it, a've been worried about ye, where a've ye been?"

"With Tam of course an' don't ask any more questions. Ah just want to sleep ahm really tired."

"Emy, there's somethin' wrong isn't there? Ah know ye, ye always tell me everythin'."

"But not tonight, tell ye in the mornin'."

Millie does know me very well, we've slept in the same room for years. I pretend to fall asleep but my guilty pleasure is turning in to a nightmare. As I sober up, realisation dawns. I've been led astray, been taken in by his kindness, his good looks, his willingness to listen. But all the time he only wanted to get me in to his bed. Job done he just went to sleep didn't even bother to walk me home. Get a bus he mumbled and turned over, lost interest in me completely, got what he wanted and I fell for it. How could I be so stupid, naive? Tears well up and run down wetting my pillow. I try to keep quiet but I must have sobbed as I felt a hand on my shoulder.

"Emy, tell me about it."

I turn over, reach up, grab her and pull her down to my level, my tears are now streaming down uncontrolled. They're not from sorrow but from frustration. I killed the first man who molested me, I got away from Proctor before his hands went any further but now I just give in without a fight.

"Emy, yas makin' me upset, what happened tonight?"

I blurt out everything, the whole evening laid out in front of her, my stupidity exposed.

"Oh Emy, move over." She squeezes herself in beside me and wraps her arms around me. I feel the heat from her body, her breath in my face. She tries to comfort me saying that I'm human, it's natural and not to feel bad, but I know she's never done it. I slide my arms around her and we cuddle, me and my very best friend, what would I do without her. I give her a peck on the nose and she laughs.

"Emy." She pauses, I wait. "Umm.., what's it like."

I tell her of my innocent anticipation. How I was completely unable to prevent him from doing what he wanted. The unexpected pain inside me, his heavy, noisy gasping and then the weight and smell of his sweating body collapsing on top of me.

"I'll tell ya it's over-rated and what's more ahm ganin round there tomorrow an' ahm ganin to cut it off!"

This sets us off giggling, then laughing out loud. She volunteers to hold him down while I wield the scalpel and then we work out what to do with it. Plug the hole in the wall, start a collection. We're having hysterics, there's a bang on the wall then a mumbled complaint. We turn down the volume back down to giggling. Eventually she slides off the bed and crawls back to her own. I smile to myself, she's able to cheer me up no matter what. I feel much happier but I promise myself that I will go and see him as soon as I finish work whether he wants to see me or not.

****

"Gone hyem to his family pet."

I stood there trying to work out how this could have happened. "Ah thought he was workin' down here an' was lookin' for a house like."

"Tam, nae chance, he likes to play the field too much. He travels all over, ah see him for a couple of days each month then he's off."

My heart was sinking fast. "But he's gan back to his Ma an' Da now?"

"Ma an' Da? Howay with ya. He's gan back to his wife an' kids."
She stopped and stared. "Oh my, you've been caught haven't ye
hinney. Look take me advice an' forget him, he's not worth it. You're a
bonny lookin' lass there's plenty more about. Ye won't go short."

I stammer a thank you and walk away. I'm numb from head to toe.
This morning I thought maybe I was wrong about him. That he was
taken over by the passion of the moment, like me, and he was now
stricken with guilt, like me. I can see the truth is a very different
picture, he planned and schemed to get me back to his room, ply with
me drink and then.... oh god.

I just walk, my brain in a whirl. I'm trying to fit the parts together.
Why he should do this? Why he should treat me with such disdain? No
respect. Obviously I'm not the first, just one more in a long line of
conquests. I feel anger rising in my chest. What a fool I've been. I'm
muttering out loud and my speed increases, surprised pedestrians
sidestep away from my headlong rush. He can't do this to me. I decide
to go and see him wherever he lives, confront him and his family, show
his wife what he's like. But how's that fair to her? It'll just bring
misery. Mind she probably knows anyway, he can't be that good an
actor. He wasn't acting in bed, he knew what he was doing all right. For
a moment I recall our love making, how gentle he was at first, how he
kissed me all over sending shivers of intense desire though my every
part. I was powerless then came the pain. I couldn't get away, trapped
beneath him. He knew what he was doing, he'd perfected the art with
so many others. Men, they're all the same, nasty, selfish, arrogant
bast...

There was a sudden shout, something large looms in front of me.
"Whooooa, get awa."

I look up the body of the horse was within inches of my face, I jerk
myself back but the following cart just clips my shoulder swivels me
round and sends me flying to the ground.

The driver jumps down, leans over me his face contorted with anxiety.

I'm embarrassed, I struggle to get back on my feet. "Ahm alright."

He looks relieved and tries to brush the dirt from the road off my uniform. Now he looks embarrassed. "Sorry Miss but ye must look where you're ganin, ye were nearly under ma wheels. Ye sure you're alright?"

"Sorry, just a few bruises."

"You've made a mess of your uniform, ah can take ye back to the hospital for a check up if ye want?"

I look down and see what he means. I'll need to wash it before I go back tomorrow. "No, ahm alright thank ye." I start to walk away but my leg gives way there's a sudden sharp pain, I shout and I stumble on to my knees.

The man and a passing lady rush over and support me.

"That's it ahm takin' ye back, yas ganin nowhere, somethin' may be broken." They both help me in to the cart and pack sacks and blankets around me. I feel a complete fool but I'm in their kind hands and I lean meekly against the side suddenly exhausted. The journey back to the hospital passes slowly and comfortably as the cart sways gently from side to side, my eyes close and I drift in and out of sleep. He is a kind man. But he's an exception.

"Oh so you've decided te come round have ye."

I hear a distant voice, I recognise it from somewhere and try to open my eyes. I see a shadowy figure, hazy, blurred around the edges. The vision focuses slowly, it's a woman in a uniform, a nurses' outfit. I blink trying to focus.

"Come on Emy ye canna sleep all day."

It's Millie. I must have overslept and try to sit up but I can't, I'm being held down. "Millie what's happenin', am ah late for work?"

"You've been out for the count since ye came in. You've had concussion an' you've sprained your ankle, ye really came a cropper. We're all worried about ye, Trudie an' Rose an' ...."

She was interrupted by a loud booming voice over her shoulder. "And about time to, cavorting about, not looking where you're going." Millie swivelled round and saw the large buxom figure of Sister looming over. "I want you out of this bed and back to work. We're short of staff as it is without all this going on."

My head feels fuzzy, full of cotton wool but I know I must do as I'm told. "Yes Sister, sorry." I struggle to sit up and start trying to pull back the bed covers.

Sister watches me and sighs. "This afternoon will do. Help her Student Nurse Hardy." She strode away her shoes clicking loudly on the tiled floor.

Millie, after ensuring Sister had left the ward, turned to Emily. "You'd better do as the old battleaxe says. I'll get back after the ward round this afternoon an' help ye back to our room an' we'll see how well ye can walk." She stood up to leave but then remembered. "That carter keeps comin' back to check on ye."

"Who?"

"The man who nearly ran ye over, ye know. He brought ye back here."

I look at Millie not understanding a word she's saying.

"Ye don't remember do ye?

"Remember what, what am I doin' here anyway, what happened?"

Millie sits back down on to the bed. "According to this man ye walked right in to his cuddy, an' his cart knocked ye over. He loaded ye in to the back an' brought ye all the way here. If it wasn't for him you'd still be crawlin' about somewhere."

I slump back on to the pillow and I try to think back but there's nothing.

Millie pulls the sheet back over me. "Don't worry it'll all come back to ye, give your brain a chance. Mind, ah don't suppose it'll be good viewin' when it does. Look, a've got to get back to me ward I'll be back this afternoon."

She pats my arm and leaves me alone with my thoughts. How could this have happened? What was I doing? There's nothing, just nothing there. I hear murmured voices and look over to the desk at the end of the ward. I see a nurse I recognise talking to a man of the same height dressed in workman's clothes, cap gripped in his hand. The nurse is shaking her head. He suddenly turns in my direction, sees me and raises his cap-holding hand. I mechanically raise my hand in return. The nurse is still talking and points to the clock on the wall, he nods and leaves the ward but not before giving me another look and wave. I don't recognise him but I wonder. I have a good idea.

Chapter 14

I was right. The nurse walks over, sees I'm awake and speaks close to my ear. "Student Nurse Mulligan, there's a very insistent young man who wants to see ye; he says he brought ye in an' wants to know how yas gettin' on. Ah keep telling him that ye need rest but he keeps tryin'. Ah hope it's alright with ye but a've said that now you're conscious he can come at visitin' time this afternoon, just fo' a short while."

With her help I sit up and feel the pain in my ankle but at least I'm thinking more clearly. "Yes of course, what time is it please an' ah couldn't have a cuppa could ah?"

"It's near enough midday an' I'll get ye a drink, no sympathy mind, walking around town dreaming. You're lucky you're still in one piece." She turns to go but not before she smiles and adds. "He's a nice lad."

Lad, the word triggers my brain, instantly I recall Tam, then my conversation with the landlady. My brain is swamped with memories flooding back in waves, my heart sinks, married, how could he? I've been such a fool. I decide I want nothing to do with men, I'm not going to see this carter man, he'll be just the same, I'll pretend to be asleep that'll teach him a lesson. Buried beneath my dark thoughts I know that he saved me and brought me here but there again what's he after? As if I didn't know.

"It's only bruised, you can go but use a stick for walking." The doctor has examined me and decided that I'm fully conscious and fit apart from a swollen ankle. He nods to Sister and walks over to the next bed. Sister glares at me. "Normal time tomorrow morning, right?"

I dutifully nod but I'm thinking I bet you wouldn't if you had this pain. I'm still feeling sorry for myself when Millie hurries in smiling looking eager obviously pleased with herself.

"Guess what, Charlotte has sent us a message. A committee member has agreed to visit the school next week to see what this camera can do.

Ah should be workin' but Rose has swopped her shift with me so ah can go."

My brain is now fully functioning. "But ah have to go with ye ah don't know if ah can, am ah workin' like?"

She grabs my arm tight. "A've checked an' it's your day off."

"So it's all systems go?"

"Wey aye, ah canna wait, I think." She stares at me. "We'll get him won't we?

"Yes we will, the two of us, Charlotte and her brotha, he's got no chance." She squeezes my hand, turns and rushes off. I shout after her.

"Millie, I'm feelin' better, just in case ye wanted to know."

Her hand goes to her mouth. "Ahm so sorry Emy she tried to look serious but failed miserably. "How are ye? "

"I died in the night."

"Oh that's bonny, see ye tonight then." She hurries away but pauses by the swing door, looks back and mouths 'sorry' before she disappears from sight.

I'm left in complete turmoil, nervous about the Beetroot plan, upset with Tam and this carter pest and wondering how I'm going to do anything with my painful ankle. I think first things first, let's see if I can walk. I swing my legs out of the bed and gingerly put my weight on them, excruciating. I stagger around my bed holding on to posts, cupboards, anything for support and then on to other bed ends apologising as I make my way slowly up and down the ward. One woman reminds me of my persistent visitor.

"Your husband is he? No, if he's owt like mine he'll be in the boozer with his pals havin' a fine ol' time without me. He's your boyfriend am ah right? Nice lad maybe needs tidying a bit." I smile and stagger on grimacing at every step.

The nurse walks over shaking her head, she hands me a stick. "Ah say this you've got some spirit. Don't mind Sister she'll understand if ye canna make temorra. Let's see how you're doin', hold me arm with

59

your left an' the stick against that ankle." We make progress down the centre of the ward, much easier. I decide I'm going to return to my digs. I feel re-assured I can manage and feel determined to start back at work tomorrow, sticks and all.

"Thanks, ah feel much better, if ah can borrow another stick, I'll get dressed an' get back home."

She gives me a doubtful look but she probably notices I'm going no matter what. "Alright then, if you're sure. I'll help ye doon the stairs an' get Student Nurse Hardy to help ye get back, alright?" I nod. "Thanks."

Dressed back in to my scuffed uniform I arrive at the hospital entrance with the help of the nurse and Millie, one each side of me. That was an adventure, hysterical laughter all round interspersed with piercing pains and explanations to fascinated bystanders on the way. We all sit down exhausted.

"Canna imagine what these people think of us. A hospital with no lifts? Ye leave worse than when ye arrive!"

Having rested and with the help of both sticks I rise from the chair, thank the nurse for her help and with Millie by my side we make for home.

"Hey what about your visitor, what shall ah tell him?"

I shout over my shoulder. "Just tell him a've been released an' gone home. Ah suppose you'd better thank him from me."

"Shall ah give him your address?"

"No."

The half mile back to my digs never seemed so long. There are so many steps in the pavement I've never even noticed before but now I have to stop at them all, concentrate and carefully lower myself down and just as carefully mount up again. Obstructions bar my way at every turn, barrows, boxes, street lights. All this among a whole city of people out and about weaving their way around us cursing and muttering. Millie helps me all the way but she's very quiet or maybe it's just me having to concentrate so hard. We finally arrive at our digs and we sit gratefully down on to the entrance steps. I breathe a sigh of relief, I feel exhausted but there's no respite, it's Millie's turn.

"Emy, you're just too bad."

"What?"

"For starters ye should have stayed in the hospital to recuperate, you're obviously not fit to gan to work temorra." She paused.

"And"

"An' ye should see this man who helped ye back, he seems very kind an' considerate. Ah know you've got a thing against men an' ah expect Tam is just as embarrassed about what happened the other night but they're not all bad."

This is the last straw, I glare at Millie, my closest friend who I know I love dearly but I can't help myself. "Ye don't know one thing about Tam, he's despicable. It's not any of your business but I'll tell ye. Ah went round to his digs an' was told by his landlady that not only does he do this sort of thing all the time like but he's married with children. He no doubt has a girlfriend in every toon in the land leavin' his wife at home strugglin' with their kids. An' this carter, whatever his name is, why do ye think he keeps coming rund? Don't ye think he has somethin' else on his mind? Perhaps, just maybe, to take advantage of a grateful, eager to please young lassie?" I pause to get my breath. "An' you're right, ah do have a thing against men an' my next step is to get that bastard Proctor."

Poor Millie is dumbstruck. Her eyes are set wide open and her mouth gapes. I struggle up on to my feet and try to get up the stairs with some degree of dignity. I get to the door but of course I haven't got my key handy. Silently Millie opens it for me and lets me in. Thank goodness no-one else is around to see or hear me and I make my way to our bedroom, the door crashes closed behind me and I collapse on to the bed. My anger subsides to intense frustration and I thrash my pillow with both hands before I collapse onto it and start sobbing.

It's some ten minutes before the door creaks open slowly. By this time I've calmed down, cried out and I can see Millie creeping towards me with a tray holding two steaming cups, the door does its usual trick and bangs shut all by itself. She turns in annoyance at the noise.

"Ye see even that door's like a man. It does what it wants no matter what." But I'm smiling at her. She puts down the tray and runs over to me.

"Oh Emy, ah had no idea, ahm so sorry."

She gives me a cuddle and I mutter. "An' so am ah, talkin' to me best friend like that. Ah didn't mean to be nasty to ye."

"Ah know." We sit together on the bed arms around each other.

"Come on let's drink our tea an' ye can tell me more about the plans for Proctor."

Her eyes light up immediately, she sits on her own bed facing me and starts. "We arrive first thing on Thursday mornin' an' gan to Charlotte's room. We get changed there an' meet her brotha with his camera. The woman from the committee arrives at eleven o'clock. She'll be shown the camera an' some of his pictures an' then taken to see Proctor at half past eleven." Millie then turns on her scheming smile. "Meanwhile just after eleven, I'll gan to his room, sent by Charlotte of course an' dressed in my best school clothes, to see if he would like a cup of tea. I'll try to show some interest in him like, wiggle a bit ye know."

I frown. "He might grab ye there an' then, it'll be far too early we won't be outside."

"No he won't, I'll dangle him on me string an' then nip out."

"Mmm, then what."

"Easy, give him time te think an' gan in ten minutes before ye do. I'll shout if he gets out of hand."

I'm not convinced, so many things can go wrong, he may hurt Millie, we may be delayed getting to his room and be too late. "Oh

Millie it's so risky, he's sly, he may jam a chair on the door an' we canna get in, he's very strong especially w...."

We're interrupted by a knock on our bedroom door.

Assuming it's Rose or Trudie we shout come in. The door opens and a small man I recognise stands there smiling.

"Millie Hardy an' Emily Mulligan?"

My heart sinks, I don't answer and look away. He's the carter that keeps appearing. Someone obviously gave him my address.

Millie looks nervous but replies politely. "Yes that's right"

"Well don't ye know who ah am?"

"You're the man who ran over me friend aren't ye?"

He grabs his hat off his head and clutches it tightly with both hands."Well yes an' ahm very sorry about that but Emily wasnae lookin' where she was g.." He stopped and I look around, he's now looking very uncomfortable but then continues. "Ah hope you're feelin' better."

Millie answers for me. "She was unconscious for a while an' she's got a badly sprained ankle an' she needs to rest, perhaps ye can come back later?"

"Errr yes of course." But he doesn't move away. "Ah came 'cause ah recognised Emily an' when ah came to see her at the hospital ah recognised ye as well."

"How, from when?" He now has both of our attentions.

"From the school. Ahm older than both of ye ah think but ah used to see ye at mealtimes an' some of the lessons. Don't you recognise me? You've got a brotha called Con."

I forget my injury and my distrust. I sit up to study him. Millie must be doing the same as he starts to blush under our scrutiny. He is small and thin with an impish face and short cropped fair hair highlighting his protruding ears. He is still dressed in the same clothes as when I first saw him in the ward. A dark waistcoat over a white open necked shirt, dark long trousers supported by checked braces and boots. All a bit scruffy and he has a distinctive smell about him which isn't unpleasant.

I think back but can't place him but Millie's eyes brighten. "Wey aye ah do, ye used to be with a lad with dark wavy hair."

He looks disappointed. "Oh, yes that'll be Seb." He shuffles his feet about and looks as though he wants to leave but adds. "Ahm Frank by the way."

I feel both relieved and embarrassed. All the time he wanted only to introduce himself. I don't want him to go. "Sit doon we can have a chat, do ye fancy a cuppa."

Millie fetches him a cup and we talk about the school, the food, the work, Charlotte and the other wardens but then we mentioned Proctor. He goes quiet and sips his tea.

He doesn't have to say anything, I know and I'm sure Millie is the same. "He molested ye didn't he?"

He nods.

"Was it bad?"

He nods again.

I look at Millie, she nods at my un-voiced question. "Frank, we had the same problem an' me brotha Con. We've got a plan to get him."

He looks up eager to hear. He sits down and concentrates on every word getting increasingly excited. When we finish he stands up. "Ah want to be there, not ye Millie he's too strong for ye. Ahm much stronger now but ah can still look like a fourteen year old."

I exchange glances with Millie. She looks put out. "No, ah can do it. Ahm stronger than ah look. Ah want me revenge just as much as ye." She pauses before continuing in a quieter tone. "You're very kind Frank but it's my idea, no way is anyone else ganin in there."

I feel proud of my friend and so scared for her. I much prefer Frank or anyone else to act as the bait but I have to stand up for her. "Thanks Frank but Millie has to be the one." Then it occurs to me that he may be able to help. "But look, come with us. Ye can be another witness like an' tell this Committee woman what he did to ye."

He kicks the ground frustrated. "Alright then." But then adds in a fierce tone. "If he hurts ye Millie Hardy, I'll kill him."

His ferocity surprises us and it dawns on me that he has a soft spot for Millie and probably has had it for some time.

Chapter 15

With our heads down we're fighting against the squally rain arm in arm. I'm still limping but have left my sticks behind. We've both been up before dawn nervously chatting about the day ahead. It could be everything to us both, three of us counting Frank. He's meeting us at the school. I know wanting revenge so much is a sin but this is different. It's not just one horrible thing between two people, we're trying to catch a serial molester and buggerer, that's a word I've learnt from Rose. We're doing this on behalf of so many children who have suffered his attentions over so many years.

Millie, my very best friend, usually so bright and bouncy, has set herself for the task. She's been so determined, so adamant and confident that we'll get him. We've hacked at her hair and given her face and neck a few dirty marks. She really looks the part but I feel so nervous for her, having to encourage him, show him she's available or rather he's available. Not that that matters to him he'll soon notice she's a girl. It won't make any difference, by that time he'll have only one thing on his mind. I think of the canes in his room. I've never seen or felt their pain, I managed to escape in time but Frank told us about them and Charlotte has seen his collection stacked neatly in his store room. She confronted him but was told that they were for 'correction purpose' only. The bastard.

We notice Frank's cart outside the school, his horse eating from the nosebag. Then we see him sheltering in the entrance. He sees us and runs over.

"Ye alright?"

"Drenched, have ye been here long?"

"Nah, anny a few minutes."

"Will yor cuddy be alright?"

"Ol' Jake, he'll stay there all day if ah let him, lazy ol' bugger." He realises what he said and looks embarrassed. "Sorry."

I walk up to Jake and pat him. My foot gives a twinge but I can't blame him, it was all my fault. I think of Tam again but chase the thought out of my mind. I give his ears and forehead a friendly rub but he doesn't seem to notice, too intent on eating.

I set my shoulders back. "Right let's do it." Millie pulls the bell and we wait for the usual small boy or girl who's been allocated the job today. I wonder if it could be Con but it's not, it's Charlotte herself. She looks very smartly dressed and different somehow. She smiles and beckons us in. We introduce Frank but there's no need.

"I know you Frank Tanner, you're welcome. Come in to my office, my brother's here already."

We follow her, almost running past Proctor's office, the door stays closed thank goodness. Then we step up the familiar grand staircase and down the corridor.

"Go straight in." Inside we see a large man with large moustache bending over the table examining a box. He immediately looks up and smiles and we can see the family resemblance.

He speaks in a low but friendly tone. "Nice to meet you people. Charlotte's told me all about it and I'm so pleased I can help." He looks over to his sister and smiles, she smiles back. I can see and feel the fondness between them. "My sister's had a bad time lately and that's got to change. Isn't that right Charlie?"

Charlotte blushes slightly and introduces us, getting her own back. "This is my cheeky brother Branwell or Brandy as he is known." Her eyebrows rise daring him to disagree. He just laughs and gives his sister a brotherly wink. "Charlie and Brandy a right pair of Sprotes aren't we?"

"Mmmm, never mind all that. Now show us your new fangled camera."

He proudly picks up the box from the table and shows it to his bemused audience. "This is the latest and best camera you can get, high speed, variable focus and see how light she is. Just point it and press the button and hey presto we have a picture. Well that's the theory anyway."

"I hope it's more than just theory Brandy. It has to work we won't get much time to fiddle about, it's a matter of: in the door, flash and out again then in that automobile of yours and away."

"Don't worry old girl it'll work and the picture will be yours soon enough but this lady from the Committee will see everything anyway won't she? A shiver passes through me as I get back to the reality of our situation.

Charlotte answers. "You would think so but this committee stick together. They stand up for each other and for the managers like Proctor. We're lucky we've got the only woman here, a Mrs Stanningly, she may have more respect. But we need the back-up, the proof of what goes on in this place."

Frank breaks his silence. "An' ah can back-it up as well."

I add. "An' so can me brotha who's still here an' Millie an' lots of others like."

Charlotte holds up her hands and concludes the discussion. "But the photo will be fool-proof." We're silent all hoping our plan will work. She looks over to her clock ticking remorselessly on the window sill taking us ever closer to our time for action. "Mrs Stanningly will be here at 11 o'clock so we've got over half an hour." She looks over to me and Millie. "I've got your school clothes. You can change in the storeroom next door. I've put a mirror in there for you. I must say your face and hair look great Millie. You've got a pretty face not unlike some boys we've had, so you'll pass with flying colours. Emily, there's no hiding for you, you're a young lady and no mistake but we'll keep you in reserve. So, off you go but come back in here after you've changed for a last check-up. Oh and by the way Millie, your name is now Billy."

In the storeroom we look at ourselves and we're back at school. The outfits are clean but shabby, worn around the edges and rough making us scratch as if we're flea infested. I tie my hair back in to a ponytail and we're ready. I give Millie a last hug before we step out on to the stage to act out this real life drama.

Back with Charlotte we find Frank also dressed in school clothes reversing his time clock back to a fourteen year old.

"How do ah look?"

We both answer in unison. "Amazin'," I continue, "but ye didn't have to change, you're not ganin in."

"Ah wanted to be with ye an' Matron, errrrr Charlotte gave me these to wear. Ah just want to be part of it, to support ye."

I noticed he was looking only at Millie, she felt the special attention and smiled. "Thanks Frank we do appreciate that."

"Yes, yes all very good. It's ten minutes before she arrives. Now off you go Billy and see if he wants his morning tea now and act the part."

Millie takes a deep breath and without further ado she leaves us to wait.

The minutes tick by so very slowly, ten minutes, fifteen. I'm losing patience, I want to scream, she should be back then there's a knock on the door. "Come in."

A small boy comes in, takes in everyone's staring eyes and blushes. Charlotte can't wait any longer. "Well what is it."

"Umm, there's a woman at the door. She says she wants to see ye or Mr Proctor."

"Where is she now."

The poor boy has found himself the centre of attention and shrinks in to his clothes completely overcome.

I understand his problem. "Don't worry, you've done just the right thing. Just tell us where she is an' ye can go."

"She's sittin' on the seat outside Mr Proctor's office."

Charlotte is first out the door. She shouts to her brother over her shoulder. "Quick and bring the camera." I follow at the back remembering to thank the boy and to tell him to get back to his job.

We run down the corridor and leap down the stairs two at a time. I've never seen Charlotte move so fast. A lady is seated on a chair. She looks very business-like with a smart black dress topped with a small hat perched above white hair scraped up in to a bun. There's a handbag by her side and a file on her lap but she's not reading. Her attention has been diverted away onto something else.

"Ah Mrs Stanningly, sorry for the wait. I'm Charlotte Sprote, the Matron." She offers her hand but it's not taken she's listening to something.

"Umm shall we go to my office?"

Mrs Stanningly finally answers in a stern low voice. "Never mind that, what is that noise." We all listen, trying to stem our fast beating hearts and short breaths. Grunting, loud sobs, a sudden crack of a stick.

I can't stop myself. "Oh my god, Millie." I stare at Charlotte for help. She has heard the noises and has set her face like rock.

"Mrs Stanningly you had better come with me, Branwell get ready." She pushes at the door, it doesn't open. She puts her shoulder and all her weight behind both arms but no reaction. She mutters it can't be locked, she feels in her breast pocket for the key. She fumbles it drops to the floor and she stoops to find it. The tortured voice is getting louder, the whip cracks more frequent.

"Out of me way." Everyone looks around Frank is running headlong towards us and the door. We step aside. He makes heavy contact, there's a splintering of wood, a crash on the other side and the door swings open. Frank stumbles, Branwell steps over, followed by Mrs Stanningly, Charlotte and me. There's a flash, then another and another.

The scene before us shows to everyone the debauchery that has been common place for years. Disgusting, demeaning, repulsive, degrading and ultimately illuminating.

"Branwell you've got what we want, get going." But Charlotte is only shouting at his back. He is already making for the front door to produce exposures for the ultimate exposure.

Proctor is moving pulling up his trousers but far too late, nothing has been hidden from view. Millie, poor Millie is bent over the desk her buttocks bare, long red wheals shouting guilty. She is still sobbing.

"What have you got to say for yourself Charles." Mrs Stanningly stares at Proctor for an explanation. She must surely know the truth.

He stammers. "Mary, I didn't know you were coming."

"Obviously."

He looks back at the still revealed buttocks "This, oh you must understand sometimes it's necessary to keep discipline, a firm hand and all that."

"I'm not looking at your hands. You are a disgrace, an embarrassment to the school, to the children and to the committee. I am now going to report what I've seen. You can be confident your days here are numbered." She looks at Millie and then to Charlotte. Get this poor girl dressed and look after her. None of this business must ever get out. Do you understand?"

Charlotte nods and Mrs Stanningly turns, picks up her file and bag and marches out of the school.

Proctor's face has been glowing bright red since we crashed in to the room. He is now trying to take control. He stares at Charlotte, points at her and screams. "You, you fabricated this, you got this boy, girl, to provoke me. You're all in it together. My report will show the committee that I was set up by a frustrated, evil, vengeful old bag, who's already on the way out. You'll never get another job no ma...."

I've had enough. "You're the one on the way out. You've made so many bairns mental wrecks over years of sexual attacks an' that includes me an'..."

I'm interrupted by a full blooded scream of "An' me". We turn to see Frank march up to Proctor. He swings his clenched fist and connects with his midriff doubling him up and then swings again and connects precisely with the point of his chin flinging him back on to the desk before rolling sideways on to the floor. Frank is now out of control venting years of pent up anger on his hate figure. He starts kicking the prone body making it jump at every contact. By the time we pull him away Proctor lay still, drooling from the mouth and blood oozing from face wounds and nose.

"He's dead."

Charlotte kneels down and feels for his pulse."No, thank goodness he's not. We'd better get him to hospital."

"Pity."

Millie's now fully dressed and surprisingly produces a broad smile but not her familiar happy, fun-loving smile I know and love but victorious, vengeful. "Ah got the bastard didn't ah?"

Chapter 16

"Ye two alright in there?"

"Alright driver, just miss the bumps."

Myself and Millie are lying back in the cart with cushions and pillows packed around us below a tarpaulin draped over a metal bar frame to protect us from the fine drizzle. I'm going back home to see my sisters with the help of Millie and Frank. They're now an item but they never leave me out and when I told them that I wanted to see Gertie and Flo, Frank immediately volunteered his horse and cart for the long journey. He did say it's alright with his boss, I just hope so, it is a long way.

Frank's reply was lost in a crack of the whip and a marked increase in speed throwing us against each other uncontrollably. Millie starts yelling at him between collisions, both of us had to hold on to something to gain some stability. A corner of the tarpaulin suddenly pulls back and a capped and scarfed Frank appears looking completely innocent of any wrong-doing.

"But madam ahm only tryin' to avoid the potholes!"

He manages to avoid laughing for a few seconds before Millie lets him know what he could do with his potholes. The cover is pulled back over amid howls of mirth. Millie looks cross but then her face changes to one of scheming devious-ness.

"Ye just wait Frank Tanner 'till ah get ye by yourself."

"Wey aye an' then what will ye do?"

"I'll, I'll....ah don't know yet but it will be painful."

I laugh with her but I know it's only words. Since we de-bagged Beetroot they've been inseparable. Frank is a man the like of which I've never met before. So considerate and caring and is never aggressive, at least not since he almost killed Proctor!

It's been over a month since that day and according to Charlotte a new man has taken his place. A strict disciplinarian but fair and, as far as she knows, has no sexual deviances. Her position in the school has been reinstated and she seems happy with that. For myself I have doubts. If we hadn't devised the Plan to reveal Proctor in his true light then nothing would have changed. It needed someone to put themselves in to grave danger. No amount of verbal or written complaints made the slightest difference. It needed action from determined people to make things happen. It shouldn't be like this but to get what's right you have to take risks and that's what we did. It's the way-of-the-world and I'm never going to forget this fact.

I think back to that fateful day. Poor Millie's buttocks were red raw. Trudie and Rose could hardly believe what they could see in front of them. Millie was not ready for the strength of the man, how powerless she was in his grip. She realised it was exactly the same as when she was a schoolgirl. Despite being older and stronger it was not enough and, like before, she gave up the struggle to stop him just to get the act finished and be released.

The physical scars are healing but I suspect will always be there, the mental scars most certainly will be. It was unfortunate that Proctor was brought to our hospital for treatment. Charlotte, bless her heart, explained to Matron as much as she could, what had happened and thank goodness we never had to work on the same ward. To everyone's relief he was released within a week. On that day we watched him leave from a top floor window. Someone collected him in an automobile, a man. Before they climbed in they both looked up at the building. I don't know if I imagined it but as if by some magnetic force our eyes met. A shuddering chill passed through me in a wave. I wondered if we would ever meet again. I desperately hoped not.

We often see Charlotte. She drops by when she's been shopping or meeting a supplier. After her first visit, the penny dropped with both of us. I turned to Millie and saw the same realisation.

"We canna call her Teddy any more."

The moustache had gone. We both gasped, hands to our mouths eyes wide open. We made jokes and laughed.

"Maybe it blew away in a high wind. She's got a boyfriend who doesn't like bein' tickled when they kiss. Losin' too much food in it!"

But although we made fun of her we both knew we didn't mean anything by it. She was now like a family aunt: helpful, friendly and comfortable and we both love her.

I haven't seen my little sisters for a long time, far too long. They must now be six years old and probably driving poor old Ettie Stephenson to distraction. She sent me a letter at the hospital and described how they're doing. This made me realise how much I'm missing them and I felt guilty that I hadn't made the effort to visit before. Ettie, right at the end, told me that she has some news but worryingly wrote no more. I wondered what on earth it could be: could she be ill, does she have to move house? The girls seem to be doing well, so it's not them.

I talked to Millie about the letter and the very next day she told me that she and Frank had arranged transport back to my village for a visit – in his cart and all three of us were going. She even swopped our shifts around so there was to be no 'ifs or buts' I was going. She managed everything except for the weather but I don't care, rain or shine I'm going home for the very first time in over three years.

Some hours after we leave I'm staring up at the cover flapping over me, hands behind my head, looking forward to arriving back at the village. The cart is rocking gently and Millie has fallen asleep. I suddenly realise that the pitter-patter of the rain has stopped and bright shafts of light were now streaking in to my hideaway. Our steady pace was slowing and I could hear a familiar sound. I sit up, crawl out from under the cover and look out. It was a beach, not any beach but my beach. The sound is from the waves slowly rising up and spreading serenely over the stones before receding back again to await their next surge. Frank pulls to a stop, I stand up and stare at the view. Nostalgia fills my very being. It's like I'd never been away. There's the rocky outcrop jutting out in to the sea unchanged and some way along, my cave our very own bat-cave. The beach itself is deserted, no, I can see two small figures with their heads down. I watch them knowing full well what they are doing. Both are young girls with head scarves tied tightly around their heads and wearing long dresses. One has a bag slung over her shoulder, the other an apron with a wide pocket at the front. They slowly make their way methodically examining the stones and every now and again pick something up and drop it in to their bag or pocket. I jump out of the cart, walk to the top of the beach and stare at the coal gatherers. I look up and down for the wheelbarrow but there is none. Surely they don't walk back to the village carrying loaded bags but then I hear another cart approaching from the opposite direction. The two girls look up and wave and start walking up the beach. One of them suddenly notices our cart on the other side and point obviously talking to her companion at the same time. They stop, the cart approaching me stops and I stare. I start slowly walking along the track towards them. I cannot believe what I'm seeing, they're not friends they're sisters. I turn off and start running, down the stony beach, half tripping, half slipping and as I get near my arms spring out and I shout to my very own twin sisters.

"Gertie, Flo."

For an instant I wonder if they recognise me. They look shocked but then look at each other to confirm their thoughts and both smile, the smiles I remember so well brightening up their pretty faces framed with blonde locks of hair escaping from their scarves. I arrive, kneel down and grab them both as one with my enveloping hug.

We chatter non-stop. My face wet with tears I garble my story of what I've been doing and both together they tell me what they've done. I can't believe how much I've missed them. How could I have stayed away for so long. I stand up and, still talking and holding hands, we walk slowly up the beach to the waiting carts. We see Frank and Millie waving on one side and Ettie waving alongside Bennie on the other. It's such a lovely reunion.

Chapter 17

Millie, myself , Gertie and Flo walk then chase, stop to show off our dresses and then walk again back along the track to the village and then on to Ettie's house. Ettie and Frank follow along behind in their carts. Our conversation is dominated by the delighted squeals, shouts and questions from the twins.

I search around to spot any changes but apart from some of the children noticeably older there are very few. All the while the tranquil, soft whooshing of the breaking waves transport me back to my childhood. I smile, pleased, despite the hard times we had, I have some happy memories. I'm surprised to find our old house is empty, Ettie tells me that several families have been in but have left within weeks. She doesn't know why, it's a mystery.

We are now sitting around Ettie's kitchen table spread with bowls of fish soup and fresh bread. Well, actually I'm on the floor back to the wall with my sisters being shown their new wooden dolls made by a local woodworker. I look around and notice familiar objects: Da's clock on the mantelpiece over the range, Brendan's model coble boat on the window sill and on the floor Ma's rag-rug she made from our old clothes. Ettie looks embarrassed but there's no need, our things are being put to good use as they should be. With the help of the villagers she seems to be coping very well. The girls go to school for a couple of hours every morning giving her time to do some paid sewing and stitching work. She proudly holds up some embroidery she's being working on. I notice the tiny, intricate needle work and wonder at the quality. Her eyes must be so sharp but then she slips on a pair of thick-lensed glasses and I understand.

News from the village confirms my visual observations that nothing much has happened. The fishermen still complain of the catches and the pitmen their conditions underground. But then comes the news Ettie mentioned in her letter. She looks over to me and smiles and prepares for her revelation. "Gertie and Flo have been sworn to secrecy so ah can tell ye mesel." She pauses and I wait, holding my breath in anticipation. "Yor Mam's comin' home in two months."

I immediately grab her hand I cannot believe it. "But Ettie ah only saw her last month an' she didn't mention anythin'."

Ettie now grabs my hand. "Your Ma told me but she didn' want to tell ye cos at that time it wasn't certain. But now it is. Good behaviour they call it." She smiles, nods and stares waiting for my reaction.

"But that's over six months early."

"Nine months actually."

I throw my arms in to the air, shout, then get up to hug Ettie, the girls grab one of my arms each grinning from ear to ear. A sudden weight I didn't know existed has been lifted and I feel exhilarated and flop back down. Millie and Frank come round to fling their arms around me. I'm so pleased, I want to cry with joy but I control my emotions and start thinking out loud.

"But Ettie where is she ganin to live, how's she ganin to cope, she's got no money. Ah could send her some an' what about Con? Can we get him out of the school like?"

"Hold on Emily pet, one step at a time. She can move in to your old house next door, the landlord will be only too pleased to let it. To pay for it she can bait lines an' gut the fish, she's done it before an' she'll do it again. As for Con, well, ah thought ye may be able to help like."

I turn and stare at Millie. "Wey aye, ah could gan an' see Charlotte, there's nothin' te stop him comin' home now."

We all gabble on suggesting all sorts it seemed all too good to be true. Ettie brings us back to earth.

"Mind Emily pet, your Ma has been through a lot in the last three years it's no holiday in prison. Ye know she's had a hard time in there, she's not the same woman as went in."

I know this, I've seen her change. She always seemed quiet, pleased to see me but reserved, never mentions the conditions or the others inside. One day I noticed she had bruises on one side of her face. She tried to hide them by sitting to one side but I'm not daft. I questioned her and she said she'd walked in to a door, as if! But I'm absolutely certain that she's craves her children and she'll soon get back to her old self.

"Ah know Ettie but no-one is. It's been over three yeors an' we've all changed." I looked over at Millie and continued in a lower tone. "An' ah 'spect Con has more than anyone." I don't go in to detail Ettie would be horrified and I don't want to upset her she's been so good to our family. She looks so pleased being able to tell me the news.

"You've done so well for yourself young Emily. Ah was so worried when ah left ye an' Con at the workhouse, especially that matron, she looked a right ol' battleaxe. But look at ye now, a fully grown woman an' a nurse. Your Mam will be so proud of ye."

I feel embarrassed and I'm probably blushing. "Thank ye Ettie but that 'ol' battleaxe' is actually very nice, we call her Charlotte, now we've left. She got us both our nursing jobs an' we still see her from time to time."

We talk and talk, about the arrangements to be made when Ma comes home, my brother Con and what the twins are doing in school. All about my family, it's only then I realise that Millie must be feeling envious: she hasn't any family that she knows of. The children and wardens at the school and now the staff at the hospital and of course Frank, are her family. She doesn't show it, she plays with the twins easily but she must feel the large gap in her life. She must wonder where her Ma is, she must have one. I have always assumed she must have been very young, unmarried, taken advantage of by some opportunist man who then disappears without trace. Mmm, I know how that feels. And where is she now? Probably no family she can turn to either. I've asked these questions so many times in my own head making up mad assumptions but Millie never speaks about her but she must wonder?

Tea finished and with Bennie and Jake in the small stable behind well in to their nosebags, we set out for a walk along the main street towards the harbour. Steps are being brushed and windows cleaned. Cleanliness has always been the byword in the village. The pitmen particularly bring in dust and clarts on their boots and it's the women's job to remove it, a daily chore. The shop is already spotless, we open the door, the bell tings and there's Mrs Maxwell completely unchanged dressed in her full length blue trimmed, gleaming white apron. She greets Ettie and the twins but doesn't recognise me.

"Alright Mrs Maxwell, how are ye?"

She looks over to me and looks puzzled, then a slow dawning. "Ruby's daughter, Emily?" I nod. "Oh my, oh my, what a bonny lass you've grown in te. Come here an' let me look at ye. She comes from around the counter, holds both my hands up and studies me from top to toe. "But you're a grown woman." She lets my hands fall and then claps. "You're the very image of your Mam when she was your age." She looks over to Ettie who nods. "An' you know she's comin' home herself soon?" I nod. "Well don't ya worry about her we'll all make sure she's right, she'll not be wantin' for anythin', mark my words." All I can do is nod again and smile before she continues un-abated. "Over three years just fo' defendin' herself an' her bairns. He had it comin' the lazy, dirty minded ne'er-do-well. Anywa' never mind about him, what you doin' for yourself now like?"

I introduce Millie and Frank and tell her all about my nursing career. She gasps and claps her hands with pleasure at my news. She's such a lovely person, always tries to see the best in everyone. I smile to myself as we leave and continue our walk down the main street. Millie notices.

"She's nice."

I nod. There's not a thing that goes on in the village that she doesn't know about. A bit of a gossip I suppose but there's nothing bad about her at all. I turn to Ettie. "Ah forgot to ask about Mr Maxwell, how is he?"

"Just the same, when he's not fishin' he's drinkin'." She peered in to the Collier's Arms which was completely empty except for ol' Stan propping up the bar in his usual place - at the far end. He turned when he heard voices, gave us a brief nod then quickly returned to his glass of brown liquid. Mr Maxwell was not to be seen. Ettie continued unshaken. "He's still a bit of a lazy bugger but ah tell ye this, he's not violent, never laid a hand on her, or anyone else come to that. More than can be said about most 'rund here."

I can't think of anything to say to this although I agree wholeheartedly. We walk on silently thinking our own thoughts disturbed only by Gertie and Flo skipping, shouting and laughing as they run on ahead. We arrive at the harbour but the small fleet of cobles is out at sea with only the odd rowing boat tied up to the wall or pulled up on to the beach alongside. The open sided gutting and packing sheds are deserted, fish cages and baskets are packed high against their walls awaiting the fishermen's homecoming. Complete silence is broken only by the soft lapping of the tide against the stone walls, the harbour flag flapping listlessly at the sea entrance and a sudden impatient call of a gull.

"It's so peaceful here." Millie has sat herself down on a basket taking in the harbour view.

A thought suddenly crosses my mind. "Ye have seen the sea before haven't ye?

"Of course, well only the once like, at North Shields. It was a school trip, ah was only about six or seven, then we went on to Whitley Bay. That was really canny, the sea was too cold so we went in to the Leisure Gardens, the Spanish City. It was amazin' but it was nothin' like this."

For the first fourteen years of my life the sea has been my daily companion sometimes calm and serene other days angry and frightening but here's my best friend seeing it for only the second time in her life. I take her by the hand. "Come on we're ganin down to the beach an' I'll introduce ye."

She looks worried. "Introduce me to who?"

I start to run, pulling her along. She's wide eyed and excited. The twins run with us, Frank and Ettie walk behind looking puzzled.

We soon reach the beach. "Right take your boots off an' your socks an' tuck your dress in to your knickers."

" What? Ahm not ganin in there, it'll be too cold."

"Rubbish." She has no choice and as soon as our legs and feet are bare I drag here in. When the first wave rolls in over our toes she tries to pull back. I realise she is actually frightened and it's not just the shock of the cold water. I keep a firm hold on her arm, then Frank appears on her other side, trousers rolled up above his knees, and grabs her other arm. To anyone looking it must look like we're going to throw her in. I turn round and see Ettie laughing at us but keeping a tight hold on Gertie and Flo. I wave and start laughing myself but in so doing completely miss a much larger wave which suddenly buries our legs under water to well above knee level. Automatically we stagger back towards dry land but are caught by the retreating surge sinking our feet in to the sand and as a group, toppling us over on to our bottoms completely soaking ourselves. We all scream and shout as one, it is so cold.

Now out of the water we scramble up on to our feet, Millie looks shocked but I know what to do. "Wey aye we'll run along the beach to keep warm an' dry our clothes at the same time." We're joined by the twins as we scamper along the sand avoiding the incoming swell of the waves. Fortunately the sun is shining and we feel warmer. Millie is now more relaxed and can now splash in to the sea without any persuasion.

"Ah feel so invigorated, can we de it again? The water feels much warmer now."

"Best if we just paddle. We need to get our clothes dry an' apart from that you'll need to learn to swim."

"Ye can teach me Emy, now." She turns to Frank. "Can ye swim?"

"Wey aye but a've never been in the sea. We used to dive in to the Tyne. It was just as cold like an' ye had all sorts floatin' about."

"Ooooh Yuk!"

"Wasnae that bad but it was best to keep your mouth well shut."

"Ooooh Yuk, Yuk, Yuk!"

Frank laughed then sat down on the sand to put his shoes and socks back on. "We'd best get back on the road if ye want to get some sleep before your shifts start."

He's right and immediately I feel sad having to leave but I'm cheered when I remember me Mam's news. Our family can be together again. I look out to sea and somehow I just knew I would see them. A white mist has formed and drifting through is a fishing boat in full sail. There's Da and my bruthers looking to shore then waving at me. They're far away but I know it's them. I wave back, Gertie and Flo do the same, we keep waving until the mist envelopes them again and then disappears leaving the horizon clear as before. I drop down on to my haunches to my sister's level and put my arms around them.

Flo whispers in my ear. "We see them sometimes an' we always wave back but we don't know who they are."

"They're yor Da an' your two older brothas. They died at sea over three years ago but ye see they haven't forgotten us an' in their way they're lookin' after us, making sure we're doin' alright. Does it make ye sad?"

"No, it's nice, we feel happy when we see them."

"Good an' so do I."

We gather our clothes together and make our way back to Ettie's home and get ready to go back to Newcastle.

Parting at the door isn't painful it's full of hope and anticipation of seeing Ma and Con again.

"Look after yourselves, it was canny to see ye an' we'll see ye again when your Ma gets home. Don't worry about these two, they're no trouble – much." She looks sternly over at the twins who are fighting over the coats.

I speak quietly to her. "You're a marvel Ettie."

She smiles. "They keep me young at heart."

The journey home is uneventful. It's dry and we sit quietly with our backs to Frank.

"Do ye always wave at the sea Emy?"

I look over to her, I can't explain what I see, she would hardly believe me. "Sometimes." I change the subject. "Millie, do ye ever think about who your Ma is an' where she is now?"

She looks surprised at the question. "Ah don't think ah did at first but the older ah get the more ah wonder. Did yor Ma comin' home make ye think about mine?"

"Wey aye, ye know maybe she's a big star on stage at the theatre or even a member of the Royal Family."

She slips her arm in to mine. "Of course she is." She laughs and then frowns. "More like she got raped by her fethor an' then told to leave home when they saw she was pregnant."

"Ye should try to look for her, no, we should both try, an' Frank. Ye never know."

She lays her head on my shoulder. "No, ye never know."

We arrive back at our digs in the pitch black of night. I thank Frank and Millie for taking me home and having such a wonderful day. I leave them outside and make my way to our room. I'm so tired, too tired to wash, I just pull off my clothes and flop in to bed. What a day, what a wonderful day that I'll always remember.

I don't remember falling asleep but I'm awake in the early hours and I have to rush to the nettie and I'm sick. I feel weak, shivery and queasy and then I'm sick again. Oh God.

Chapter 18

"Mills, Emy let me in."

I hear repeated loud, persistent knocking on our door and Trudie shouting. I must be dreaming, I turn over and bury my head in the covers.

"Hawa it's half past seven ah want to show ye somethin'."

I tense up, I'm not dreaming, this is actually happening. Then I hear movement in the room, Millie is getting out of bed, thank goodness she can deal with it. I can relax and stay under the covers.

"Mornin' Millie, did ye have a canny day yesterday?"

I hear Millie opening the door to let in Trudie then lighting the gas for the kettle. "Wey aye It was a greet day Tru, hey, wait a minute, half past seven, we don't start 'til nine."

"Sorry Mills ahm just off to me bed but ah want te show ye this." She sits on the end of my bed. "Come on Em, ye too."

I hear all this and I'm pretending to be asleep but now I'm interested and peer out over the covers.

"Well, look at ye, have ye been on the razzle or what?"

I must look terrible, I remember last night's sickness and my stomach immediately turns over again. "Sorry Trudie ah feel a bit sick. I'll be alright in a minute." I struggle up to a sitting position and she hands me a leaflet. She doesn't give us time to study it before she reads a copy herself.

"A meeting is to be held on 'Woman's Suffrage' outside the Free Trade Hall at half past three this Friday. The speaker is Lady Constance Dunlop of the WSPU."

My brain suddenly wakes up. I've read about this organisation, they don't just talk but act. They've been breaking windows, shouting down speakers at political meetings then getting arrested and thrown in prison for their troubles. I really want to go and I try to remember when I'm working.

"Ah bet ahm workin' on Friday, I'll swop with someone. What about ye two?

Trudie smiled. "A've already swopped with Rose for Saturday. She wants a night on the toon wi' her lover boy."

Millie looks forlorn. "Ahm sure ahm working that day."

I'm absolutely determined. "Well if ah canna swop ahm ganin anywa. They'll have te de without me for a few hours like."

Millie looks worried. "But Emy what if the Ward Sister finds out an' she will." She pauses then continues. "Alright look, I'll try to cover for ye but ye must tell me everythin' about it."

I've forgotten my sickness and jump out of bed and give Millie a hug. "Thanks, ah don't deserve ye as a friend."

"No, ye don't."

****

Friday morning dawned and the nausea returned. I've suffered it every day since I got back from visiting my home. Sometimes it lasts all day and sometimes just for an hour or two. Then it dawns on me – this is a real reason for having time off. I've been struggling along doing my best but it can't be good having a sick nurse in a hospital ward. My mood lightens I feel justified. With a sudden spring in my step I wash and dress and begin what could be an eventful day in my life.

Typically it's raining cats and dogs. The pavements are full of puddles, we're getting splashed by the spray from passing traffic on the road, my boots have given up trying to keep my socks and feet dry and the noise of the rain on our umbrellas shuts out most other sounds. But saying all that we just don't care. Earlier, after a bit of over-acting, Ward Sister told me to get back to bed until I get over my 'hangover', what a cheek! In fact today's nausea disappeared quickly in the morning thank goodness and I'm eager to hear what Her Ladyship has to say.

We arrive at the Free Trade Hall on time but obviously well after hundreds of other women. The square outside is full. We squeeze in to the hubbub our umbrellas strengthening the overlapping waterproof roof. Below, the maelstrom of bodies is making a cacophony of sound silencing the pitter-patter of the rain above.

I feel excited and I can see Trudie feels the same. I shout trying to make myself heard. "How are we ganin te hear her, or even know she's arrived?"

My question was answered immediately. There is a rippling of voices saying the same thing, 'she's here'. On cue the rain slows to a drizzle, the umbrella roof dismantles revealing a sea of hats, scarves and bonnets. Banners appear held high by women closer to the front. They read: Votes For Women, We Want Equality, Social Justice and many just had the abbreviation WSPU. I look around and notice we're surrounded by police.

I nudge Trudie and point them out. "Perhaps they're expectin' trouble."

Trudie shrugs. "They might get some."

I hear a shout nearby 'there she is'. I follow pointed arms to the front of the square and I see three women mounting stairs to gain a height visible to everyone. Two are dressed in black with white blouses and small black hats. The lady between them is shorter but stately. She's dressed completely in black with a large feathered hat held on by a white scarf tied around her neck. She holds up her hand and the crowd grow silent. She looks to the sky and notices the clouds chasing each other away eastwards then holds the tannoy to her lips and in a low contralto voice she booms:

"Even God is on our side."

The crowd laughs and claps enthusiastically. She unties her scarf and removes her coat leaving them by her feet. She may be short but she has a regal presence. She starts speaking, slowly at first describing the lies and deceit of the politicians. The promises made, the delays, postponements, the excuses, all the political manoeuvrings to avoid having to make unpopular and difficult decisions. She speaks clearly and emphatically so everyone can hear and understand.

It's obvious that everyone is now already on her side and she raises the tempo:

"The Women's Social and Political Union has been formed to take action. The time for talking is over, it hasn't worked. The Movement has become a laughing stock. Well I can tell you now this is going to change. We're not going to be that annoying group of gossiping women which is satisfied by a few throw away promises and forgotten a few weeks later. We're here to stay until we get what we want and we want parity and respect."

There are great cheers and shouts, banners are waved and small groups are demanding 'Votes For Women'. The police are listening, watching expressionless. They know when to react, when violence is incited. Lady Dunlop hasn't finished:

"Our aim is to make our politicians uncomfortable. We'll be knocking on their doors, we'll be at their meetings. They won't be able to turn without seeing what we're doing, what we're demanding and we will not rest and it will not stop until we women win."

More cheers, Trudie and myself join in lustily. I feel such solidarity, such determination. If this is happening all over the country we have to win! I'm glowing, I know our time is coming. No longer will we be at the beck and call of men for sexual favours, limited to breeding and drudgery. We must have the vote, to own property and be social equals. My hands have closed into tight fists and I thrust them high and shout with everyone else. Lady Dunlop holds her hand up for silence. She lowers her tone and speaks with steadfast determination.

"I can promise the politicians and the policeman around about us now, that we will not intentionally cause hurt or injury to anyone. But I

89

can guarantee, you will know where we are." After more cheers she lowers her voice and studies her audience and continues. "There is one important action to be taken now. We need your help, we need you to join our growing army of suffragettes. If you're with us then come forward and sign the form. Thank you so much for listening."

People shuffle forwards to sign, all the time the cheers and clapping seems to go on and on. We chat to our neighbours, excited, eager to help in whatever way we can. Eventually we get to the front and write down our details on the form. There must be hundreds of names. We're now all members of the WSPU, ready to change the lot of the women of our country. We begin our short walk back to the hospital when a familiar voice calls my name. "Student Nurse Mulligan." I recognise it immediately, it's my Ward Sister. She looks ferocious. "Be in my office in half an hour, is that clear?"

"Yes Sister."

I stand still completely stunned. I watch her marching away head held high, chest out. My feelings of high excitement and anticipation sink like stones.

"Oh God, ahm for it. I'll be up before Matron an' no mistake."

Trudie takes hold of my elbow. "She canna moan at ye for bein' here pet, she's here herself, she's one of us."

I look down at the ground beneath my feet wanting it to swallow me up. "Ah know but ah lied to her. She told me to gan to bed, she assumed ah was hung-over from a night out."

"The truth is that ye haven't been well for the past week. Tell her that an' say ye were ganin te yor bed straight after the meetin' here an' that ye didn't want te miss it. She'll understand, she's a supporter. Hawa we'll gan straight there, get it over with."

We walk on slowly. Trudie is still in full flow but I need to think what to say. I love my job in the hospital, I'm determined not to lose it. I'll do extra hours for nothing, do the dirtiest jobs, scrub the latrine floors, anything. But there's one thing I'm not going to do and that's give up my WSPU membership.

"Come in and sit down."

Sister is sitting behind her desk, back ramrod straight, uniform starched, perfectly in place, hands clasped in front and her face is set like stone.

"Well?"

"Ahm sorry sister, ah really have been feelin' sick but ah didn't want to miss the meetin'." I gabble on and on until she holds up her hands up silence. I stop mid-sentence.

"Never lie to me. I feel certain Mrs Sprote drummed that in to you at school." I nod. "So don't let her or me down again." I shake my head, I've used up all my powers of speech. She relaxes her shoulders and unclasps her hands. "Any more lying and I'll have no option to report you to matron." She paused. "You're an excellent student and you'll turn out an excellent nurse, so don't spoil it."

"Ah won't sister."

"The WSPU is worthy of your support, and mine, but keep their activities in your own time." I nod again. "There's another thing. A man called this morning asking for you and Student Nurse Hardy. He wanted your address. I didn't give it but I suspect he'll work out where you're staying."

My eyes shot up. "My heart leapt uncontrollably. "Did he give his name, was it Tam, Thomas, was he Scottish?"

"No he didn't." She paused. "He sounded very refined, he was older than me." She looked at me quizzically and saw me slump back in to the chair obviously disappointed. There was another pause, I looked up and saw her still looking at me. "How long have you had this sickness?"

"All week like."

"Any other symptoms?"

I look at her and wonder what she was getting at. "It's usually in the mornin' but sometimes all day, worse if we have cabbage for lunch." I don't know why I mentioned this but the very thought of the smell of cabbage makes my retch, even now.

"Is Thomas a friend of yours?"

"Yes, well no, not now."

She closes her eyes, I don't understand why she's asking me these personal questions.

"Go home now and if the sickness continues then you'd better consider your position." She gets up from her chair, "I have to see matron – about other things, off you go."

I leave confused and go and see Millie. She's in the ward above. I climb the stairs wondering what sister was getting at. I've just eaten something, or drunk something, that's all it is. And what's Tam got to do with it? I stop dead, my hands fly to my face. "Ah canna be, ah jist canna be." I flop down on to the stairs devastated.

"Emy, what's wrong." Millie finds me and jumps down the stairs and stoops down.

I look up, tears in my eyes. "Millie ahm pregnant."

Chapter 19

"Ah did wonder". Millie is now sitting down beside me holding my clenched hands.

"It's never crossed me mind. The first an' only time an' ah fall for it. What's ganin to happen to me job here?"

"It's not certain yet but if ye are, we'll have to sort somethin', both of us, Trudie and Rose. We're your friends we'll look after ye. Hawa a've just finished let's gan for a walk."

Everything adds up, morning sickness, familiar smells now making me retch. I've even gone off my old favourite – a cup of tea. Millie has led me down to the river and along the well trodden path running alongside. The river's always busy with boats of all sizes but I don't see or hear them. Instead I see Tam walking towards me, smiling, hands stretched out to me. We're kissing gently then more urgently. His hands are sliding over my clothes then searching underneath. We're both gasping, moaning but I don't know what to do, I'm putty in his hands, I know I won't be able to stop him, I don't want to stop him. Then we're both naked on his bed, his deep inside. He's thrusting, withdrawing , thrusting again on and on. It's hurting me but I feel a deep sensation I've never felt before. He's body is damp, I can smell his body odour. I want to push him away but he's too heavy. Then he stops his eyes are closed, he groans loudly and I feel him coming. We cuddle each other tightly waiting for the intense sensation to subside. When it does he withdraws, gets dressed and walks away. He's now laughing, his head thrown back as if in victory, rubbing his hands proud of his success. The bastard.

Someone's talking to me, I look up. Tam is nowhere to be seen he's been replaced by Millie.

"If ye are pregnant ye should tell Tam. He should look after ye."

I look at her as if she was speaking in a foreign language. "Oh wey aye, find his house an' explain all this to his wife an' bairns. She's sure to understand. Millie there is no way ahm ganin to see that bastard again. If ah am pregnant then I'll look after the bairn somehow. Ah was stupid enough to fall for his sweet talkin', it's my responsibility alright?"

I can see I've shocked and surprised Millie but she adds quietly. "An' your friends will help."

My anger subsides and I hold her hand. "Sorry Mils." I feel bad for shouting, I add, "an' thank ye, ah think I'll need it."

Weeks have gone by I just know I'm pregnant, my breasts have grown larger and my hips seem to be spreading but at least the daily nausea is receding and I can now drink a cup of tea and enjoy it! Only my close friends know although I'm sure my Ward Sister is well aware. I keep working as if nothing has changed. I do feel worn out by the end of my shift and my social life outside of the hospital confines is growing less. Despite the absent father I'm actually looking forward to seeing the baby. Mentally I gloss over the giving-birth bit. I'll worry about that nearer the time.

My ten hour shift has ended and I'm making my way back to the digs. The Ward Sister has a word with me on my way out. She tells me to put my feet up and eat good food. She knows full well. All I can do is smile sheepishly and say: "Ah will, thank ye."

It's only a ten minute walk but there are no lights and at night the usual direct route is pitch. I consider taking the well lit route along the main road but decide against it, I want to get home. Just a couple of minutes along it dawns on me that I'm normally accompanied with someone and very rarely do I come this direct route in the dark by myself. I start to hum and sing to myself. I notice a shadowy figure coming towards me at a run. I back up against the side of a building. I find I'm holding my breath and trying to bury myself in to the brickwork. The shadow is approaching fast, it's almost upon me and then realise it's another nurse

94

probably late for her shift. My breath is released like a tornado. My shoulders relax and I move away from the wall smiling to myself. I think stupid woman, get a gr----. A bright torchlight is suddenly flashed in to my eyes. My hand automatically covers them.

I shout. "Who's that? Is that ye Millie?

A man's voice replies, a voice I remember only too well. "Well, well, Miss Mulligan. I'm so pleased to have found you."

"What do ye want ye creep."

The torch is still full on straight in to my eyes, I can't see a thing.

"Now that's not a nice thing to say to your school headmaster. The person who helped you get your job here."

"There's only one thing ye taught me – never trust a man, he may well be like you, a pervert."

The torch light suddenly swung away and I could suddenly see his silhouette. He's walking forward quickly his arm in the air. The torchlight is swinging back towards me, I duck low, the light swings over my head and I charge him full in the chest and push him against iron railings and he crumples down at my feet. The impact releases the torch, I reach down, grab it and point it at him. His face is contorted with rage. Even in the glare I can see it's turned a blotchy, deep, red beetroot colour. I make the mistake of staring too long. He grabs my ankles and sends me flying banging my head against the brick wall opposite. I clutch my head in pain but he's on me in an instant grabbing my neck with both hands.

"I'm going to teach you not to mess with me you bitch."

His grip is getting tighter, I go for his wrists and realise I'm still clutching the torch. With all my strength I jab in to his face and again and again as hard as I can. I feel myself choking but at last he releases his grip and tries to grab the torch. I pull it back, he misses, I swing it round and catch his head side on. It catches him off balance and he rolls over. I get up and shout for help at the top of my voice.

He's up on his feet and makes a grab for my coat. "Oh no, you won't get away with it this time."

I feel a punch to the side of my face that sends me flying in to the railings and I scream and scream.

"Scream all you want, there's no-one here to hear you." He pulls his arm back to punch me again but another torch light appears, wavering, being held by someone running. The wonderful sight of a policeman appears. He grabs Proctor's punching hand.

"What's ganin on here then."

Proctor tries to release himself but he's held firm. "She's just a whore. I'm a respectable man she's been trying to accost me."

The torchlight switches to me still up hard up against the railings. He sees what I'm wearing.

"This young lady is a nurse. You're the one who's doin' the accosting. Ye better come with me to the station."

Proctor pulls hard with the strength I know he has. The policeman is now struggling to hold on, with his other hand he manages to pull out his truncheon and clubs him hard to the side of his head. The blow careers Proctor in to the brick wall head first. He slumps to the ground out cold.

The policeman examines him. "Ah don't think he'll be givin' ye any more trouble miss." He walks over to me and examines my face. "That's a nasty one. I'll accompany ye back to the hospital."

I cover the bruised and sore side of my face with one hand and point to the still figure of Proctor with the other. "What about him."

"Don't ye worry about him young lady, he's dead."

Chapter 20

"Yes!" Millie punched the air, her face full of unbounded joy.

"Millie, how could ye?"

She rocked back in her chair by my hospital bed. "Easily, A've dreamed of this day an' now it's happened." She punches the air again completely unashamed.

My frown slowly turns in to an embarrassed smile, then in to a joyous laugh and I join her in throwing both my arms in the air in jubilation. I should have been horrified. I was at first but then realisation followed. Retribution, revenge, vengeance, years of scores settled for countless children.

"Oh Millie, this is just too bad bein' so pleased that someone has deed."

But I can't stop smiling. One side of my face is swollen and all colours and there are bruises around my neck but it was worth those few minutes of utter terror. The policeman had just left him where he fell and took me back to the hospital. I was stunned, I asked him what was going to happen. "Resisting arrest an' you're my witness an' your injuries are the proof. His next of kin will be notified an' they will make all the arrangements from there on in. I'll have to make out a short report but all ye have to do is get better. By the way did ye know him?"

I explained that I did, who he was and briefly why he wanted to kill me.

He shook his head. "Ah think ah did the world a favour." He added. "Look ah realise this was a particular circumstance but it may be better if ye chose another route back to your digs at night or at least gan with someone else, safety in numbers an' all that."

"Yes, ah will." I thought I never want to go that way ever again.

The Ward Sister herself patched me up and had insisted that I used one of the beds to recover. She gave me a look of concern and warned. "There are no broken bones, these injuries will soon disappear but we have to consider someone else don't we?"

All I could do was nod and say thank you. My friends came round today one after the other so I had to relay the story each time. Then Millie, just starting her shift, ran in. "Ah was so worried when ye weren't in yor bed this mornin'. Ah thought there must have been an emergency here but when Rose told me what happened ah couldn't believe it like."

She hasn't stopped smiling since.

Last night I relived the attack. I was proud of myself how I stood up to him but I realised if the policeman hadn't arrived I would have been very badly hurt if not killed by the madman. I owe him my life, I'm deeply indebted. I got very little sleep. Every time I drifted off the horrific image of his enraged face appeared before me larger than life. I can still see it and probably will for many years to come. His wide open, staring eyes, skin covered in deep red blotches with bubbling spittle around his mouth. I recalled his heavy breathing, gasping from his exertions and that manic, victorious smile when he thought he had me where he wanted me. I was pleased when the nurses changed shift and the curtains were drawn allowing the soft early morning light to light up the familiar ward furnishing. The Ward Sister came to see me before she left. She told me that I'd have some visitors, Charlotte Sprote and a policeman. "He's going to interview Miss Sprote and then you, but not to worry I've already had a word with him, it's just routine."

The nurse has sneaked me an extra cup of tea and just as I take a sip I hear a rapid clip clop of heels on the hard floor. I somehow knew who it was. I look up and take in the lady striding towards me dressed in a smart full length brown wool coat and black hat, I was right. "Hello Charlotte."

"Oh my dear, how are you pet? That must have been a nightmare."

"Yes it was but he's now dead, He canna de any more harm."

She sat down next to the bed and held my hand. "Thank God for that. But how did he know you were here?"

"He's obviously been searchin' for me an' Millie. He knew our names an' tried his luck here an' he hit the jackpot. He must have been watchin' us comin' an' ganin, gettin' to know our routine an' lurkin' in the shadows like. He was lucky to get me by mesel. It makes me shiver to wonder what would have happened if the poliss didn't heor me shout for help."

"How creepy, what a sick man. But there's plenty about Emily. You take another route in future pet."

"Don't worry Charlotte ah will."

"Good, now, how are you getting on? That face looks sore."

We chat for a while until I see the same policeman from last night escorted in to the Sister's office. I point him out to Charlotte.

"I was asked to come here to corroborate your story I suppose. It'll confirm the motive behind his attack on you."

Sister came out and waved at Charlotte to go in. After she had left I was waved in for my turn. It seemed to be a clear cut case but I wasn't so sure. It reminded me too much of the cover-up when I killed Uncle Joseph and Ma had to take the blame.

I quickly step out of the hospital slipover and into my nursing uniform still complete with the dirty marks down one side. The policeman is much younger than I'd realised. He stands up when I enter and gives a nervous cough and at the same time he points to the chair.

"Thank ye Miss, err Mulligan. I won't keep ye long. Please tell me what happened last night, in yer own words, from the beginning."

As I relay my story yet again he's busy scribbling down everything I say in his notebook. I finish and wait for him to complete his writing. "Also ah want to thank ye for savin' me, ah think he would've killed me."

He immediately blushes crimson and gives me a fleeting smile that suddenly lights up his solemn face. "That's alreet Miss." He coughs again, and puts away his notebook and pencil. He rises from the desk and reaches for his coat.

"Is that all, will there be a trial?"

"I canna imagine so. I'll give the report to my Sergeant at the station an' he'll decide." He gives me another quick look, he still looks flushed but continues. "It's an open an' shut case in my view. I don't think ye'll hear from us again. Umm, how's your face Miss?"

"Sore but it's only bruising it's not as bad as it looks."

"Good, right... I'll be goin' then. Goodbye Miss."

I follow him out the door. "Goodbye an' thanks again." I watch his back thinking he's a nice man. He turns to me as he goes through the door and gives me another flashing smile before he disappears. "Yes he is very nice."

Chapter 21

I have heard nothing more on Proctor's death, my bruising has gone and I'm only left with the continually recalled image of his face contorted by madness. Like the image of Uncle Joseph lying dead in my bedroom I have to assume this will fade in time.

I must be three months pregnant now and I feel just great. No sickness nausea, no aversion to smells or my cup of tea, thank goodness. I'm looking forward to seeing my baby. It's morning and I'm chatting to Millie in our digs about the meetings we've had with the WSPU. In particular our recent demonstration outside the Council offices held to coincide with a much larger demonstration in London.

The Conciliation Bill was drawn up to give certain women the right to vote at a General Election but it failed despite the promises of the Prime Minister. We held banners high, we shouted abuse at the politicians and to the police surrounding us. Unlike in London there was no fighting, no stones thrown or anything like. We were both surprised how little support we got from the people of Newcastle. Most upsetting to me was the abuse from women suggesting our place was at home and not to meddle with men's affairs. How narrow minded, how disrespectful to your own sex. I realise that to change beliefs held for generations past, will take time. But you have to start somewhere and this is that time.

The police cordon was tightly controlled preventing us getting close to the main entrance but we could see faces at the windows, press reporters and photographers taking notes and photos of our leaders. We were making our mark. Our leader made a short speech and thanked us for supporting our demands before we started to drift away. The police cordon broke up and we all mingled together as if nothing had happened. It was only then that I noticed a familiar smile. A policeman with his helmet held under his arm approached us.

"Hello Miss Mulligan, how are ye."

Millie looked surprised but I smiled back at him. "Much better thank ye."

"Good, good." He didn't know what to say next and blushed. "Umm.. no more problems ah hope."

"No, ah always take the main road route back to my digs now."

"Good, good." There was another silence. "Well ah must be ganin, bye Miss."

"Goodbye, oh, by the way what's your name?"

"PC Symonds, er Stanley Symonds, Stan."

"Goodbye Stan, ahm Emily by the way."

He smiled, popped his helmet back on, said goodbye, smiled again before he turned and walked briskly away.

Millie was dumbstruck, but not for long. "Well you're a dark horse, who was that?"

I told her that he was my hero who saved my life. "Did ye spot that smile."

"Ye canna miss it, but ahm not sure ye should be fraternising with the enemy."

"Oh don't be daft, he's not the enemy, he's just doin' his job."

"But you was fraternisin' all the same."

I pretended not to know what she meant and we laughed about it all the way back, but I didn't deny it.

"Ahm coming in, decent or not." Our door flies open and Trudie marches in complete in her uniform ready for her shift, she sees us lounging on our beds still in our nightdresses. "It's alreet for some! Here Emy, I met the postie, this is for ye." She throws the letter at me. I grab it in anticipation an' try to recognise the writin'.

"Come on, there's only one way to find out like."

I break open the envelope and start reading the letter, just one page. "Ah don't believe it. It's from Ettie. Me Mam's comin' out Friday next week."

"That's great news Em but ye knew she was due out."

"Ah know, ah know. Oh my goodness I'll have to meet her an' then take her home an' then get Con out of the school. How will she cope after all this time? Oh dear, oh dear." My eyes widen, a reflection of so many un-answered questions.

"Em, one step at a time. Ye need another cuppa an' we can talk through it with ye."

"Have to leave me out for now a've got to get ganin but ahm so pleased for ye Emy." Trudie gives me a hug and rushes out the door with a last 'see ye later' thrown over her shoulder.

Myself and Millie talk through all the arrangements that have to be made. Travel to the prison in Durham by train and an omnibus back to the village. I'll take some time off to settle Ma back and help her cope with the twins. In her letter good old Ettie says that she has already managed to secure our old house and made some enquiries on work down at the harbour. By the time we're dressed for our own shifts my panic has subsided and I can look forward to making a new life for my family. There are so many uncertainties of course. I know you can't possibly take over from when you left off as if nothing has happened. How will the twins feel, how much has prison changed her, how will she feel about her daughter being pregnant and then there's Con. So many uncertainties but I feel a warm anticipation spreading through me. I know we'll all pull together and have the warmth of a family life again. It hits me hard how much I've missed it. I so want it back.

It's Friday, the day has dawned and I wait patiently under the huge canopy of Newcastle-on-Tyne Central Railway Station. Each time I travel to see me Mam I sit on a platform bench and marvel at the size of the building particularly the great arch spanning over the numerous railway lines and platforms. I still jump at the sudden whistles and I smell the coal burnt by the shiny, bright green mechanical monsters clanking by. They're wreathed in clouds of steam and smoke with the words 'North Eastern Railway' emblazoned on their sides. They pull long rakes of coaches full of passengers on their way to York or London, Manchester or Scotland. I see a destination label for Edinburgh and my heart jumps. I feel for the swell of my growing baby inside, still indiscernible by anyone else. I wonder if Tam has any idea, does he ever think about me? As if. And what will Ma think about it? I sigh: will she be disappointed or even ashamed of me? I sit lost in my thoughts and in a mist of white smoke drifting past.

I jump as a railway man shouts nearby, 'All aboard for Darlington, Durham, York and London.' My train has pulled in. I spring up and join the crowd pressing forward to choose their seats for the journey. I manage to get a place by a window and with all other seats in the compartment filled the locomotive whistles and we set off slowly but surely. The station platform and offices and all the people left behind on the platform drift backwards. I always have a desire to wave goodbye but I resist, allowing my hand to just lift a fraction before bringing it down on to my lap feeling silly. Free of the station I gaze at the familiar sites of Newcastle until they too are left well behind and we're rolling along through the countryside occasionally misted by drifting clouds of steam. I settle down ready to enjoy the journey and mentally prepare to meet me Mam.

Leaving the hubbub of Durham station I'm soon approaching the prison in what I thought was well in time. The prison itself is a vast complex of large factory size buildings making my workhouse school look small and insignificant. I know the way to the entrance gate. The roads are quiet here with few people about. I see a lady standing outside wearing a long black coat a bag by her side. She's looking around and seems to be lost. As I get nearer I recognise her, it's me Mam. Oh no, I'm late. I run the last fifty yards, she sees me and smiles.

"Sorry Ma, ah didn't think ah was late."

She doesn't answer but returns my hug tightly. We stay clasped together for a long time, I can feel her shaking. It's the first time we've been able to touch each other for over three years. I wasn't ready for this, uncontrolled tears flow down my face, it's so wonderful she's free and with me. I pull myself together and pull back and we examine each other. Both of our faces are streaked with tears. I see again how she's lost weight, her face is gaunt and her coat now looks too big for her shrunken body. She looks much older than her forty three years not helped by the severe cut of her hair.

"Ye look well pet."

I smile. "Thanks Ma." I add, "an' by the time a've finished with ye, so will you."

"Do ah look that bad?"

"Ye just need fattenin' up a bit."

"And ah need to be with me family."

"Oh Ma." I can't say anything else and we just hug again.

Our journey back on the train is filled with me chattering about my job, the twins, Ettie and the house and of course Con. She nods and smiles and in between times she just stares at the passing scenery. I've already decided to take her back to my digs and catch the omnibus back home Saturday morning. Millie suggested it saying she can bed down with Trudie and Rose. "She'll be tired an' bewildered. It'll give her time to re-adjust before the next stage of her homecomin'." And she's right, Ma clung on to me tightly while we zigzag our way through the crowds at the station in Durham, her eyes darting around trying to take it all in. Conditions in the prison must have been terrible to endure for over three years but she had a routine and now suddenly she's turfed out in to a changed world.

Newcastle is even busier of course, a place she hasn't seen since she was courting with Pa. I have to explain about the rising popularity of the new noisy motor cars and omnibuses that seem to go by themselves followed by clouds of acrid smoke. I proudly show her the hospital where I work and try to paint a picture of what it's like inside. She nods and smiles but still with her arm firmly grasped around mine.

"An' this is where ah stay. It's full of nurses, they come an' go at all times of the day." Even as I speak two girls in uniform burst out of the doors and run down the steps towards us.

"Hi Emy, gota rush, see ye later." They notice Ma by my side.

"This is me Mam."

"Oh, hello Mrs Mulligan, nice to see ye." They smile and rush on.

Mum nods and watches them rush away half walking, half running. "They look so smart in their uniforms."

"An' so do I!"

"Ah bet ye do." She gives my arm a tug. "Ahm so proud of ye."

I immediately feel guilty. She's put me on a pedestal but she doesn't know what a predicament I'm in. What a stupid thing I've done and here she is, just finished over three years in prison for something she never did.

"Thanks Ma but not as proud as I am of you."

I open the door to my room expecting the usual post-earthquake jumble of clothes and bags and find to my amazement a clean and tidy room. Beds are made, the floor empty of debris, everything in its right place. I can hardly believe it, for a second I wonder if I've entered another room. I see a note on the table leaning up against a teapot.

"Come in Ma an' take a seat. I read the note:

'Hi Emy, how about this for a room, I swapped it for our old one! I might be able to pop in before you leave tomorrow morning, Millie.'

I think how wonderful it is to have such a friend. I behave as if the room is always like this. "Like a cuppa Mam?"

She nods and smiles. "Yes please pet." She looks around the room and keeps smiling, I guess why but still ask.

"An' what are ye smiling at?"

"Ye must have quite a friend, unless of course yiv changed since a've been away."

"Ah don't know what ye mean, ahm sure. I'll gan an' get yor tea."
Before I leave, I turn round at the door and laugh. "You're just too bad
Ma, as if ah was ever untidy."

For the rest of the afternoon we sit and chat. She wants to know all
about the workhouse school, what the conditions and the staff were
like. For the most part, after the initial shock at the beginning, I enjoyed
myself. She seems pleased. Of course I don't mention the downsides;
the strict discipline, the punishments, Proctor. Whenever I think of him
I feel the guilty pleasure of knowing that he won't be molesting any
more children and that I helped to end his reign at the school, and of his
life on this earth. Then I think of Stan.

I've decided that one of my main aims is to feed her up, get some
good food down her but it's not easy. Her appetite has vanished. I lay a
sandwich down in front of her for tea and prepare a proper meat stew
for dinner but she just pecks at the food.

"Now Ma, ye know what ye used to tell me". I try to emulate her:
"Now lass, get that scran doon ye, what ye don't eat now you'll get at
the next meal, an' the next 'till it's gone, alright."

She laughs and she tries a few more mouthfuls but the empty plates
she leaves are as a result of my help, I now have the appetite of a horse
and I think I know why.

The nights are drawing in and I have to light our gas mantle. We get
ready for bed early, I can see she's tired and I help her in to her
nightdress, I recognise it from years ago, at home, but she's now lost in
it, she must be half her weight. I'm determined to make sure she gets
back to as she was. I feel our roles have been reversed, I'm the carer
and she's the child. I wonder if she can gain control of her own life
again. She's in bed looking at me getting ready, studying me. I feel
embarrassed, I know I've developed since I was fourteen and
particularly now I'm pregnant but my stomach is still flat she can't
possibly know of the baby growing inside. I realise that I have to tell
her sometime soon, but not yet. She's not ready, nor am I.

I turn down the light and we settle down and say good night. I can somehow sense that Ma is deep in thought and it's no surprise when she starts speaking.

"Emily?"

"Yes Ma."

"Who's the father?"

Chapter 22

"Pet, ye don't have to explain. Ah got pregnant with our Brendan before we were married."

I'd started to tell her my story, the ugly truth behind my condition, when she interrupted me. I'm shocked, it was out of the blue, so unexpected. "I didn't know."

"We had no choice but to get wed, both our parents saw to that. I'll always remember me fether's face. He wasn't angry, he didn't shout an' rave, he just looked so sad. Ah had let him doon an' he blamed himself, not me or yor Da. Ye see he thought it was his job to raise us in his treasured Catholic beliefs. So there were no histrionics, no threats, just a quickly arranged weddin' an' a bairn four months later. Mind we had to move awa from Seaham, it was only a weeny place then like, an' don't get me wrong they were canny folk, but that sort of thin' was shameful an' ah would never have coped wi' the looks an' gossip."

"Ahm not ganin to get married an' certainly not to Tam. He's just a handsome, smooth talkin', selfish bastard an' ah fell for it. Ah pity his poor wife."

"Emily love, he's a man an' that's what they de. Your Da was bettor than most. Oh he had his faults, mostly the drink, but he did love his family an' he supported us until he died. Many a man falls short of that."

"But Mam, what do ye think about me?"

"That's easy. You're a determined, hard workin', carin' hinny who's been caught. But ah know ye have the strength to carry on an' by the sound of it ye want to make some changes. But pet, ye have to be canny, yas tryin' to change a world run by men. Why should they let ye? Despite our old Queen rulin' for so many years, the power of men remains the same. You'll have to ruffle some feathers good an' proper to make a difference."

"An' that's what ahm ganin to do Ma, make a difference, no matter what it takes. Ahm ganin to have me bairn but that's not ganin to stop me."

"Good for ye an' I'll support ye where an' when ah can but, for me, just for now, ah want to gan home to look after yor sisters an' brotha."

"Thanks Ma. Good night."

"'Night pet."

I'm so relieved. I feel the burden of pregnancy has been lifted. No recrimination, histrionics and crucially Ma showed no disappointment. I haven't let her down. Thank goodness I don't know how I could have coped with that. I can now relax and look forward to tomorrow's trip home.

Someone is up at five o'clock blundering about in the dark. Still half asleep I think Millie has come in from her night shift. Then coming to, I realise it's me Mam.

"Ma, what ye doin' out of bed it's too early?"

"Hawa Babs, get up, we're late, we'll get locked in."

I spring out of bed and grab her. "Mam, you're not in prison, you're with me, Emily, in me room in Newcastle."

Her eyes are staring at me but unseeing. "Barbara, what ye doin', come on, get dressed."

I try to speak calmly but assertively. "Mam, you're sleep walkin'. Ye must get back to bed now." I take her by the hand and try to lead her back to bed. But she's tense and fighting to get away from my grip, she shouts. "Na, na, come on we've got to get ganin." I hold her firmly by the shoulders and manage to sit her back down on to the bed. I sit beside her. I say soothing words trying to comfort and to re-assure. Eventually I feel her relax and she lays back down on to the pillow. She's still mumbling, mostly incoherently but the odd word comes out crystal clear: latrines, jankers, solitary, beat me 'rund the face,

Gertrude, Florence. I lay down beside her and cuddle her like a baby until all I can hear and feel is the soft breathing rhythm of sleep.

I'm still in her bed and I can see the glow of the early morning sunshine lightening up the sky. I haven't been able to get back to sleep. I can't help but wonder what she's been through and all for me. How much love can you have for someone to suffer so much. I'm overcome with emotion and tears roll down each side of my face and dampen the pillow. I ask the same old question: Why is it always women who suffer so much and men just.... . My tears dry, I stare at the dawn-lit ceiling. Silently I vow to change it or, God help me, I'll die in the attempt.

I'm in that half awake, half asleep time when reality and dreams overlap. I hear a knocking. I lie in bed wondering where it was coming from then: "Emily." Then another knock, my eyes widen, it's my door and someone's calling me. I sit up suddenly pulling my arm from under Ma causing her to roll over. "Emily," more urgently this time, "are you awake?" I swing my legs out of bed and put on my dressing gown. I know that voice, it's not Millie, Charlotte! I run to the door, unlock it and swing it open. The sight before me is something I have never dreamed of. Two people, one was my beaming, buxom, moustache-less friend Charlotte Sprote bundled up in a long wool coat, hat and scarf. The other holding on to her with one hand and the other holding a swollen cotton bag is a skinny young lad, beaming from ear to ear, his lovely familiar and well scrubbed face almost hidden within a cloth peaked cap, my Con.

I gaped, I can't speak. I just open my arms wide, he releases his bag and his hold on Charlotte and throws his arms around my neck gripping me tightly.

"Millie's told me all about your Mam coming out and you taking her back home so we thought.... well, here he is."

111

"Oh Charlotte that's wonderful. Look ye must come in an' have a cuppa." I feel a hand on my back, I turn to see Ma just behind looking at Con. I step aside out the way of their reunion.

"Hello me son."

Con's eyes are staring, for a second he doesn't recognise her then. "Ma?"

"Yes ahm your Ma."

Still unsure he walks towards her, she pulls him to her bosom and cuddles him tightly, head on his shoulder, her damp eyes closed. Con's arms respond and he flings them around her waist. "A've missed ye."

I try but I can't hold back the tears myself and I grab hold of Charlotte's arm. I realise she's also crying moping her face with her hankie.

I didn't hear the approach of someone behind but I hear a laugh. "Well ahm so pleased it's a happy reunion."

"Oh Millie." I attempt to wipe my eyes on my sleeve. "Look ye must all come in we'll have a celebration cup of tea.. an' ah might have some orange juice." I look at Con who's now overcome with emotion looking from one woman to another but still maintaining his firm hold on Ma's hand. He can only nod.

"Oh Ma this is me friend Charlotte Sprote the school matron an' this is Millie who ye can see is also a nurse. Millie was also at the school. She normally sleeps in here. It seems these two together have planned this without tellin' me anythin' at all."

"Ahm so grateful to ye both, all three of ye. Ye don't know what it means to me."

Millie took charge. "Look, all ye make yourself at home, I'll bring the tea an' juice in." She smiles and walks off to prepare the drinks in the kitchen.

Soon we're all sitting on the un-made beds facing a table full of drinks and a special tin of biscuits. We talk about the school, the hospital and about our journey home. Ma doesn't say very much but I

112

catch her studying me and Con. I'm still shocked at how thin and pale she looks but most importantly she's looking happy. I hope her long term in prison fades in her memory and she can get back to what she wants more than anything else – to care for her children.

Chapter 23

I'm staring out the window of our omnibus, I'm looking at the sea but not seeing it. My mind is elsewhere with Ma and Con. They're sitting in front, they've been chatting for most of the journey. With time Con has overcome his bewilderment and loosened his vocal chords. He seems to be back to his old self. No mention has been made of Proctor of course. He's been put to the back of his mind but I'm sure he's there lurking ready to knock him sideways. I know how important it is for him to talk about it and try to release the demon. I've been so lucky with Charlotte, Millie and my other friends. If I'd had to keep it all inside I'd be a mental wreck by now.

I've decided. I'm going to speak to Ma before I leave, explain everything. She has to know because she'll have to deal with it. She'll need to talk it through with Con. It's the only way.

Con suddenly points out of the window. "Look Ma there's our beach with the bat cave. Emy look."

All three of us stare out at the familiar scene. I wonder if my sisters would be there but there was no-one. The tide is on the way in, coal gatherers need a retreating tide for the best results. But I know they would be ready with their barrows and carts, some things will never change.

We arrive at our house, the street was empty save a young lad who sees us and scampers away in to the distance and down one of the alleyways. The driver slows and stops right outside and we all jump down with our cases and shout out our thanks. We watch the omnibus accelerate away, noisily at first but quietening as it gathers speed and then silence as it disappears past the far end of the village. The door opens to reveal a smiling Ettie Stephenson.

"Welcome home Ruby pet."

I can see, peering around the door, are two curly blond haired six year olds. "Come on ye two, who's this?"

Ma's hand goes to her mouth smothering her gasp of surprise. "Gertrude, Florence?"

They both nod in unison.

Ma bends down on to her knees and holds out her arms. "I'm your Mam, do ye remember me?"

They nod again but are uncertain. Ettie waves them over and they step slowly forward until they are just out of Ma's reach. But Ma steps forward and envelops them in to her arms and she holds them tightly, her eyes now tight shut. I can see the girls relaxing in her grip and they start giggling at being squashed. Ma releases them and they both give her a kiss on her bony cheeks.

"And girls look here's your brutha Con." Con approaches awkwardly. I can see he can hardly believe the change in them. But he bends down and gives them a kiss on the tops of their heads.

I say to them. "Come on you two give him a big cuddle you've not seen him for over three years, don't ye recognise him?"

Gertie looks put out. "Yes I dee." Bravely she steps forward and puts her arms around his waist, Flo follows suit not quite so certain.

"It's been a lang time Ruby. It's canny to see ye."

I hear a door opening down the street and a smiling woman steps out and walks towards us. Then a door on the opposite side opens and a woman with young children behind cross the road and approach us. Then I can see Mrs Maxwell look out of her shop door, she sees us and smiles, strips off her apron, throws it inside and almost runs to us, then another and another until it seems the whole village is on the move. I've never seen anything like it. It's a tidal wave of familiar faces all smiling, all so pleased to see and be a part of Ma's homecoming.

Ma is completely overcome, she's crying and greeting and laughing.

Ettie shouts above the voices. "There's some scran on the table, you're all welcome." She turns to Ma. "An' ye can stop yor bubblin',

115

there's a cuppa waitin' an' your favourite chair." She takes Ma's hand and leads her in to her house.

Our house was cold and empty the last time I was here. But now, I look about me, mouth agape. All her old furniture is back, pictures on the shelves and dressers and her old range is alight and warming the rooms. Our kitchen table is buckling under the weight of plates of sandwiches, sausage rolls, cakes, juice and of course several large pots of steaming tea surrounded by cups. Then I see a large wooden board hanging above the range. It's a sign and on it are large painted letters they read:

'Welcome Home Ruby'.

****

It's been two days since I took Ma and Con back home. I'm now on the omnibus back to Newcastle and I'm re-living the reunion and keep smiling to myself recalling images of delight and surprise. I just know my family are in good hands. Ettie had done so much to welcome them and the rest of the village all helping out. It gives me a warm glow inside reaching out to the top of my head to the end of my toes. I have to go back to the hospital but I will return. I want to see Ma fatten up and Con of course.

My kid brutha......he was so pleased to be home. He would look around the house, the backyard, his little sisters and he would just smile. He couldn't stop himself. It was as if he never thought it would happen, that he would be in the workhouse forever.

This morning I sat with Ma in the kitchen while Con and the twins were getting Bennie ready. I had to physically sit her down, stop her fiddling. Then, as best I could, I told her of Con's years of torment at the hands of Proctor. She said nothing except when I'd finished she thanked me for telling her then put her hand on mine and added 'Ah understand pet, it goes on in all institutions.' Leaning out of the omnibus window waving to everyone waving back I saw that Ma was holding Con tightly by the hand. It was then I knew he was in the best

116

hands, with someone who understands and, I suspect, has suffered equally.

We bump our way on the rough road above the beach, our beach. I remember my coal gathering of yesterday, probably for the last time. Me, Con, Flo and Gertie were in the cart with Ma driving Bennie. How we children ran down to see the cave and re-told our favourite scary stories, then paddling in the breaking, freezing cold waves. I knew it would happen: there was our coble, 'The Henry and James' with Pa, Brendan and Patrick waving. I looked back and saw Ma had walked half way down the beach and was also waving out to sea, she was smiling, happy, at long last.

The beach is soon lost to view but I have my memories forever. Living in a small mining, fishing village can be tough, unrelenting but the community spirit is binding and the air here is clean, fresh. All is far removed from Newcastle's squalor of smoking chimneys, sooted factories buildings and the constant, nose to tail traffic on the roads. But this is where I'm heading and where my future lies and this is where I can help make a change for the better.

Chapter 24

1911 – The policeman's Story

"Here's yor scran love an' a've given ye a couple of biccies, on the quiet like."

"Thanks."

"If ye divvint mind me saying like, why do ye do this in yor condition?"

"Ahm pregnant, it's not an illness. Some things you've got to stand up for an' me an' my girl are both doin' it, alright?"

"Alright, alright don't get narked." The policeman turned and went to leave but before he left he asked. *"How do ye know it's a lassie?"*

"Ah just know."

He smiled and banged the cell door behind him, turned the key and looked through the grill. *"Sleep tight."* He walked back to his office past the other cells shaking his head. He couldn't understand what this suffrage was all about. His wife was happy at home looking after their three children, she didn't want to vote. She doesn't understand politics, she wouldn't know who to vote for anyway. He settled down behind his desk and stared at his steaming mug of tea reliving his day - and what a day.

It had started quietly enough: they were ordered to accompany a group of demonstrators outside the Free Trade Hall, nothing new there. The women dispersed around mid-day and they left to get on with their regular work. Then, in the middle of the afternoon, the alarm was called. There was a disturbance along the High Street, every man had to drop everything and get over there fast.

He recalled the tempestuous scene before him: the shouting, the crowds of onlookers then a crash of glass, more shouting. A group of three policemen were trying to restrain a woman, she was like someone

118

possessed. At first he assumed she'd be a normal working girl getting off shift from one of the factories and then taking on too much booze, but no. She was well dressed and middle aged she could have been a lady. Then he heard another crash of glass and another just to his left. He turned and ran hard towards the woman who was already shaping up to smash more windows at the next shop. He grabbed her arm but she turned and with her other hand belted him to the side of his head sending his helmet careering off in to the watching crowd. He blew his whistle for assistance but not before she recovered and smashed another window sending shards of glass in all directions. It took three policemen to restrain her.

When she realised she was caught she stopped fighting and started shouting at the top of her voice 'votes for women'. He noticed bleeding cuts to her face from the flying debris but he couldn't help. His job was to get her locked up in the station, she'd have to be treated after.

Shouts and cries from other skirmishes could be heard but his hands were more than full as his small group marched the short distance to the waiting cell. On the way the crowds cheered, for the police or for the woman in their grip, he didn't know which but he did remember some women shouting abuse. 'Stupid bitch', 'silly cow, she's got what she deserved'. It was obvious they didn't have full support from their own sex let along from men. He thought then they've got no chance.

Once in the station, the prisoner and others in their gang were led to the cells. They were quiet, refined and walked with dignity. He noticed a younger lady who was heavily pregnant. She was a canny lass, head held high, he wondered what her husband will think of this.

He reached for his mug and drank deeply. At the same time he noticed the clock showed his shift was nearly over. It was almost time to go home to his family. But there was this nagging question in his mind, does his wife support these suffragettes? She's never mentioned it at all but he did catch her reading the newspaper. It reported on a fracas at an MP's house. He hadn't read it himself but the headlines

119

were blaming the Suffragettes and this Pankhurst woman. A chill passed through him when he considered his wife might do something so stupid. His reverie was broken by his replacement arriving, PC Stanley Symonds.

"Wakey, wakey, time te get back to your lovin' family."

"Oh it's ye Stan. Right ahm off home, been quite a day."

"So a've heard, how many in?"

"Over a dozen."

"Any problems."

"No, good as gold. They're different from the usual riffraff we get. Well spoken, almost polite. Oh an' there's a pregnant one in cell six."

Stan eyes widened. "What's her name?"

"Hold on it'll be on the sheet er....Emily Mulligan." Why, d'ya know her? He looked at Stan quizzically

"No, of course not, how could ah?"

"Anywa they're all yours, they've been fed, ahm off home 'to me lovin' family'." He picked up his still muddied helmet and his coat and left the station. He was tired but he still felt annoyingly uncomfortable about his wife.

As soon as Stan was left by himself he went down to the cells. The women were quiet, some still eating, others reading on their beds but he was only interested in one cell, cell six. He unlocked the door and entered.

"Oh Emily."

"Don't 'Oh Emily' me. Ah told ye what ah was ganin te do."

"But ah didn't think ye would. Are ye hurt anywhere?"

"No, ah came quietly. Stan ah believe in what ahm doin', it's the right thing. Don't waste your time in tryin' to persuade me otherwise."

"Look ah can get ye released, compassionate grounds an' all that."

"Don't ye dare Stanley Symonds. We want to see the newspaper reporter." She quickly changed her tone an' walked over half smiling. "Stan, would ye try te get one here, for me?"

120

"Don't ye try to get rund me, I'd get myself in bother."

"Please?"

Stan got flustered, he always did in her presence. He thought the world of her ever since the day she was attacked near her digs. Even when he learnt that she was pregnant it didn't make a bit of difference, he hoped that she liked him, just a little. In fact he knew she did, they'd had some great times together. They had done no more than kissing and cuddling, he understood why, it was frustrating but he couldn't bear to lose her. Now he could feel himself colour up. "I'll see what ah can do." He gave her a peck on the cheek. She responded and caught his face in her hands and gave him a full kiss on the mouth, then whispered. "Thanks Stan."

"Ye are, now what's the word that writer uses? Ah yes, 'Incorrigible.'" He gave another of his face lightening smiles and left the cell shaking his head. He didn't lock the cell, for him it wasn't physically possible.

Chapter 25

1911

I feel anxious. I'm now in bed after a really nice day: a pleasant shift in hospital and a fun evening with Stan at the Empire Music Hall but the morning will herald a very different day.

My Stan, he's a lovely man, so patient and understanding. He doesn't mind that I'm pregnant by someone else. I think he'll do absolutely anything for me but I can't give him what he wants. I have had to tell him that I'm not interested in getting married yet. I can feel he's been working up to asking me so I thought it kinder for me to let him know what I think. We do a lot of cuddling and laughing but nothing more, mind, it would be difficult to do anything else in my condition. I can see people look at us and notice how we enjoy ourselves. They must assume we're husband and wife with our family on the way, little do they know.

We said goodnight on the steps outside. I told him about the demonstration tomorrow morning and the march along the high street in the afternoon. He supports me of course but he looked concerned especially about the march. He'd heard of problems elsewhere in the country and he admitted that there'll be a large police presence, just in case. He kept repeating that I shouldn't do anything daft, just march nothing else, I just nodded and held him close so I couldn't look him in the face.

Millie was waiting for me propped up in bed reading under the flickering gas light. I know she can't come tomorrow, her ward is short of staff and she couldn't get the day off.

"How's the Bow Street Runner then?"

"I assume ye mean Stan, yes he's canny, on good form."

"It's a wonder he can get anywhere near ye with that great bulge. Talkin' of babies, I'm worried about what you're ganin to do temorra."

"Oh don't ye start. Stan's been naggin' me as well. I'll gan to the meetin' outside the Free Trades an' then see what happens in the afternoon like. I'll probably just wave our banner an' shout."

"Emmy ah know ye too well, you'll be up with the rest of them. You'll get caught an' locked up."

"That's good comin' from ye, if ye were comin' you'd dee the same."

"Maybe but ahm not pregnant."

"Good." I turned my back to her, stripped off my clothes to get ready for the night but then just laid face up on top of the bed. I felt hot and upset.

Millie, looked over at my profile and smiled. "Ye look like a beached whale!"

I looked down at myself and laughed then took out my pillow and gave her a good thwack with it.

"Ah wish ah could be there. It's so darin', such a scary thin' te do."

I feel the same. I wonder if I really have the nerve or will I just walk away and melt back in to the crowd. I slip on my nightdress and get under the covers. I feel tired but sleep's impossible and I just stare in to the darkness. I drift off eventually but in what seems like minutes I'm woken up by Millie getting dressed for work. She whispers in to my ear. "See ye tonight an' look after yourself."

I can only grunt and wave a hand in the air. As the room grows lighter and my head clears last night's anxiety starts to flow through me again. But my nervousness now comes with excitement. We're going to get noticed and show that we mean business. I'm pleased the day has come and I almost spring out of bed but I stop half way remembering my extra unbalancing weight. I mutter, 'easy does it' and lift myself up, 'there's no rush, just take yor time'.

****

The morning's gone well, a demonstration at the Free Trades Hall and now I'm with Lady Dunlop and others in a top room above a tailor shop in the main street. We've been planning over dinner, just a snack really, and I can't wait. Everyone here is older than me and most are from a different class, very posh and well spoken little trace of a Geordie accent but they're very friendly and feeling nervous, like me.

Lady Dunlop rises, her poise and assertiveness commands the room. "This is the time ladies, the banners and bags are downstairs. Always remember: Don't put people's lives at risk, including your own. Make sure everyone knows why we're doing this and hold your heads high. Keep thinking that we're doing this not just for us but for every woman in the country."

There are cheers and one by one we start to leave the room. I'm one of the last lifting myself out of the chair when I feel a hand on my shoulder, it's Lady Dunlop.

"Emily my dear. I would fully understand if you don't want to participate and so would everyone else. So please don't feel you have to, having your support, holding your banner high would be sufficient."

I'm thinking, no way am I going to be left out. "Thank ye Lady Dunlop but this is somethin' ah feel very strongly an' I'm...." I patted my bump, "...we're ganin to be there with ye."

She reaches out and holds my hand. "I'm very proud and honoured that you're with us and by the way just call me Constance, we're all equal here."

I'm blushing with the attention of someone so famous. All I can say is "thank you". I leave the room and join the others picking up a bag and a banner. It's quiet, everyone preparing themselves mentally. Just before we leave we wish each other good luck, hug and kiss and then we're out in to the din of Grainger Street and disperse in different directions.

I'm following Nancy, a feisty lady, she's holding her banner high and shouting at the top of her voice. I can hear her even above the constant traffic noise. People look and stare, some stop, some shake their heads others just wonder. She stops outside a haberdashery, reaches in to her bag, pulls out a stone and without a second thought throws it with all her might at the glass window. It shatters on to the pavement in a million shards. People suddenly back away shrieking, hands to their faces, then look back in horror. Nancy moves to the next shop, a chemist, and repeats the process and then the next. By this time the pedestrians understand what's going on and shout at her to stop. They try to grab her arm but she's too strong, too determined, they're no match for her strength. A fourth window slumps to the floor in pieces, she's running now and with her last stone the huge plate glass of a dress shop disintegrates. With her bag empty she marches defiantly along the edge of the pavement holding her banner high so that all can see, pedestrians, cyclists and drivers.

People are shouting at her, pointing back at the carnage. I look myself and see thieves taking advantage of all manner of goods exposed and unprotected. They run off at full speed with their pockets bulging and their hands full. A wave of disappointment fills me, their actions are fuelling the reaction against us. Our aim is to demand and achieve equality for women not to benefit the dregs of society.

My bag feels heavy around my shoulders. I know it's my turn no matter what the circumstances. I walk on skirting the damage of the last broken window and head for the next shop, I hear shrill whistling above the shouting and traffic noise, I reach down and grab a stone from my bag, I take aim and pull back my arm but I see a woman behind the window, she's frightened, she's now turned her back to me trying to protect her confectionary wares. I stop, I can't do this, she could be injured, this is not right. I drop my arm, immediately I'm grabbed from behind and roughly pulled away, both hands now gripped tightly, my banner falls to the pavement. I'm pulled away from the scene, I realise

I'm fixed between two burly policemen. I start to struggle but remember Lady Dunlop's words. I relax, straighten my back, hold my head up and walk calmly and I shout at the top of my voice 'Votes for Women'.

The policemen say nothing, their grip relaxes when they realise I'm not trying to escape. People step aside before us and stare and gawp. Some jeer, there's the occasional voice of support but mostly they just look and wonder. At the station there are no questions asked I'm taken down some stairs and deposited in a cell. They leave immediately, locking the cell door behind them. It's eerily quiet but then a voice calls me.

"Emily, Emily Mulligan?"

It's from another cell. "Wye aye, who's that?"

"Elizabeth. Are you ok? How did you get on?"

"Ahm afraid ah didn't manage to break any windaz, there was a woman standin' right behind it an' she looked so scared, I just couldn't an' before I could get to the next one ah was hauled away". Sorry."

"Don't you dare be sorry, you were there, you did your bit with us. I just hope the newspapers report it."

At that moment another woman is brought in and she's locked in another separate cell. I recognise her but didn't know her name. She's much older than me, older than me Ma even and she looks distressed, dishevelled and frightened. Elizabeth tries to comfort her but I could hear her quietly whimpering. Within an hour all the cells seemed to be full with obviously two or three in some. We chat and laugh to start with but as the excitement fades we go quiet. I'm now wondering what effect this will have on my work, on Stan, will he be so disappointed? What would Ma think? The fact that she had to put up with this isolation for over three years, it hardly bares thinking about. I know it was her determination to get back home to look after her children that got her through. She had an objective and so have I. This is what I want to do more than anything else and my thoughts turn to getting the newspapers involved. If no-one else knows what we've done here, in a street in Newcastle, then it will have been a waste of time and energy.

The police treat us with respect but they don't understand why we're doing this. They see a group of well dressed, well spoken ladies from comfortable homes creating mayhem in the streets. It's all a mile away from their well set, indoctrinated ideas that a woman's place is to support her husband, keep a clean, warm home and of course to give birth and to raise his family. Why should we want parity, why do we want to vote in elections? It is a massive change in perception and it will take years but it's coming, there is no doubt. I can foresee hard times – abuse, incarceration, pain and loss but in the end we will achieve what's right.

Being locked up gives me time to think without diversion. I can set down my priorities in my mind. My baby is important, I'm going to ensure she'll be well cared for and loved but she'll have to come along with me on my journey, my crusade.

A rattle of keys brings me back to reality. I look up and see Stan outside my cell.

"Oh Emily."

I immediately rile at his disappointment. "Don't 'Oh Emily' me. Ah told ye what ah was ganin to do."

He unlocks the gate and comes and sits down on the bed beside me and we argue but in hushed tones. I feel sorry for him, he's upset, hurt, but a light switches on in my brain. I ask him to find a reporter who wants a good story for the newspapers. After some persuasion he promises to try, he leaves, turns and gives me one of his stunning smiles and my heart bleeds. How can I be so manipulative, so shameful.

Actually, it's quite easy!

Chapter 26

"Well student nurse Mulligan I assume you're well aware of why you're in my ward? Or perhaps I should say our ward. "

All I can do is nod I don't want to move an inch in any direction.

"No matter the good intentions, what you did was totally irresponsible. You put the life of your baby and yourself at risk and you're not out of the woods yet. You know the routine as well as I do, basically plenty of rest. The nurses will do what they can and I'll keep a close eye on you."

Sister went to leave but twisted around and laid a newspaper on the chest of drawers alongside my bed and spoke quietly. "You may like to read the front page." Then after a fleeting smile she strode away down the ward to her office.

If I physically could, I would have hugged her. She's been my saviour. Again I think back to yesterday's demonstration, the incarceration, the journalist who took our stories. He was such an innocent young man. He had no idea what he was in for when he arrived but it soon became frighteningly evident. Face to face with Lady Dunlop herself and in full flow. It was almost a dictation and with a gentle but unmistakeable threat of a damming call to his editor if he changed any of the facts.

But then at some early hour of the morning, still in my cell, came the pains, excruciating, gripping, intense agonies from my womb. I could only lay on my bed, grip my bump and bellow. Thank goodness Stan was still on duty. One look at me was enough. He ran back to his office and arranged an immediate transfer to the hospital. I was carefully carried out of my cell and out of the station with the shouted support from all the other arrested demonstrators still ringing in my head. Poor Stan had to remain behind. I wanted to grip his hand, I was frightened, I knew what could be happening but all he could do was whisper some supportive, kind words. I understood why. The pains thank goodness became less severe and by the time I was examined at the hospital, my hospital, they had subsided. All appeared to be back to normal, no bleeding, blood pressure, pulse all as it should be but I was dreading a repeat performance. I was taken up to my ward for 'observation' and given a sedative. I realised I was being given special treatment rather than be sent home and told to rest. I was so thankful for it.

I was awake by midday and almost immediately confronted by Sister. I know she is a supporter and like me a member of the WSPU but she has drawn a line at joining action demonstrations. Perhaps under the circumstances I should have done as well. I know if my baby is safe I've been so lucky, there is a time and a place. I pray for forgiveness and thank providence that the benefits of my nursing status have allowed an increased survival chance for both of us.

I reach over, take the newspaper and get comfortable ready to take in our story. I've no need to hunt for the right page. There it is and there I am slap bang on the front page standing alongside Lady Dunlop, my pregnant lump plain for all to see. I colour up and look around to see if anyone else notices: No-one. I study my face, mmmm, not bad, I look determined with hands clutched supporting my bump. Mmmm, yes, not bad at all. I think back to my persuasion tactics on Stan and immediately feel guilty, but only a little. What a man!

For a whole week now I've been hidden away in a quieter part of the ward and apart from a few scary twinges my baby has settled down and is hopefully thriving. The hospital staf have been so supportive. My presence is like a massive conspiracy that everyone knows about. Nurses seem to tread lightly over, whisper questions and bring extra cuppas as if they're smuggling black market goods. Matron purposely completely ignores me as if the bed was empty, thank goodness but even the doctor spares a few minutes of his time to check on my progress. I believe I'm the world's worst kept secret and I'm so grateful.

Despite all this care I would just love to see Ma but I know this is impossible, she has no way of getting to Newcastle. She will be aware that I'm near my due date and I know she'll be thinking about me, worrying and maybe praying. Maybe this is why I feel so much better. By my calculations I'm now within two weeks, of course she could come at any time now, but I'm so relieved to get this far. There is now every chance of a successful birth.

I settle down for the night, relaxed, optimistic and happy. I wake hours later, my eyes flick open and they focus on the shadows on the ceiling and I wonder why. I don't have to wait long. A searing pain stabs my body, my eyes widen, I clench my stomach, hold my breath and shut my hands into tight fists. This is different than before, I know it is, I hope it is. The steel grip of pain releases and I can breathe normally. I know that if this is my time the pain will come again. It does but over an hour later. I grimace but behind the face is a hidden smile I just know my birth contractions have started. I reach over and grab my bell it rings so loud it has to wake everyone in every ward in the hospital. Within seconds I hear clicking of heels on tiles, childbirth has started and so begins another phase of my life.

Many hours later in the afternoon of the 11th June 1911 Mhairi was born. I hold her close. She has the most amazing head of hair any of the nurses have ever seen. Curly jet black hair not only covering her head but over her ears and down to her eyes. I've given birth to a monkey! A quote from Millie later that morning. What a cheek! I spend my time twirling the curls round my finger then brushing them in to patterns. She's beautiful and slowly but surely I'm forgiving her for the last two hours of absolute agony.

In the latter stages an intake of gas-and-air coupled with my own choice of birth position came to the rescue. My chosen position, really the best I could find from a bad lot of alternatives, had never before seen on the ward – on my knees face down on to the pillow! I can only imagine the chatter in the restroom. I may never live it down. The nurses were so calm and reassuring. Their repeated requests to push, push again, and again were in reality not needed. My body was in automatic mode and push it did whether I liked it or not, I had no control. I will never forget each emotion: the relief when the final excruciating pain released my girl, the wonderful fulfilment of holding her in my arms and the creeping exhaustion taking over my every fibre. A once in a lifetime experience - maybe, maybe not - but I'm not going to think about that. Presently I'm just sinking in to the pillows, Mhairi in my arms and a cup of tea beside me. Despite the soreness and the bone weariness, I'm thinking it doesn't get any better. Breast feeding, where to stay, returning to work, telling Ma, these are all problems to sort tomorrow. I'm just taking time to enjoy this special moment.

****

Sister allowed us five days in the ward and my friends had planned everything for when we left. I'm so lucky to have them. In similar situations a mother giving birth to an illegitimate baby would be thought shocking, a disgrace. Many would land up in the Workhouse, my best friend Millie a prime example.

In fact I haven't moved and still stay in my room in the nurses' quarters, Mhairi sleeps in a borrowed crib at the end of my bed. I'm still sharing with Millie. She has to put up with the disturbed nights, steeping nappies and the bouts of upset and yet manages to continue her nursing duties uncomplaining. To be fair Mhairi is not over-noisy or fractious. Maybe it's the cosiness of the surroundings or Millie's tuneful lullabies but life for me is relaxed and carefree. But nothing stays the same.

"Guess what Em."

It's a Saturday evening and Millie has just returned from a night out with Frank, she looks pleased with herself. I'm sitting reading and feeding Mhairi.

131

"Gan on then pet."

"Well what do ye think?"

I put the book down and study my friend. Her face is split by an ear to ear smile. I can guess in fact, I knew it wouldn't be long.

"He's asked you and you've said yes."

She looks surprised. "How do ye know?"

Mhairi has actually dropped off to sleep so I lay her back into the crib and gave my friend a big smile and a hug. "Congratulations, I somehow guessed. Have ye set a date?"

"Before the end of the year and we're gettin' a house just doon the road. Frank knows the people there and they've agreed to let it to us." She looks at me wide eyed expectantly. "What do ye think."

"I think it's canny news ahm so pleased for ye both."

She's now in full flow and words are spilling out like a river in spate. I am pleased for her, they are such a loving couple, made for each other but I feel a pang of jealousy. It's stupid I know but we've been inseparable for four years now and I know I'll miss her company something terrible.

"We'll still see each other and I can still babysit. Ye can bring her rund when ye gan out with Stan."

There's no stopping the flow and we chat into the night until the early hours before I have to insist on getting some sleep before Mhairi wakes for another feed. But I lay awake and wonder how my own life has to change. I have to return to work which means I need to find someone to look after my baby. Deep down I know I want to continue nursing and my support of the WSPU but the thought of leaving Mhairi wrenches my heart. Only when I decide to talk to Stan about it can I drift off to sleep but I know the wonderful routine of my life for the last few months is coming to an end.

****

"What do ye think pet?"

I'm pushing Mhairi fast asleep in her pram back to my digs with Stan. We have just met with Mr and Mrs Roberts the owners of the house where Stan rents his room. Stan had the idea that they would be keen to look after Mhairi when I was working. They are a childless couple but he knew they adored children and he was right.

"They seem very nice, very homely. They certainly got on with Mhairi and she was very relaxed with them."

I now live alone with Mhairi in my quarters and I know I must return to work both to pay back the hospital staff for helping me through last year and my own need to earn my keep. I am also keen to rejoin the fight for women's rights. I've been sitting on the sidelines watching the very real progress being made but that's not enough for me, I want more. Despite this I've been dreading the thought of leaving my baby with others no matter how nice and homely they are. I realise I can't do everything but this doesn't make it any easier.

"I'd like to give it a trial like. Don't forget they've had little experience, they may panic if she's starts off."

In my heart I'm certain they will cope, no matter what.

Chapter 27

1913

I'm on the platform of Newcastle-on-Tyne Central Railway Station. My friends have squeezed in to the waiting room, standing room only. I can't bear the crush, the close proximity of others inches away from my face, so I'm braving the arctic conditions outside. The station seems to funnel the wind along the railway track freezing everything in its path tingling the skin on my face and legs. I stamp about keeping life in my limbs. A steam locomotive shrouded in steam and smoke rumbles towards me and stops quite close, the driver sees me and waves me over.

"Step inside lass an' get a warm."

I 'm taken by surprise and stare at him. He shrugs and turns away but even where I'm standing I can feel the warm pillow of air around the cab. I venture forward, grab the handrail and step on to the footplate and shout at his back. "Thank ye."

"He turns back to me smiling. "Get yourself over here lass by the fire, we're ganin to be here for a few minutes."

I see for the first time another man, he's looking out the other side. He sees me, smiles and touches his cap. I look around the cab. It's full of hissing pipes and odd churning noises but it's warm and I can feel myself thawing out.

The driver is older, his face is weather-beaten and crinkled like an orange. I notice a thin pipe stuck out the side of his mouth and without removing it he asks me a question. "Ye off to the smoke?" I must look confused, he continues this time taking his pipe out and jabbing it in the direction of the track. "London?"

"Wye aye, ah am, the first time."

He asks me what I'm going to do there and tells me all he knows about the capital, which isn't much. It turns out he's never been. He

134

does all the talking and I smile and nod at the right places. "There's ganin to be a war ye know, mark me words." I've seen the headlines in the papers but not taken much notice instead concentrating on WSPU issues.

The WSPU has taken over my life. I know that myself. I don't need Millie or my nursing friends to tell me, although they do. Everything else has been relegated down my list even my Mhairi. I always seem to be dumping her on Mr and Mrs Roberts, but I can see they're fond of her and are always willing to help.

And then there's Stan. He would make a loving husband, caring, thoughtful everything most men aren't, but not for me. We've been together now for over a year. He must be so frustrated. He adores me and we cuddle, sometimes lie in bed together naked but we never make love, I just can't. But he says everything is ok and that I'll come to love him. He might be right, I do love him in a way but he's up against something much stronger: my desire to make a change for women and the last thing I want at the moment is a marriage and more children.

"Sorry love, the signal's off we've got to get ganin."

I'm brought out of my reverie, the warmth of the fire has driven out the shivering and allowed my thoughts to drift away. "Oh sorry, thank ye very much. Ah feel much bettor fo' the warm."

I step down on to the platform and wave at them as they slowly chug away down the track and out the station. I pull my coat around me to try to keep in the newly gained heat. Soon my friends from the WSPU join me.

Nancy gives me a hug. "You must be frozen out here Emily, you should have come in with us we would have made room."

Another friend, Celia, speaks out. "If ye ask me she's been better out here. Ah was right up against a little man who kept his eyes on me the whole time."

Nancy, whom I've known since the early days of the Group, examined her up and down. Not surprising, you in that dress, it pushes everything up and out. He was lucky he didn't get his eyes blacked."

"You're just jealous."

"Too right."

We laugh out loud shouting more ribald comments making us relax before our long journey south and, for a while, forgetting what our intentions are when we get there. We're a group of five volunteers all older than I am. Maud and Dorothy must be over forty, fifty even, well brought up, well dressed, definitely upper class but they're not averse to swearing like very posh troopers. Nancy is younger, very thin with sharp features making her look fearsome to those who don't know her. She normally wears trousers making her look manly but she belies her appearance and is kind and very supportive to the younger members. The last of our group is Celia. She is the closest to my age and background. She's smiley, bubbly and bouncy and always seems to be well presented, smartly dressed and never without her white face powder and rouge. She's married and always talks of her husband in glowing terms but this doesn't affect her enthusiasm for the WSPU. I wonder if she's pregnant. Then there's me, twenty years old, the youngest.

Lady Constance Dunlop chose us from a long list of volunteers and we all feel utterly determined not to let her down. Our job? Well we don't know. The WSPU national committee has asked for support from local groups like ours but the details have been kept secret. Our instructions are simply to meet in the old Wool Exchange in Bermondsey. Accommodation inside has been booked for two nights and, all being well, we return the next day. We have nothing to show our allegiances, no banners or badges. We're just a group of ladies travelling to London. It is so exciting.

Our train enters the platform the locomotive tilting to the curve. Coach after coach follow the hissing engine, it has to be the longest train I've ever seen. We find our reserved compartment, a whole compartment to ourselves. I feel very special amongst so many others having to race up and down trying to bag a seat. We settle ourselves in and before long a shrill whistle portends a jerking start to my adventure in 'The Smoke'.

We swop seats on our journey so each of us has a chance to be by the window. I soon get my chance and almost immediately I see the familiar sight of Durham cathedral alongside the old Castle. I immediately think of me Mam at home. I've been to see her, Con and the twins many times with Mhairi. She's filled out and looks as good as new. She works hard – at the harbour and looking after the family – but I can see she's where she's always wanted to be. Friends keep calling, checking on her wellbeing. On my last visit a man arrived on horseback. He was a miner from the next village. He said he just wanted to check if Ma was wanting on anything but he was in his Sunday best and his face and hands were well scrubbed. I smile remembering both his surprise when he sees me and Ma's embarrassment. She fussed about pretending to be busier than she was. We had a disjointed discussion punctuated with knowing looks and sudden bursts of laughter. Ma didn't have to explain, I could see how well he got on with the children, how relaxed they were in his company and how casually they called him Bobby. When he had left I looked at Ma and she looked at me. We both smiled, nothing was said, nothing needed to be said. Just before I left for the omnibus I gave her a hug. "Davey seems canny." She answered coyly. "Aye he is."

"Oh, a've left me sandwiches at home, a've got nothin' to eat for the journey." Celia is searching through her case looking distraught.

Nancy answers putting her mind at rest. "Pet, we're on the Flying Scotsman, there's food on the train and we've been given some money from WSPU funds remember? In fact let's wander through to the restaurant car now."

Celia slumps back in the seat. "Thank goodness ah thought ah was going to starve." Then she realises what Nancy has said. "The Flying Scotsman, ah never dreamed the like, hawa let's get ganin" She immediately springs up from her seat and headed for the door to the corridor. "Hawa ye lot."

Maud looks at Dorothy then at Celia. "We'll go later, when you get back. Someone should be here to look after our luggage."

Celia looks surprised. "Do you think there are thieves about, I don't want to lose me clothes."

Nancy answers. "You never know, mind they'd be surprised finding the likes of your underwear."

"Cheek, they're the latest fashion ye know."

"Mmmm for a whore!"

The compartment rocks with laughter but Celia blushes bright pink and looks uncomfortable.

Maud comes to her rescue. "We're only joking. You youngsters go... and leave some for us."

Our walk or rather our stagger through the train was bewildering. The noise is terrifying especially at the connections between the coaches. Here they seem to be swaying in different directions at the same time and you can see the track below rushing by at a dizzying speed. It all changes when we reach the restaurant car, everything here is calm and serene. Well dressed passengers are served at their tables by smart waiters carrying food on silver trays. This is another world.

We are showed to our table and our chosen food is brought without fuss or bother. Other diners smile and nod a greeting.

Celia whispers. "Ah bet they wouldn't smile if they knew what we're ganin te do.

Nancy answers again in a whisper. "I wish we knew what we're going to do."

All three of us think of the possibilities. Demonstrating, causing some kind of disruption maybe blocking roads, more window smashing or perhaps something we've not done before. The thoughts of breaking the law and the inevitable consequences stifle our jollity and our conversation dries up. We eat our meals quietly.

The remainder of our journey is filled with periods of discussion about suffrage and the WSPU, dozing to the clickety clack of the wheels and reading books and magazines. We arrive at the terminus, Kings Cross, in the late afternoon and we stretch our legs walking down the platform and to the buses to complete our journey to Bermondsey. The old Wool Exchange is a large brick built structure in amongst huge square blackened warehouses serviced by a grid of surfaced roads filled with delivery wagons. The familiar sounds and smells of docklands surround me like a blanket and comfort me. On arrival we are immediately taken to a small room where we meet our 'Action Leader'. She is tall, elegant and well spoken. Formalities are short, our action for tomorrow morning is explained and we are given a hand-drawn map of our operating area.

"I'm sure I don't need to repeat that secrecy is crucial. Tell no-one, not even a WSPU member, is that clear?" We all nod our understanding. "You can of course eat in the canteen here and sleep in the dormitories, they're quite comfortable. One more thing, the timing, it is so important, it has to fit in with our other diversion activities so don't be late." She rose from her seat. "The canteen is at the end of this corridor on this floor; from there someone will show you to your quarters. I have to see to other groups now but remember keep to the schedule and ladies, the very best of luck to you all." She kisses our cheeks and leaves the room leaving us completely stunned."

Chapter 28

"God in heaven I didn't expect that." Dorothy is the first to speak all our thoughts.

We are sitting together around a table in a very noisy echoing canteen. There are groups of chattering women all around, cutlery is crashing and seats scraping. It's reminiscent of school day meals only louder. We're all eating some sort of meat pie and vegetables, no choice but it's good basic food and very welcome after our long journey south.

"Nor me, I thought we would be just demonstrating or obstructing the traffic or an event or something but never this."

Celia looks at the older women from one to the other. "But what if we get caught like? It's against the law, we'll be put in prison."

Nancy adds. "Again."

"Oh dear." Celia looks shocked. She's the only one out of us five who hasn't been in prison. "I would hate to be locked up an' fed gruel." She looks at all of us wanting some re-assurance.

"If it all goes well we'll be away before anyone notices."

I can see she is not convinced. "Hawa Celia pet let's gan an' see our room, maybe there are showers like, a freshen up will do us all good." I want to bolster her confidence, there's a danger she'll panic and back out. I stand up and pick up my bag ready to leave motioning her to do the same. She does and we walk out. I call behind us. "See ye in the dorm ladies." They smile and nod.

We're both in the large shower room standing under comforting warm flows, even soap is provided. There are other women doing the same. I look at Celia. I can see she is not relaxed. She's facing away from me. I just assume she's not used to washing with others but then I notice the marks. Long ugly purple black diagonal wheals cross her back from her buttocks up to her shoulders. My hand flies to my mouth in shock. I walk over to her and gently turn her around. Her arms are covered in blue bruises, grab marks from large hands. Her bare breasts have been scarred by something sharp, there are more grab marks at the top of her legs. I can't take it in, as a nurse in a hospital I've seen many a damaged body but not on this scale of physical violence. My gaze lifts and I stare at her neck and face, I can't stop my automatic reaction. "Oh my God." The soap has washed off her make-up revealing more bruises to her cheeks and her high necked dress covered yet more savage bruising around her throat. She stands, head bowed, ashamed.

"Who on earth did this to ye?"

She just stands there, water cascading over her battered and bruised body. I gently place my arms around her. "Is this yor husband."

She nods.

I mutter audibly. "The bastard."

She steps away and starts to speak, quickly, eyes wide open. "No no it's not all his fault, it's just that he always wants te....ye know. But sometimes, ye see, ah don't want te but ah know ah have te but ahm sore inside an' it hurts an'...." She peters out and starts sobbing. I bring her back in to my arms.

"Look, finish washin', get dressed an' we'll get back to our room."

We sit on my bed. She's still defending her husband's actions. I wait until she runs out of steam, stops talking and just holds her face in her hands.

"Celia, listen to me. Ye must leave him."

"No no ah canna, ah love him."

"Celia, ye canna possibly love someone who does this to ye. Ye must leave him an' ye must leave him now. You're not ganin back to him, I canna let ye. He'll kill ye."

"Ah canna leave him, he'll find me an' then, an' then he'll...." She flops down on to the bed, turns her face in to the blanket and sobs. I make a decision there and then.

"You're ganin to live with me an' Mhairi . He won't find ye there. You're ganin to have to find another job in another town, I'll help ye."

We sit in silence with the odd sniff and sob from Celia. I'm trying to understand how someone can put up with such vicious violence and still pretend to love the perpetrator. I wonder if my plan is possible, is she too much under his control? But then it dawns on me, of course she can. I see in an instant that she does have the determination, the guts, to change her life. Hasn't she signed up and dedicated herself to the WSPU and how does she maintain her pretence of being happy go lucky all the time with a loving husband? Inner self belief, she must have it in abundance. I realise now that she won't be backing out of our operation tomorrow. She's nervous, we all are, but she will go through with it, of that I have no doubts.

We dress in to our nightgowns and slip in to our beds.

"Thank ye Emily."

"Don't worry pet I'll look after ye." I feel like she's a younger sister and I feel responsible for her. I now have to work out how I can look after her. It will be difficult, a challenge, but it's the right decision. This level of violence and lack of respect for women by men is not uncommon but this is what we're fighting against. The WSPU exists principally to win voting rights for women but the movement goes so much further than that. It will eventually reach out to all classes of society, all the way from the aristocracy down to the poorest slums of the cities.

Chapter 29

The sounds of dockyard workings wake me. I swing my legs out of the bed and make for the window behind. No-one else is stirring in the dormitory. The view is dominated by large warehouses but between their hulking masses I see a glimpse of the winter morning sunshine lightening the horizon. It heralds the start of a very different day.

Below me, the road is still lit by the gaslights flickering illumination on to the sparse traffic. Mostly horse drawn carts and men on bicycles. The enjoyment of our journey down, the surprise of our WSPU operation and the shock of Celia's mutilated body are in the past. Nerves have gone. My mind is set on the task ahead. It's too early for the building's heating system to warm the large room and there's a chill in the air. I slip back under the warm bed covers and go through in my mind the details of the master plan for the day ahead. Our Action Leader seems to have covered all eventualities. The timetable is clear, the location of the materials to be collected, how to carry out the action and the method of escape. Now completely at ease with what we have to do, I swing myself out of bed again.

There is by this time some activity. From our group Maud and Dorothy are dressed and ready, Nancy is away having a shower but Celia bless her heart is still tucked up in bed fast asleep.

"Come on sleepy head, breakfast is waitin'."

Her eyes spring open and in one movement she sits up looking confused. Realisation spreads across her face. "Am ah late, oh God, have ah missed anythin'?"

"Yes pet, we've done the job an' we're ready for our dinner."

She turns and stares at me, then seeing me smile she relaxes and slumps back down on to her pillow. "Ah diddn't get to sleep for ages, too much snoring an' coughing. Ah think a've only had a couple of hours."

"Ye need a cup of tea an' some breakfast, hawa let's see what they've got." Without thinking I strip off her covers revealing her bare bruised arms and neck and then throw them back over hoping no-one else has noticed. I whisper. "Sorry pet."

She looks embarrassed but manages to dress herself discreetly and we all leave for the canteen. There's little conversation between us. All our minds are focused on the day ahead. Surprisingly our Action Leader appears at our table, she has someone with her. "I have another for your team, this is Hilda, she'll help with the demonstration but will link in with you and warn of any problems or necessary changes. I'll leave you together to get to know each other."

Hilda sits at the spare seat around our table. She's very petit with a small sharp face and darting eyes. She speaks with a broad cockney accent. "Don't mind me ladies, I'll be makin' sure ya won't get disturbed. I kna the chuffin' area well so's I can lead ya there, awright?"

We all find it hard to understand all she says and she has to repeat her questions several times. She obviously hasn't been briefed fully about us and she takes notes. "Thanks ladies. Right this is what we does so earwig up. We've gotta take the train ter Greenwich and from there ter the pick-up point is a ten minute bowl of chalk, er that's a walk to you. We meet me mate there, e's got a cart and e'll 'elp load and then we take it to the back door of the 'ous. You'll be awright no-ones in. 'e'll 'ave all the ovver bits ya need. After you're done you're on your own, I suggest you scarper back 'ere."

Nancy asks the time of the train.

"It leaves Bermondsey station at five minutes past eleven, I'll be wif ya, it's only two stops. You'll be at the 'ouse at abaht midday. Good timing for the demonstration at the front. You got a watch aint ya?"

We nod.

"Good, clock ya outside 'ere at quarter to eleven." She gets up and looks around. "I fink I'll grab sum grub while I'm 'ere."

We sit quietly taking in what we have to do. Maud frowns and looks at Dorothy. "I don't know about you Dot but I'm not built to hump stuff about. Dorothy also looks worried.

I look at Maud, she's small, well dressed and I can see she wouldn't be used to this sort of work, I answer. "Celia, me an' this mate of Hilda's can load up the cart, ye can help us at the other end like."

She looks relieved. "Thank you Emily, mind I do want to do my bit."

"Whey aye, you'll be with us all the way."

We congregate outside the Hall, the street is now a hive of activity. The carters, unused to seeing so many women in one place, stare, some smile and raise their caps, others just wonder and scratch or shake their heads. The station is in view further along and on the other side of the street. Hilda is already waiting dressed in grubby grey trousered overalls.

"Come on then ladies, the station's over there, not far, folla me."

I look at my four friends, they seem overawed. I grab two of them by their arms and start walking after Hilda. "Come on girls, head up, smile, look confident." They follow my lead, three of us in the front, two behind. There are more stares and laughter but we don't care. We're here to do a job for women's rights, proud and determined and no-one's going to stop us.

Our journey on the train is short and squashed. Apart from our group there are many other women with banners and cotton sashes all making for the same destination. Everywhere we're stared at, people going about their normal business wondering what's about to happen. I am too.

Shortly after leaving the train Hilda leads us off the main route and down a side street of terraced housing turning to stores and warehousing as we get nearer the river. We stop at a block of wooden stables. Hilda tells us to wait and quickly steps over the cobbles to the rear of the building. We have a good view of the river. There's a gentle ebb and flow against the wharf wall. The early morning sunshine has disappeared behind leaden skies, its gloom reflecting on the water surface making it too look grey and heavy. I can see activity in the docks behind, large freighters being unloaded by swinging derrick cranes. In the river itself barges and lighters are tied together in groups awaiting their next turn of duty. Over all of this is the all pervading smell of the sea. A chill wind blows in from the East. I pull my coat tighter around me to keep in the warmth but I shiver, a combination of the cold and nervousness of what we have to do.

Hilda returns. She looks cross. "That lad should be 'ere with the bleedin cart by na." She looks along the track running alongside the river. She takes out a watch from her breast pocket and tutts muttering darkly to herself.

"Is there a problem Hilda?" Dorothy looks worried.

"Nah na we'll be awright, 'e only lives in Woolwich it ain't far ter come." She keeps staring down the track. "And there 'e is na."

I peer down the track myself and see movement in the distance. I can make out a horse and cart moving towards us at a gallop. In a few minutes it draws up in front of us, the cob breathing hard. A young lad no more than twelve years old jumps down.

"Sorry Ma, I got stopped by the coppers. They're all over the place. They wanted ter kna where I'm garn."

"What d'ya say?"

"I said I was ter pick up sum tarps."

"Good lad, we can put them over the top of the stuff." She looks over to us and waves her hand. "Ok ladies, this way, we'll load up and get on our way."

We follow her to the back of the stables to a store-room, doors already open. Inside was 'the stuff'; timber planks of different sizes, a basket full of kindling wood, a can of petrol, some cloth and some matches. We all know what we have to take but seeing it brings it home and sends shivers down my spine. Loading takes little time and we spread a dirty brown tarpaulin over the top, I pocket the matches.

Hilda looks over the cart making sure everything is in place and hidden from view. "Sorry abaht the transport ladies but it's not too far. We'll take it easy, rushin' it will only raise eyebrows, kna wot I mean." She settles herself in her seat alongside the lad. We're sitting on some old dirty blankets to ease the bumps. Poor Maud and Dorothy look appalled but they follow us and make the best of it they can. Our journey follows the winding river but behind the buildings. Compared to the main route it's deserted with only the occasional movement by the warehouses.

Hilda turns round and shouts above the clip clop of the horse's hooves and the rattle of the wheels. "We're coming to the 'ouse from the back, we'll keep away from the main road. By this time the coppers will be 'avin' their work cut out lookin' after the demonstration."

We leave the riverside and approach the back of a row of houses overlooking the main road. I look for a large detached building, the home of the politician, our quarry. He is a vociferous opponent of the WSPU and a thorn in the side of the Bill to change the voting laws. It is a dangerous mission but we are comforted knowing that the complete household is away in Scotland. There will be no danger to anyone's life.

I see the building, I recognise it from a photograph we've been shown. I point it out to the others. Hilda and the lad are already well aware and we make our approach to the yard to the rear of the house. I feel the tension building, my heart beat is increasing. There is no talking only the slow clip clop then nothing. We focus on the back door recessed in to the wall. We jump down and one by one we start moving materials in to the recess, paper, kindling, cloths and finally large lumps of timber. We tiptoe backwards and forwards, our faces are set, our heads are forever turning this way and that looking for discovery. Hilda has the petrol and slops it over our pile. I reach for the matches, the

147

others step back. I light one and throw, nothing, I light two together and throw, a sissle then nothing. I kneel down light another and set it to the paper, it glows, the flame grows catches the petrol soaked kindling then a flash and a crump as a fireball engulfs our stash. Smoke billows out the recess quickly covering the rear face of the building and up and up into the sky. There it's gathered and directed by the breeze over the house and along the main road. It's now clear for everyone below to take notice.

Our group stares mesmerised by the sudden spread and the intense crackling of the fire. Hilda brings us back to reality with a shout. "Back in to the cart ladies, quick, the coppers will be 'ere any time."

The boy is already taking up the reigns and is waving frantically at us. We have to help Maud and Dorothy but the rest of us jump aboard. I get up last and we're off. The fire has spread alarmingly in just a few seconds. Waves of smoke engulf the cart hiding our getaway. I thank God that no-one is home. A ground floor window suddenly becomes clear through a hole in the gloom. To my horror I see a small girl behind the glass. She's wide eyed, confused, the window is shut tight, there's no escape. I scream. "Oh my God ah have to get her out." I slide off the end of the cart. The others see me and bellow above the din.

"No......."

Chapter 30

The sudden reveal of the window has disappeared and I'm blundering around lost in the grey billowing cloud. My eyes are watering as I peer through the acrid fug. I slap my hanky over my mouth and nose but my lungs still fill with smoke making me cough. Finally my outstretched arms feel the rough texture of the stone wall. I sidle one way, reach the corner, curse under my breath and begin the search in the opposite direction. I remember too late the garden ornament and trip over leaving me on my knees. I realise then that at ground level the air is clear and gasp in wonderful clean air. I spy a stone, grab it and still crouched as low as possible I continue my search for the window. Above the crackle of the raging fire I hear voices nearby, someone in authority is shouting, demanding the fire brigade be called. I can see no-one but I feel a window sill. I stand and without thinking I crack the glass with my stone, and again, and again until it shatters and shards fall at my feet. Immediately there's a shriek from inside, smoke is sucked in to the room but the air is still clearer and I can see the girl. She looks terrified as she backs away from me. I must look like a wraith or some other ghostly figure she only dreams of. I shout.

"Over here, I'll get you out." She hears me but doesn't trust that I'm here to help.

I lower my voice to sound calmer. "Ahm Emily, it's alright ahm here to help ye. Come on jump up an' I'll help ye out the window away from the fire."

She very slowly starts towards me. There's a bang from somewhere in the house which startles her making her jump in to a run. I help her climb on to the window frame and lift her down to the ground. Hand in hand we walk carefully away from the house and out of the smoke.

"Is there anyone else in the house?"

She's too shocked to answer. She just stares at the burning inferno.

"What's yor name hinney?"

She looks at me confused then in a surprisingly calm voice. "No, my name is Mary."

I try again. "Mary, is there anyone else in the house?"

"No, my aunt's gone shopping."

I am so relieved, I give her a hug. "Come on, let's git away from here."

I stand up but I feel a presence behind, a large hand grips my shoulder.

"Not so fast you two."

****

"Mrs Emily Mulligan?"

"Miss."

"Right, ... now what's your name young lady?"

"Mary, sir."

"Mary, Mary what?"

"Mary Herbert, sir,"

The Sergeant asking the questions looks completely shocked. "Do you live in Charlton House."

"Yes I do, sir."

"But I was under the impression all your family are holidaying in Scotland."

"They are, sir, but I was unwell and stayed at home with my aunt, ummmm, sir."

"Oh, and where is your aunt now."

"Shopping."

The sergeant beckons to another policeman. They whisper out of earshot culminating in the second policeman grabbing his helmet and rushing out of the station. The sergeant turns back to Mary.

"I've sent someone to fetch your aunt. Please sit over there." He indicates a bench in the far corner before turning back to me.

"Now Miss Mulligan, come with me." He grabs the top of my arm and leads me away from the desk and towards a room behind.

"Where are you taking her?" Mary was standing up and looking anxious.

"I'm going to ask her some questions. You just stay there. I'll get a drink of water for you if you like."

She runs over shouting. "You can't lock her up, she saved my life. I would have been all burnt up."

The sergeant looks confused and releases me. I squat down to Mary's level and hold her hand. "Don't ye worry about me pet I'm just ganin to answer some questions. Ye stay over there an' wait for yor aunt alright?" She looks at me with her round, sad, blue eyes staring in to mine. As I get up she says.

"Thank you for saving my life."

I smile back then turn and walk in to the room followed by the sergeant. The door closes behind us but another opens and leads me down in to a dark, punishing time of my life.

Chapter 31

I have no energy, I lie on the bed exhausted, I just want to sleep. My hunger, initially painful, aching, debilitating, has disappeared replaced by a deep lethargy and an emptiness filling my very being. The bed is narrow and hard, the pillow is harder but I feel little discomfort. I recall the experience of the past weeks: the initial kindly treatment of the police sergeant. His questions answered clearly, truthfully and my motives explained but all met with head shaking, incomprehension and the inevitable arrest and custody. My trial, just one of many for suffragettes, the judge going through the motions, same words, irresponsible, dangerous, anti-social, incarcerated for the public good. Now imprisoned, locked in solitary confinement in Holloway, a hell's den. There cannot be a worse place on earth, so barbaric and cruel. No respect shown between warders and prisoners, we're treated like degenerates, the scum of the earth.

Food is brought every day usually thrown on to my small table to slide and clatter against the wall spilling its contents accompanied by threats and sniggers. One hour later the same plate is collected, the food untouched, more threats and, if I don't pretend to be asleep, a stinging slap to my head in punishment. It is that time today. I hear the rattling of the key in the door, the door creaking open and shuffling of boots. I open my eyes and see not one but two warders looking down at me, their faces sneering, mocking.

"Shame you haven't eaten Mulligan, get up, you're coming with us." Then in a lower threatening tone, "It's dinner time."

****

Doctor Eric Grimston examined his constructions. All self-built to his own designs. He smiled to himself remembering how he had convinced the authorities of the assured success. Now was the day he could show them off.

152

The full apparatus was spread out on the table before him ready for yet another test. He spoke quietly to himself. "This must work, there must be no mistakes, no coming apart, no mess." He looked at the clock. "Good I have still ten minutes before the prisoner is brought in. I have time."

His eyes and hands combined in intense concentration for the examination. Firstthe rubber tubing, he measured the length, tested its flexibility and checked for blockages. He checked for the perfect fit of the thin steel funnel to slide in snugly to the end of the tubing. Alongside was his back up, a wide glass syringe with its own tubing, to be used only if the gravity system fails. All perfect.

His eyes then flicked over to his masterpiece, his new, steel, hinged clamp complete with rubber padded jaws to prevent crushed bones, always a nuisance. Strutted between the jaws was a screwed threaded bar on which a wheel could be turned to adjust the patient's mouth. He gently twisted the wheel between two fingers. He smiled thinly as the bar extended slowly pushing the jaws further apart.

He rubbed his hands together in anticipation of success. He looked over to a steel pot half full of grey, fluid porridge, an immersed, wooden spoon was lying against the rim. He gave the mixture a stir checking its consistency and to check for lumps. There was none, nothing his apparatus couldn't cope with.

He jumped as his serenity was shattered by the steel door of the room crashing open slamming in to the brick wall behind. Three women entered offering no apology for their sudden, noisy entry. The two warders, dressed head to toe in black, keys jangling on their thick leather belts, looked severe, threatening. Their hair scraped back in to tight buns topped incongruously with a white lace bonnet. The woman between was smaller lost in the standard shapeless prisoners uniform picked out with arrows. He was jolted by her demeanour, she stood upright, calm but proud. Her face pretty, wide mouthed framed by untamed locks of curly dark brown hair. He felt his emotions stirring

153

and looked away immediately. Why is she here in a place full of the criminal classes she should be treated with respect, dignity?

"Are you ready doctor?"

Without looking round he answered. "Of course, sit her down." His mind clicked on to the reason he was there. His priority was the success of his apparatus, nothing else. He stared back at the table, his eyes wide open his mind concentrating, filtering out all unwanted, unnecessary feelings. He waited giving them time to manoeuvre her in to position. There was no noise, no fight, no tussling just a small squeak as the chair adjusted itself to the weight.

He gently gathered the jaw clamp in his hands, turned and approached the chair still looking down. The patient's feet came in to view. He looked up their eyes met. He couldn't look away. She was so young and yet so calm, so pretty. Oh God.

"Are you alright doctor?"

"Er, yes, yes of course."

"Well get a move on, we've got two others to feed.

"Right."

The doctor held the clamp in one hand and with the other, lightly held the prisoner's lower jaw. He paused, then in a weak voice asked her to open her mouth wide.

"Oh for goodness sake, come on Mulligan open up." Without further ado she thrust two fingers inside her mouth and pulled down hard. In an instant the prisoner bent her head and bit in to the fingers as hard as she could. The warden's eyes lit up and she bellowed in agony. The second warder reacted with a solid, swinging punch to the prisoner's head sending her flying off the chair and on to the floor into a heap.

The two warders, one still in agony lifted her bodily and threw her roughly back in to the chair. The prisoner was now semi-conscious, her cheek was cut and blood was oozing from her mouth, the warders blood.

"You little bitch. Come on doctor, get that wretched thing fitted." She grabbed the prisoner's hair and jerked her head back and squeezed her cheeks to bring down her lower jaw, this time with no resistance.

The doctor had stepped back in shock but now obediently crept forward. The prisoner was groggy and allowed her mouth to be emptied and swabbed clean. The clamp was fitted and the rubber tubing complete with its funnel was slid in between the steel jaws and slowly, inch by inch, pushed down her throat. Her shoulders and legs were held tight by the warders as the doctor slowly poured the gruel in to the funnel. From experience the warders lent back as far as they could to avoid any blowback from choking. But the prisoner was semi-conscious; her muscles were relaxed allowing the food to slide down her throat and in to her stomach. The job done the tube was pulled out and the clamp removed.

"Ok doctor, we'll get rid of this wretch and bring in the next." The warder started to lift the body out of the chair when there was a sudden low rumble and belch making her twist round in perfect time to meet head on a projected stream of stinking, blood flecked, vomit.

"Ahhh, you dirty bitch of a whore." She released the body which collapsed on to the floor her head bouncing off the solid brick wall then lay motionless.

****

I'm walking along a beach, weightless, enveloped in a misty but ethereal light. I'm able to glide without effort, it's easy, perfect. I see but don't feel the touch of the pebbles. I notice some are black, I stop and stare and wonder. I realise what they are and touch one to feel its texture. I smile pick up the piece of sea-coal and hold it in my hands. My fingers curl round and I grip it tight. I can feel something, an energy pulsating in to my hand, up my arm and then fills my whole body. I feel a presence and I look up. There are men, women and children walking, no, they're gliding towards me. I don't understand what they're doing or who they are. I wait, they're getting closer, I see they're smiling at me, some waving others laughing. They must know me, but I don't know...yes,yes, I do know them. My whole family, Da, Ma, all my brothers and all my sisters, they are all here. They stop except for Ma, she stretches out her hands, I feel their touch on my shoulders. She speaks softly, slowly.

"Ahm so proud of ye pet, we all are ....but it's time for ye to gan home, home to your bairn, your daughter."

My daughter? I feel confused what is Ma saying, daughter, bairn, my bairn, Mhairi. Oh my God, Mhairi. My hands open, the piece of sea-coal drops to the beach, tears fill my eyes. I feel a growing pain in my head, throbbing, crashing, thumping. My hands clasp around my head to stem the agony, I want to scream, the light is fading. I look up, Ma has gone, all my family have disappeared I see only a wall a few feet away. I realise I'm alone back in my cell, alone with this pain. The tears are still flowing, dampening my cheeks, dripping from my chin then seeping and sucked dry by the folds of my rough prison tunic. Another noise but not in my head, a tapping, a light insistent knocking, then I hear a low, whispered voice.

"Emily."

I sit up slowly. I wonder if I'm dreaming again.

"Emily, are you awake?"

It's someone in the next cell. I struggle to sit up and, still feeling groggy, I search around for something to tap the wall, I remove a shoe and use the wooden heel.

"Who's that?"

"Celia."

I felt shocked but also pleased it was someone I knew. "But ye escaped."

"Ah came back ah was worried about ye."

Our conversation is disjointed. I'm feeling dizzy, my face, my whole head is still throbbing fit to burst. I try to concentrate on her story. It seems that when she saw me return to the house she slipped off the cart herself to follow me but then lost me in the smoke and haze of the fire. She assumed I joined the demonstration on the main road and mingled in. But from being initially peaceful the march degenerated in to a sea of violent confrontations with the police. Celia and many others were arrested and ended up in the same police station later on the same day. This is her first week in Holloway.

There is a sudden rattle of a bar against our doors followed quickly by a warder's bellow. "Be quiet you two or one of you will be moved."

We stop, my eyes close craving relief from the intense throbbing but I can still make out another tap, much lighter than before, then a barely audible whisper. I lift and rest my head against the wall.

"Never surrender."

I tap back and whisper the same. "Never surrender."

I'm suddenly gripped by a sharp, stabbing pain. I collapse back down on to the bed head in my hands, I want so much for it to stop, I cannot stand anymore. My body is seized by a creeping numbness, relaxes and my mind slips away down a long dark tunnel to a much more peaceful place.

Chapter 32

I'm flitting in and out of memories, some restful and comforting, others so scary, even terrifying. I'm reliving scenes in my life. My re-assuring days at home with my family all around me, laughing and pulling faces but in an instant my vision is in turmoil, I'm swirling, screaming, the faces are changing into hate figures. A leering Uncle Joseph takes shape, alongside him appears Charles Proctor, sweating, threatening. I want to run, I want my family, I turn away I can't look. I see my bat cave and hide. I know they won't find me here, they've never been. This is my hideaway. All is quiet. I can make out the sound of the surf running up the beach and pulling back, repeating, never ending, consoling me. I can hear a new melodic sound far away it's not the familiar cry of gulls or the pik-pik-pik of the oyster catchers. I try to concentrate, it's getting louder. I peer out of my cave and listen. Someone is singing, the voice undulates smoothly sometimes blending with the surf and then reaching a crescendo above everything else. I must be in another world, maybe this is heaven. If it is, I love it and want to stay. I feel calm, I lie back against the cave wall, then slip down on to the pebbles and let the sound envelope me. The singing stops, my eyes flick open.

"Hello Em it's about time ye joined us in the living world."

I shut my eyes, I want to listen to the singing some more but it's gone.

"It's me, Millie, ye canna hide from me. I'm not leavin' ye, ahm here to take ye home."

My eyes flick open. I see someone sitting beside me. The vision is indistinct but the voice and name are familiar, I know this person. Who can it be? Why is she here in my cave? I try to focus, the mist clears from her face instantly I connect the face with the name. It's my very best friend Millie Hardy. I can smile but I want to stay where I am.

"Millie, it's so canny to see ye."

She's smiling at me. "An' it's so canny to see ye pet."

"But what are ye doin' here in me cave?"

She reaches over and touches my arm tenderly. She whispers. "Emy, you're not in your cave you're in hospital an' you've been here fo' two weeks. The doctors say you've been in a coma all this time. We've all been so worried."

Hospital, I'm in a hospital? I look around and I take in the bed I'm lying in, the white walls, another bed alongside. I'm confused, I try to raise my head, it feels so heavy.

"Steady on ol' lass I'll help ye sit up." Millie slides her arms under me and pulls me effortlessly in to a sitting position, lies me back against the back rails slipping a pillow between.

I want to help her but I feel so weak. "Sorry ah must be a ton weight for ye to lift."

"There's nothing of ye. First thing ah have to do is feed ye, ye leave that to me." She pauses and examines my arms and face. "You've been through a very bad time, do ye remember anythin'?"

I shake my head and look down at my thin bony arms and hands. I don't understand. My hands go to my face and feel the jutting cheek bones. I twitch as I touch the side of my head. "What's happened to me Millie? ah feel so weak, what have ah done?" Tears roll down my cheeks. I can't help it I'm so confused.

"Move over Em ahm comin' in." I feel her sliding under the covers and we sit squashed together, my head drops down to her shoulder her arm holds me tight. She starts singing softly in my ear, the same singing I heard before in my cave. My eyes close again still wet with tears and I drift off into a dreamless sleep.

I wake to the clatter of a ward trolley. I feel rested but my mouth is dry, my stomach aches and my throat is sore. I remember Millie, I look around but she's gone. I feel disappointed.

"Like something to drink love?"

159

The trolley has stopped at my bed, a woman is looking at me expectant for an answer. I nod. "Yes please."

"I've got some broth if you want dear although the sister says you can't 'ave too much at the moment."

I nod again. "Thank ye."

"I'm so pleased to see yer awake, you've been in the coma for ages."

I can't think of anything to say so I just smile back. I try to pull myself up to a sitting position. Seeing my struggles the woman helps me and positions the pillow behind. "Thank ye."

"You jist get this down ya, it'll build you up." Then she continues in a lower tone really speaking to herself. "And my goodness ya need it."

I look at the bowl of broth and my stomach clenches. I try the mug of tea first, it's only warm but it slips past my sore throat and I can feel it run down into my stomach, weird. Strong hunger pangs grip me enticing me to try the broth. Slowly at first then enjoying the taste I speed up until the bowl is empty. Almost immediately I feel sick. Dispirited I lean back hoping the feeling will ease. It does over time and I start to wonder where I am and why am I in hospital. The ward door swings open and there's Millie striding towards me beaming.

"Emy, you're awake an' you've eaten somethin'." She gives me a big hug and sits down beside me. "Well how are ye feelin' pet?"

"Better thanks Mills but ah need some answers." I trip off all the questions that have been churning in my brain. She holds her hands up to slow me down.

"I'll tell ye what ah know like. Ye an' several others of the WSPU were arrested fer breach of the peace or riotous behaviour or somethin' like that. Ye were sent to Holloway an' you, stupid so an' so, went on hunger strike." She looked at me accusingly then continued. "Then the prison warders tried te force feed ye. It didn't work an' ye ended up knocked out somehow."

160

"Ah remember bein' on hunger strike but how did ah end up in here an' where am ah anyway?"

"Well all ye WSPU prisoners were released but ye were in the prison sick bay in a coma an' you had to be transferred here, Islington it's called. Ye know you've been away from home fo' five weeks."

"What?"

"You're catching on, an' for the past two week you've been out cold. Ah can tell ye, you've been worrying everyone, including people ye don't even know."

"Ah don't understand."

"Ye know ye wanted the newspapers to spread the 'Votes for Women' word. Well you've certainly done that, you've been front page news. Your bonny wee face has been on all the billboards."

I don't know what to think. I try to take it all in. "But has it changed anythin' an' how come you're here in London an', an'.... what about Mhairi?"

Millie grips my hand to quieten me down. "The government have released all WSPU prisoners, ye lot were givin' them a bad name. The WSPU, Lady Constance Dunlop herself would ye believe, asked me to come doon to look after ye. They've paid me fare an' put me in their house in Bermondsey an' everythin'. They're very proud of what you've done. Ah told them you've come rund an' they'll be here today to see ye – if you're well enough of course."

I stare at Millie and shake my head in disbelief, then look up. "Mhairi, what about me daughter."

"Oh she's in safe hands with Mr an' Mrs Roberts." Millie immediately fiddles about in her bag. "A've kept the newspaper article an' photograph for ye, look here it is." She thrusts it under my face.

My eyes widen. There on the front page is the headline 'Suffragette Still in Coma'. I read the article and study the photograph. There's one of me wearing my nursing hat obviously taken in Newcastle. Another of other WSPU members leaving the prison, I recognise Celia but they

161

all look ragged and unwell certainly not jubilant. The article tells of our hunger strike trauma and accusations of brutality leading to my coma. There's a comment from the hospital doctor; he diagnoses internal bleeding to the head from repeated heavy blows. My symptoms include severe bruising and facial lesions, he suggests my life is in grave danger. I see at the bottom of the page in bold is a comment and a small photograph. It can't be, it's Emmeline Pankhurst herself. I can't believe it, she even mentions me by name:

"I am totally disgusted at the treatment handed out to Miss Mulligan. She is a political prisoner not some common criminal. This has got to stop, the authorities have to recognise the difference between. We are all praying for her a full recovery but our action shows our determination to succeed. The Government must stop making worthless promises and meet our demands for equality."

"Oh Millie what have ah done?"

"You've done what ye always wanted to do – you've made a difference. Ye should be proud of yourself. The WSPU are an' so am I."

I'm forced to stay in the hospital for another four days. I don't complain, I feel so weak and just the thought of the long journey north exhausts me. By the morning of the fifth day I'm feeling so much better, the staff seem surprised at my recovery. The doctor thinks I have 'A robust constitution' and is genuinely surprised at my recovery.

"I have to say Miss Mulligan I was fearful of your condition. I've administered to others with fewer problems who didn't make it. However I advise you to take care, walk don't run and plenty of rest periods, you're not out-of-the-woods yet. Do you understand?

"Yes doctor an' thank ye very much."

"Well I'll say goodbye and I hope, in the nicest possible way, not to see you again." He smiled and continued his round followed by the sister and Moira, a nurse.

I watch the group switching from bed to bed discussing each patient in turn. With the last patient examined the doctor and the sister leave the ward. Moira turns on her heels and darts into the kitchen and comes out with a promised steaming cup of tea in her hand. Over my stay we've become friends. Like my ancestors she's from Ireland, unlike me she has a lovely broad sing song Irish accent. We have a lot in common, both nurses, both single parents but in her case she was asked to leave home with her new born. Coming from a large, strict, Catholic family she was in disgrace. Her father's last words were that he never wanted to see her again, charming. She's seen the newspapers and she knows about the WSPU and my involvement and we've had long conversations on the objectives. She's in awe of what the Union have done, Emmeline Pankhurst and her daughters, Emily Davison and me. I smile thinking that in her eyes I'm on the same level of these leading lights.

She gives me the tea and pulls over a chair. She seems excited. "I've got a few minutes. Guess what?"

"What?"

"I've only gone and signed up now haven't I."

"Oh Moira, that's great pet. But what about yor wee bairn, he needs ye."

"Ah 'e'll be gran so. Anyway dat sounds good comin' from yer!" Her face suddenly turns a shade of embarrassed pink. "Sorry oi didn't mean it ter come out dat way."

I close my eyes, I'm also embarrassed. I see a sudden vision of my daughter and a wave of longing flows through me. "Ahm the one who should be sorry. Ahm not the one to tell ye what to do."

"Yer must miss her so much."

"Yes ah do."

We sit together quietly. I sip my tea. I know people who know, must think I'm irresponsible leaving a child so often and for so long. They're right of course and I know this, I've thought about it long and hard

163

many times before. But each time I decide what I do is right. I will make a difference for women in the future, and I have done. My actions, with all the other supporters, will improve the country for all women and that goes for Mhairi as well. And I know she's well looked after and loved as part of their family, not wanting for anything....my heart is gripped, but I don't cry. I've wept so many times before. I've cried enough.

Chapter 33

My journey back to Newcastle is very different to our adventurous journey south. There's just the two of us, Millie and me. I'm comfortably wedged between my best friend on one side and the side of the carriage on the other. It's not The Flying Scotsman but still very fast and, as usual, I'm mesmerised by the countryside whizzing past just outside our window. There is so much to see. I've begun to understand the scale of the country. At home in my village I thought Newcastle was a place far away maybe even at the edge of the world, my world. I'd learnt at school about foreign countries across the sea and from me Da back from his fishing trips but I could never ever imagine going there. They were in different worlds.

I'm tired from our eventful journey from the hospital to the station. All the cheery, smiley farewells to the patients I got to know, the staff and Moira. She reminds me so much of myself in many ways, determined, energetic. She has the same burning desire. I just hope she can fulfil her dreams. Now I'm relaxed looking forward to seeing my friends, my family and my Mhairi. I feel I've done my bit for the WSPU for now. I believe I've made a difference and it's time I spent time on myself. I want to carry on where I left off. Millie has told me that my position at the hospital has been kept open for my return. The concerns of Matron and the doctors have been strongly laid to rest by my ward sister who is now, it seems, one my keenest supporters.

My thoughts turn to my family at home and wonder if they've seen the newspapers. Me Ma is a poor reader. I learnt in the short time I was at school. I tried hard to pass on my knowledge but after an initial interest she would get bored, shrug her shoulders and say daft things like: "What good would it do me?" and "I don't need to read to feed the family or to keep me house clean." Typical reactions from someone in her position. It occurs to me that education or rather the lack of it

165

doesn't help the women's liberation cause. They're unaware of what's happening in the world, they have no basis to even form an opinion. Men make all the decisions, have all the power. Women just get on with life as it is and put up with everything that's thrown at them. I sigh, my thoughts just reinforce the view that real equality will take years. Men's position is entrenched. Few will want to change, to share responsibility with the 'weaker sex'. I smile remembering the WSPU personalities I've met; strong willed, independent, determined. Weaker sex indeed. We will win, it'll take time but win we shall and I'm so proud that I've played my part in this revolution however small.

We arrive at a station, Doncaster. Some passengers have left and a group of men have taken their place, noisy and boisterous. They all immediately light up cigarettes, a new and growing habit. The compartment starts to fill with acrid smoke. A large lady opposite, who had been reading her book, coughs and glares at the group. She stands up muttering and lowers the window for ventilation as the train sets off out of the station. The group ignores her completely and continue their conversations. They seem to be well educated. One takes out a newspaper and starts reading an article to his friends but at a volume that everyone in the compartment can hear. To my horror it concerns my release from hospital. It's an article I've not seen myself. I can sense Millie tensing and she reaches over and holds my arm.

"Best thing is to lock her up again, keep her out the way. She'll only cause a nuisance somewhere else. Who does she think she is anyway?"

Another man answers. "She's probably just a whore wanting to make a name for herself." There's a murmur of agreement amongst them.

Millie's grip on me tightens. I can sense she's bursting to lay in to him. I silently grab her hand, she looks round and I shake my head.

"Whore or not she's got more guts and more common sense than all you lot put together. She's stood up for what she thinks is right. I can't see any man doing that."

I'm completely shocked at the eloquence of the speaker. It wasn't Millie but the lady opposite. She has put down her book and now stares at the men daring them to argue. They back down, they go silent, the man with the newspaper turns the page and nothing more is said. The lady looks triumphant, looks and smiles at us then returns to her book. I whisper to Millie. "Never Surrender". Yes, I just know we will win.

The men get off at York and the lady opposite prepares herself for the end of her journey at Darlington. Before she leaves she speaks to us the only other people left in the compartment.

"I'm not sure I agree with what you do but you're a brave and courageous young lady. We will eventually get the vote, mark my words."

All I can say is to thank her before she leaves, closes the door behind her and gives us a small wave before she walks off down the platform. I lean back surprised but so pleased. I smile at Millie.

"How about that, she recognised me an' she was so... so assertive."

"Like ye are now."

"Ahm not, well, ah certainly don't feel it sometimes."

"But ye are."

"Well ye are too."

"Oh no ahm not."

"Oh yes ye are."

Our voices increase in volume uninhibited in our empty compartment.

"We sound like one of those new pantomimes."

We act out a version of Mother Goose eventually collapsing in heaps of laughter. I realise I hadn't laughed for a long time and it's taken my best friend to help me through the torture of the last few weeks. I can't think what I would do without her.

The train terminates in Newcastle and we must be the last people to leave so avoiding the crush on the platform. Assertive or not I'm in the hands of Millie. I know she'll look after me. I trust her completely. We walk slowly through the familiar route through the town to our hospital digs and to my own comfortable bed and almost immediately I fall in to a deep restful sleep.

****

I woke this morning to what should have been an exciting brand new day and a start of the next stage in my life. I felt relaxed and with a large plateful of breakfast inside me my hunger pangs were just bad memories. I felt stronger and eager to get going. My nursing friends have called and we chatted for ages, too long, before they hurried off late for their work and probably straight in to trouble. Later my Stan appeared. He was in uniform looking smart and handsome. We clutched each other in welcome, I could feel he had missed me but there was something else. His smile was there but I could see tension in his face, he was holding something back.

"What's wrong?"

He released me, held the tops of my arms with his outstretched hands and silently looked in to my eyes.

"What is it Stan? Tell me. Is it Mhairi?

He didn't answer. I broke away from his grip.

"What's wrong with her, is she ill?"

"No, she's healthy but the Roberts, ye see," He paused obviously struggling to put something in to words.

"What Stan?"

"They've left Newcastle, an', they've taken her away with them."

I didn't understand. "For a holiday?"

Like a dam bursting the words came flooding out. "No love they've just disappeared. Ah went back after me shift one day last week an' everythin' had gone, well the furniture wes still there but their clothes, photographs, books had all gone, an' so was Mhairi.

"Gone? Gone where?"

"Ah don't know. Ah asked the neighbours, friends, the local shop, nothin'. Ah went to his work at the loco sheds in Gateshead. They told me he just left, didn't give any notice. One day he was there in the fitters shop the next he was gone. He didn't even tell his mates.

"But they canna do that, she's my bairn. Stan you've got to get her back." I slumped down on to the bed, head in my hands.

"A've reported them missin'. The polis in Edinburgh, York, Manchester even London have been brought in to help. Being a railway man ahm certain they've taken the train. Ah also know that her sister lives in Scotland somewhere so my guess is that they've taken her North."

"Well a've got to gan an' look myself." I looked around in panic not knowing where to start. Stan sat down beside me and gripped my hand. "Emy, the polis are in the best position. Ganin' up there with no leads is a waste of time, leave it to them."

I ranted and raved. I blamed him. I thought living there he must have heard something, seen them making preparations, packing or something. But he just sat there, shaking his head.

"Look, a've got to go. The polis do find people, that's what they do, that's what ah do. So we have to leave it with them. I'll see ye tonight."

He put his hands on my shoulders, I shrugged them off and walked away, I didn't want him there I just wanted my baby, my little girl. He left closing the door quietly behind him.

My day has been turned upside down. I feel my heart has been ripped open, laid bare. Mhairi got me through my dark days in prison and now she's gone and maybe gone forever. I try to banish these negative thoughts but the task of trying to find her seems so impossible. If you want to disappear you can so easily, so many do. I close my eyes but I see a vision of her face, tears well and fall with me in to the depths of despair. I slump on to the bed, tears of a failed mother stream, soaking in to my pillow. My life is wasted, I cry until I can cry no more and fall in to shallow, troubled sleep.

Chapter 34

1914

It's a warm summers day, too warm, but Millie and I have managed to gain temporary possession of armchairs in the staff canteen. We usually lose out but with a bit of determination we succeeded albeit having to ignore barbed comments from the normal occupants. For me it's been a long, tiring, non-stop morning in my ward having to cover for a suffering student nurse who's managed to get herself pregnant. With my hands snugly curled around my mug I lean back, close my eyes and enjoy the warmth and the comfort of the tea as it circulates around my exhausted body. Millie's sitting up enthusiastically reading a newspaper. She has become addicted to international events. Every so often I hear gasps and mutterings.

"Oh no, I bet that'll upset the Serbians."

My eyes flick open. "Pardon."

She looks over demanding my agreement and support. "They've been given an ultimatum by the Austrians,"

I cannot think of an informed response. "Oh, that sounds bad. Is it?"

"Wey aye of course it is. If they don't retreat from Albania there'll be a war out there an' Russia will be drawn in."

I have no idea what she's talking about. She is strangely fascinated by the shenanigans of European politics despite the fact that she's barely ventured more than twenty miles from Newcastle. I always try to understand but my heart is on much more parochial matters: my Stan, my family, the WSPU and most of all my lost Mhairi.

"Is that so bad? Where's Albania an' Serbia anyway?"

"Oh Emy you're hopeless. There's ganin to be a war an' the government think that we may be drawn in to it because of our treaty with France an' Russia."

I know war is very bad. I've heard and read stories of the Boer War and the much earlier battles of the Crimean War. They were horrific but they were always in places far away. Life went on un-affected. This recent news sounds to me to be no different.

"Sorry Millie, ah was miles away."

Millie's frustrated expression disappears replaced by a frown of understanding.

"They'll find her, ahm sure they will. Ye know what Stan says an' my Frank says the same."

"I know."

I take another sip of tea and remember the news nearly two months ago when I was told the police in Scotland had found the Roberts. I couldn't believe it. The very next day I took the early train to Edinburgh and then a tram to Leith. All the way there my heart was racing, I was so nervous. What should I say? Will Mhairi want to come home with me? Leith is very like Newcastle, like most coastal towns, blackened buildings, warehouses, busy bustling streets and the all pervading salty smell of the sea. A policeman accompanied me from the station to a haberdashers shop just off the main Leith Walk. The Roberts had moved in to rooms above.

I can still recall my stomach clench, my heart trying to burst out of my chest, the long echoing walk up to the first floor and my light tap on the door, nothing. The policeman then banged loudly it produced noises, voices from inside. The door opened slowly and an unfamiliar face appeared. She looked frightened, nervous. She agreed that, yes, she was Mrs Roberts and, yes, she had a daughter Mhairi . I listened and stared she looked nothing like my Mrs Roberts and she spoke with a broad Scottish accent. There was movement behind the woman's skirt and a smutty, round face appeared gazing up boggled eyed at the policeman. She was her Mhairi not my Mhairi.

I just couldn't believe it. All my hopes had been dashed in seconds. My apologies, my journey home in a blur of wretchedness, crying

171

myself to sleep, it all passed as a bad dream, a nightmare. I've relived that day so many times, it seems so unfair. I still live in hope but for now I lose myself in work in the hospital and with the WSPU.

Millie spoke again jolting away my black thoughts.

"Come on pet, how about us two ganin dancin' this weekend. We haven't done it for months? Frank won't mind an' we could ask Trudie an' Rose. It'll be a canny crack, like old times."

The thought of being on my feet all night had no appeal at all. "Oh Mils ahm too tired. All ah want to do is get to me bed at the end of the shift."

She was not to be put off and was now full of enthusiasm. She folds up her newspaper and sits on the edge of the chair. "Look ahm ganin to get a big ham joint. I'll leave a plate for Frank an' bring the rest over. Ah can help ye get dressed. When ye get back after yor shift have a soak in the bath an' by the time ah get there you'll be rejuvenated an' raring to go, alright?"

I look over to her smiling, eager face. She's so good for me. She's happy, married to a kind loving man but still has time for her friends. From somewhere deep inside I feel a twinge of a growing excitement, I relent and smile back. "Alright Mrs bossy boots Millicent but If ah oversleep an' ahm late for work I'll blame you."

"Wey aye!"

"I'll be rund at six with dinner me lady." She adds in an excited hushed tone. "A've heard they're ganin to play Tango music. Ahm dyin' to try it. It seems so...umm...darin'!" She springs up and tries some of the steps to her hummed rhythm. She beckons me to join her. I'm less than enthusiastic but she grabs my arms and pulls me up. The resultant chaotic manoeuvres are a disaster but it amuses our surprised audience. We collapse back in to our chairs amid some ribald comments.

"Ah don't think me body can stand the strain, ah think I'll stick to a waltz."

Millie's holding her side. "Ah think you're right, A've got a stitch!"

We both know, no matter what effect it'll have on our bodies, we'll be having a go.

Chapter 35

The dancing at the Palais was great fun of course. Trudie and Rose came along leaving their boyfriends to fend for themselves and the four of us had a ball. The band leader taught us some basic tango steps and told us that we have to look sultry. No chance in hell, we would dissolve in laughter every few seconds.

There was one obvious change from the last time I was dancing. Many of the men were looking very smart but this time in their soldier's uniform. It was only when we were walking home I mentioned this to the other girls and learnt that we were now at war with Germany.

"Emy, don't ye read the papers? It's all over them. Germany has invaded Belgium an' we have to protect them, France as well."

I feel embarrassed at my lack of knowledge. Millie assumes it's her duty to take me through the build up of this announcement and we're now sitting on the two beds in my flat discussing what could happen.

"So all these soldiers will be ganin to Belgium to stop the Germans an' to push them back?"

"Wey aye that's the general idea. Ah was talkin' to the one with the fancy moustache."

Trudie interrupts smiling. "Ah bet he tickled your fancy!"

"Certainly not, nobody comes anywhere near my Frank."

"Of course not!"

"Anyway what ah was saying was....um....."

"He did tickle your fancy didn't he?"

"Alright maybe just a bit," Poor Millie looks embarrassed." Anyway stop interruptin'. They're from the local brigade an' they're all off trainin' for three weeks on Monday.

My head is full of questions. "Supposin' they cross the North Sea an' invade us?"

Millie answers immediately full of confidence. "Not a chance, our Navy is the biggest in the world like. We'll just sink their ships."

"But a lot of soldiers an' sailors will die."

All four of us go quiet before Millie answers. "Ahm sure the Royal Navy will save them an' bring them here as prisoners. Anyway it won't get to that stage. He says it'll be over by Christmas."

My mind is in a whirl of incomprehension. I visualise soldiers charging at each other, ships sinking, people drowning. I wonder how on earth this has come about. Through it all I foresee injuries needing attention by nurses and doctors. Hospitals will get busier. If we don't get more staff I'll be working day and night. The very thought drains my energies and I slump back on to my pillow.

"Ye alright hinney?"

"A've just realised we're ganin to be busier than ever until it does finish. Ah just hope it is over be Christmas."

We look at each other. The truth is dawning on each of us. Everyone now looks sad and depressed, I realise I was the cause and try to cheer them.

"Hawa girls we're lookin' on the black side. It might be all sabre-rattlin' an' nothin' will come of it. We've had a grand evening, learnt a new dance an' ahm just ganin to put the kettle on for tea all rund how's that?"

The atmosphere lifts and we discuss the war no further. Rose and Trudie leave far too late and Millie asks if she can stay the night, lucky thing she's off tomorrow.

"Wey aye ye can, ye can make sure ahm up for me shift."

We lie in our beds chatting until we finally say goodnight.

"Millie do ye think it'll all blow over?"

"No."

I sigh. "Goodnight Mills"

"Night Em."

Chapter 36

1915

Millie was so right all those months ago. Our boys marched in to France and onto the battle lines strung out through Belgium. Almost immediately war casualties arrived in England. Initially we received refugees fleeing from the German invasion. They were such a dispirited, confused collection. Kicked out of their homes, transported to a foreign land where everything was different; the food, the way of life and most of all the language. Many were farmers and had been for generations. For them life hadn't changed much in their lifetime and now they were in England but it could have been the moon.

At first they spent some time in reception areas and from there were taken in by families willing and able to help out. The sick spent time in hospitals to speed their recovery. Lack of nutrition, distress and desperation had taken their toll. Most only needed care, some loving and time to take stock of their situation. None could speak English and none of us can speak Flemish but as nurses this was our job and we set about their recovery with enthusiasm. As Millie reminds me my single minded determination from my WSPU days took over and like many other nurses I spent more time with them than perhaps I should have done. I sat at their bedside or walked in our small garden areas and made them laugh at my attempts to converse by pictures on paper and books, sign language and even animal noises.

I firmly believe our care and attention surrounded by the friendliness of the Geordie people made their recovery a foregone conclusion. They want to return, of course they do, but they're seeing a new world and I can sense their excitement and wonder of it all. When they talk about their homes back in Belgium their love for their homeland is plain for all to see. They do want to return and I'm certain they will but what will they find? It will have changed, war decimates areas sometimes forever. Life will inevitably be very different for them one way or another.

The battlefield casualties are a very different set of patients.

All of them have been through the Casualty Clearing Stations close to the front line and were given 'Blighty' tickets for their recuperation in their homeland. They arrive in Dover or maybe Southampton and then walk or are carried to one of the new hospital trains to whisk them North, some to our hospital here in Newcastle. Generally they're a cheery lot so pleased to be home no matter what injury or illness they're suffering. They can have lost a limb or two, have severe mutilations or are coughing fit to burst but they're smiling through their agonies. It can only reflect on the horrors they've escaped from. To be happy, smiling and joking when your body is in pieces, it's un-natural, surprising. It's only when you hear of their experiences do you understand why. We try to be calm and efficient, making sure they're comfortable, well fed and washed, professional, but we are shocked at their stories, their courage. In quieter moments you hear of their fears and anxieties. Nightmares are common, evidenced by sudden piercing shrieks and shouts or bellowed warnings followed by tears.

Two full wards have been set aside for our brave war wounded. Some are released quickly back to their homes for convalescence others have taken several weeks. Some, just a few, are considered by their unit doctors as being fit-for-service and are returned for further active service. These boys sadden me. In my view, I believe every one of them should have some proper respite. Some may have recovered from their physical injuries but the mental stress of fighting and then the shock and pain of being injured take longer to ease. But it's never my decision. I smile, give encouragement, hide my inner grief, wave goodbye but I can see the fear in their eyes. I wonder how long they'll last.

I call them all 'my boys' and boys some of them were. Pte Michael Macilheron arrived with his left leg amputated below his knee and lacerations all over his left side from his buttocks to his face after being caught in a shell explosion. His notes tucked under him in a folder described his injuries and the treatment given. The label on the front read 'No.2186 Pte M. MacIlheron, 7th battalion Northumberland Fusiliers aged 17. Without looking at him I read the notes as he was lifted from the stretcher and onto the fresh, clean ward bed. My eyes flicked over to my new patient, he was smiling up at me, my heart missed a beat and I gasped.

In front of me lay a fresh face full of freckles with the biggest pair of bright sparkling blue eyes I had ever seen. I grabbed the notes again and re-read the age. Yes it said seventeen, clear as daylight. Wanting some re-assurance I showed it to my student nurse. She did a double take on the boy as her own eyes took in the information. Her hand went to her mouth and she shook her head at me. Before us was a young lad, certainly no older than my brother Con, desperately injured in a battle he most certainly should not have been fighting. I wondered three questions: what on earth had made him volunteer? How come his parents allowed him to? Why oh why did the army accept him?

I said nothing about it, instead we changed his dressings, washed and cleaned his wounds and made him comfortable in one of our gowns. He enjoyed being looked after by the nurses, he was spoilt rotten, we were all his aunties. The surgeon was pleased with his progress. He was a young, a very young lad, big for his age and fit from helping his father on their farm near the Scottish border. But my heart ached for him. The realisation of his injury, particularly the loss of his leg, would change his life forever but this was still to dawn. No longer would he be able to help his father, play football, run and compete with his friends. No amount of love would alter that. He'd be a cripple until he died and as the years go by he could so easily change from being the happy, smiling young lad I can see before me to a depressed, resentful unhappy man.

But here I am helping him walk along the ward with the help of two crutches. He's trying so hard to make it work. The other patients are cheering him on and he smiles and smiles, so triumphant. He tries to wave a crutch in their direction. I hold him tight to stop him keeling over. We get back to his bed. He's exhausted, I'm exhausted but we have done it and I know we'll do it again tomorrow and the next day and the next, whatever it takes. We're not going to let him down, this is our job and I'm determined not to be found wanting.

His mother comes down on the train from Berwick. On her first visit I took her in to my office to explain his physical and mental injuries and to emphasise what on-going treatment he needs when he arrives back home. I pulled no punches. In no uncertain terms I said it was going to be a slow process but worthwhile in the end. I suggested an artificial limb was possible and described how amazing advances had been made and the costs, although still very expensive, were reducing.

In my eyes she was a typical ruddy faced farmer's wife, stocky build, strong arms, large square hands and un-responsive. I hoped she was taking in my advice but I had doubts. She would stare at us as we walked arm in arm down the ward and thump him on the back when he returned to his bed. I could picture her doing the same to a recalcitrant animal on the farm.

Like so many other war wounded Michael had repeated nightmares. Most involved grunts and groans and thrashing about in the bed but sometimes he would shriek a name, it was always 'Charlie, Charlie'. I never forced any issue of talking through battle experiences but last week he especially wanted me to listen. We settled in our 'garden', a small area off the ward but his favourite place to talk to his aunties. He started slowly, still uncertain if he should unburden himself but eventually his story unfolded in all its horror just outside a small town called St Julien.

"We had to attack jerry trenches with other battalions. On a whistle we followed the CO over the top. Immediately the CO himself and many others around him fell back dead from machine gun fire but we all had to follow behind. As soon as I was over I dropped to the ground and crawled in what I thought was a forward direction but I could have been going anywhere. There was bullets whistling overhead and beating up the ground around me. I got to the point where I couldn't move anymore and just curled up in a ball. I didn't fire my rifle at all, I was shaking, I had my eyes closed. After I don't know how long it went quiet. I opened my eyes but my face was flush down to the mud so I had to turn sideways. I could see tufts of grass inches away, on top was a helmet, not mine someone else's. I thought, good, I'll keep that as extra protection but then I heard that awful whistle. It was a shell coming my way. The ground lifted everything all around and under me, high in to the air and slapped me back down again. I lay there as before but now covered in dirt and in shock, I couldn't feel a thing. I didn't want to move. I wanted to stay there forever. I was camouflaged, safe from being discovered.

I don't know how long I was there alone before I felt a hand on my shoulder and a voice at my ear shouting my name, I recognised my mate. I looked up but he slammed my face back down. He whispered clearly and urgently to keep my head down. He said he'd drag me back to our lines. He took a firm grip of my arm and we crawled or rather slid like fat khaki-clad snakes an inch at a time.

We could only have been twenty yards away but it took so long but then there was our trench. There was a man inside he shouted 'who's there'. My mate rose to speak a shot rang through the air and he slumped down a bullet through his brain. I looked behind and saw the hun sniper taking aim for another shot – at me. The shot came but it was for the German, he fell forward, a victim of our own sniper. With a supreme effort I lifted myself over the last few feet and fell in to the trench and in to another world of silence, tranquillity and peace."

I couldn't speak, I couldn't cry. This fourteen year old telling me his story of the battlefield one of the many in this war created by greed and power lust of world leaders who can't live together and get others to fight for them and to give up their lives. Why not them? Why don't they have the balls to fight each other face to face, to the death if necessary? Why do millions of others have to suffer because of their psychotic bluster?

We sat quietly holding hands until I had to ask the question I already knew the answer to. "What was yor mate's name?"

"Charlie." Tears streamed down his face. "He lost his life saving mine." He dropped his head on to my bosom and sobbed long and hard. I held him to me until I could feel him relax and now free of the desperate story held for so long within.

Chapter 37

Our lovely boy Michael went home just four weeks after he arrived. His progress was astounding. From a stretcher case to a fine upstanding fourteen year old walking in perfect timing with just one crutch. He was popular with the staff and patients alike, always smiling and helping his 'aunties' to help other amputees to walk or eat. He was, as the saying goes, just what the doctor ordered. A pretty nurse has always been known to raise the spirits of the boys but to see such progress in such a short time gives other amputees great hope and encouragement for their own recovery. The frustration in some can lead to verbal abuse, temper tantrums and depression but with Michael he smiles through everything. He just ignores the insults and shouts as if they never happened and continues his encouragement. We all want him to stay for the duration. He has been an asset to the ward, irreplaceable.

His mental condition has improved. Many fewer nightmares, no shouting his grief for Charlie. His story has been told and he now looks forward to the future. My previous concerns have been washed away by his positive attitude, his love of life. I know, one way or the other, he will succeed.

The arrangement was that we take him to the railway station and make certain he catches the right train. His Mum will meet him at the other end. Myself and the very same student nurse that treated him when he arrived waved him off from the platform. It was now up to his parents to accept him and love him for what he is. He promised to write, we're going to miss him tons.

****

The hospital trains can arrive every week or up to a month apart dependent on the level of fighting on the Western Front. Our workload therefore varies from week to week and our ability to take time off also varies. In this year of 1916 I have worked continuously for four weeks, seven days per week. Millie and most others are the same. I really needed a break and on the spur of the moment I asked for three day leave to see my family. As it happens poor Trudy my friend from student nursing days has just learnt that her Mum is ill and has had to take compassionate leave to look after her and her younger brothers and sisters leaving us short on one of the wards. Despite this, Sister has allowed me to take the days off to visit my family. We're a real team in the hospital and by taking leave I'm loading more work on the over-stretched nursing staff.

I'm walking back to my flat along with Millie. "Don't be so daft, take advantage, we'll cope. Anyway ah don't think the next train's due 'til next week so we'll be fine. Ye gan off an' see your family. You've not seen them fo' ages."

"Since last year. I'd love to see how they're gettin' on, but we do write an' we've got lots of bad cases in all the wards. Oh ah don't know."

"Em, just gan."

I really want to go and thanks to Millie I feel more comfortable I'm not letting the staff or the patients down. By a lucky co-incidence Stan has time off at the same time and the two of us are now on the omnibus leaving Newcastle behind and looking forward to seeing Ma, Con and my sisters. On my last visit the changes in them hit me hard, in a good way. My sisters now 12 years old are just beautiful, Con is now a man, broad and strong and helps crews in and around the harbour and as for Ma the transformation is complete in fact she looks younger now than I can remember. She positively glows. Gone is the fear of beatings, the worry of enough money to feed the family. She's a different woman with a face that shines with happiness and contentment and all because of Davey my step-Da. They act like happily married newly-weds, holding hands, cuddling and planning for their futures. I am so pleased for them all, they deserve it. I have to admit my teenage years of rebelling against all men have moderated since I've met some really lovely people. My Stan is one of them although I know I don't deserve him the way I treat him sometimes. He has met the family and in typical Geordie fashion he was welcomed with open arms and immediately treated as one of us.

With just a quick glance at my coal gathering beaches and a smile at the bat-cave we get off the omnibus and immediately breath in the fresh sea air devoid of traffic and factory smog. I haven't been able to warn them of our arrival and I'm hoping someone will be home. I knock on our door but there's no response so we try around the back through the close and in to our yard to try the kitchen door, again no response. I walk in, I know the doors are never locked. The kitchen is warm and the decoration and the furnishing are clean and comfortable. I feel as though the house has clasped a welcoming blanket around me encouraging me to make myself at-home.

I boil the kettle and we help ourselves to a pot of tea and some home-made biscuits and sit down and wait. There's a quiet knock on the back door and after a while it opens slowly and a face appears around the side. It's Ettie, she sees us and shouts her greeting. "Emily and Stan, it's so canny to see ye. I didn't know ye were comin'."

I gave her a cuddle, she looked pleased to see me but I could see she's been suffering with her legs as she could only hobble over. We explained about the short notice and having no time to write.

"They won't be back 'til temorra. They all went on a special charabanc outin' to Holy Island an' guess what, they're ganin to stay in tents, campin'." She smiled wickedly as if people of their age never did this which of course they don't very often at all. "It's that Davey he's always up to somethin' different. Mind it works on yor Mum. A've never seen her so happy." She giggled like a school girl telling tales.

We gossiped around the table filling the teapot as fast as it emptied. "Look ah s'pect there's plenty te eat in the larder. Why don't ye have somethin' an' stay the night then you'll be around when they get back ah know they would hate to miss ye." She looked at Stan and added conspiratorially. "And ah think they keep a bottle of beer in the larder for visitors an' ah know there's a bottle of Sherry somewhere. Davey doesn't drink but ah know yor Ma likes a tipple. Anyway I'll leave ye to it." She rose slowly and painfully and made her way to the door swaying from side to side. "Tara hinney fo' now."

"Bye Ettie, see ye temorra."

She bangs the kitchen door shut and we hear the yard gate open and close squeaking on its hinges. "She walks as if she's already been at the sherry herself!"

I give Stan a kick under the table. "Watch it ye, Ettie saved this family, kept us together."

"Ah know, you've told me already. She's a canny old girl. Also a bottle of stout would gan doon right well."

I laughed. "Let's have a look then." We found two bottles as described. "There we are one each."

We were both tired after the journey and the beer made us relaxed and happy. Stan emptied his quickly and held my hand and whispered in my ear. "Do ye fancy a cuddle then."

"In the middle of the afternoon?"

"No time like the present."

"Alright then ah can't argue with a poliss."

We slip out of our clothes and bury ourselves under the bedcovers. We cuddle tightly to keep warm and kiss gently. We have never made love, it's my fault, I don't deserve someone who has such patience but now I feel a difference. I feel somehow free, liberated and very sexy. He kisses and nibbles the side of my neck causing me to close my eyes and to gasp in ecstasy, his hands slip down to gently caress my heaving breasts. He must feel the change in my reaction he can sense that this is the time and he has the presence to take his time, floating kisses all over my aching, arching body driving away any last thoughts of resistance. I'm all his and he knows it and for the next half an hour we make love deeply and intensely. The experience is so different from my only other time and I realise what I have missed over all these years, what a waste.

We repeat our love making many times and by the morning I feel so relaxed, so loved and so deep in each others' arms. It occurs to me that this is what Ma must feel now in this very bed. How wonderful for her and now how wonderful it is for me.

I must have dropped off to sleep as when I wake I'm alone in the bed. I feel disappointed and call his name. There's no answer, then I hear the back door open and close and I call his name again.

A face appears around the door. "Mornin' ye sexy Suffragette."

I laugh. "Mornin' yourself ye cheeky Peeler workin' your wicked ways on me. Where have ye been?"

"A've been to see Mrs Maxwell at the shop an' bought some breakfast for us. Ah didn't want te raid your Ma's pantry."

"Oh ye sweetie, don't forget the pot of tea."

"Ahm at your command me lady."

I hear unpacking and cooking noises from kitchen. I feel like a lady and slide back down in to the bed and stretch my body under the cool sheets. It feels so luxurious.

I hear a shout. "Are ye getting up?"

"No, ah want breakfast on a tray please with a napkin."

I hear a laugh. "I'll give ye a napkin alright." He comes in to the bedroom looking devilish. He strips off the sheet leaving me naked before his eyes but he stops and stares and then smiles. "Ye realise you're the most beautiful girl in the world don't ye?"

"You're not so bad yourself." I start wriggling and writhing on the bed as tempting as I could.

"You're just too bad." He pulls off his shoes and slips off his trousers and shirt and joins me on the bed. We start kissing and cuddling very gently. It feels so decadent and I could feel both of us getting aroused for more love making but we're interrupted by a strong smell of burning from the kitchen.

"Our breakfast."

"Oh my God." Stan springs out of bed, "I forgot. It's all your fault." I'm left alone again and in frustration I grab a pillow and cuddle and squeeze it tightly but I smile. I feel so happy. I know I shouldn't be doing this but I deserve it and I'm going to enjoy it, while I can.

Chapter 38

Before my family returns from their trip we tidy the house and we have time for a long walk along the main street to the harbour. Then back along the beach as far as my bat-cave and then returning to our starting point. We have even taken Bennie for a walk in the fields and mucked out his stable. The poor old boy is creaking at the joints but looks as though he's enjoying his retirement. With his ears pricked and his head nodding I firmly believe he still remembers me. He has nothing to do now. I know the children's coal gathering days are over. I can see a good stack in the backyard but this is delivered directly from the pit – a perk of any miner's job.

Apart from Ettie and Mrs Maxwell I introduce Stan to some of the other ladies and retired men. Everyone is pleased to see us and like on my previous visits they give me a kiss and a squeeze.

Along the beach Stan stops and looks at me. "Ye know these village folk don't forget do they?"

"How do ye mean?"

"Ah remember the first time ah came back with ye, they were all so proud of what you've done. You'll go doon in village folklore as the one who made a difference for Women's rights. You're a heroine in their eyes, an' mine of course."

I don't know what to say. I am proud of what I've achieved and hoped that it did make a difference. But it has affected my life and not all for the good. I can never forget my Mhairi. If I was less single minded on the one crusade I would still have her with me and my heart wouldn't break every time I think of her, which is every day.

I smile up at him. "Thanks me love, but ah was just one of many an' we've still a long way to go." I look over to the horizon. "Somewhere over there men and women are fightin' an' dyin' on both sides an' for what? Do ye think this would be happenin' if women had more of a say in politics? Greed an' power are the curse of today's world. Ah believe women can bring some balance, some conciliation in to the world's equation an' make it a better place to live an' the sooner the better."

"It'll take generations pet."

"Ah know but this is a start an' ahm lookin' forward to the end of this stupid war." I turn to Stan, "an' be able to vote in the next election."

He takes me in his arms and we just kiss for the hundredth time, a couple caught in love blown by the fresh sea breeze in our faces and chilled by the soft swirl of the tide at our feet.

****

Ma, Davy and the children come back in the late afternoon. They've obviously had such a great time. The girls are on to me the second they get through the door. They're older, now almost teenagers but they haven't changed and still bounce about talking continuously both at the same time. Ma is flushed, smiling and healthily plump while Davey is the same quiet, smiling, thoughtful man as before. Con has grown. He is tall as Stan as broad as Davy but still shy and hangs back behind the others. I can see he is pleased to see us and I give him a big hug, hold his hands and kid him on about his growth.

"Oh Emily pet ye should have told me you were comin', we could have gone next week."

"Sorry Ma but ah got leave at short notice. Anyway Ettie made us welcome an' we've made ourselves comfortable an' had a canny day. Now tell us about Holy Island, did ye enjoy it?"

"It was champion we..." She was immediately interrupted by the twins who gave us a quick fire run-down of what they've done and where they stayed. It reminded me of the happy memories of the last time my family, including me, took the charabanc to the same place. It was before the twins were born so must have been nearly twelve years ago. Pa was in such a good mood, so unusual. I can't recall seeing him so happy since that day. Davey is such a different man: kind, loving and caring and, such a big thing, he doesn't drink beer or spirits. Ma so deserves him.

Stan and Davey have many interests in common but the one that stretches their minds most is 'The Toon Army', the support of Newcastle United Football Club. Even now when all professional matches have been stopped for over a year while the war is raging they can still talk for hours on the subject. So Stan with his bottle of stout and Davey with his cup of tea have retired to the backyard to continue their debate. I'm only too pleased to walk along the beach with Con just by ourselves. But what he's saying distresses me completely.

"So what does Ma think?"

"She's not pleased."

"Well of course she's not an' ahm not. A've seen the casualties, a've heard their stories. Don't believe all them posters about loyalty to King an' Country, you'll just be canon-fodder an' nothin' more. Some soldiers are heroes but the vast majority come out disillusioned, injured or dead. Anayway you're too young, you're not even seventeen let alone eighteen."

"Some of my pals have volunteered like an' they got in an' they're the same age."

"Oh Con, ah know this goes on an' ah see it often enough where ah work but why not wait 'til yor old enough, next year?"

"It might be all over be then."

I shout in exasperation. "Well bloody good job if it is."

Con goes quiet and we walk on in silence. I look to the horizon but all I can visualise is a line of crippled, beaten men stumbling along in a single file of defeated humanity and at the end of the queue is my boy Michael Macilheron on his crutches. I wonder if they would have joined if they knew what would happen to them and how badly the rest of their lives would be affected.

I sigh and quietly weep for I know that for these young men there is a compulsion, fed by the government, to sign up and fight for their country and not be classed as cowards, outcasts shunned by all society. 'Are you a man or are you a 'conchie' that is the question you should ask yourself. Can you live with yourself if you reject your country?'

I can say no more but hold his hand and walk back home. My heart so carefree and happy before is now gripped tight with anger and foreboding.

****

"Oh Stan, are all our young lads ganin to suffer 'cos of this damn war?" I stare unseeing out of the window of our omnibus taking us back to Newcastle. Stan takes a while to reply.

"They're calling this the Great War. Ah suppose 'cos it's the biggest that's ever been, it's dragged in every country of the world an' it's still ragin'. Who knows when it's ganin to end." He grips my hand tighter. "We just have to hope an' pray that it does end an' soon. With any luck yor Con will survive it an' help make sure there's no more, ever."

He slides his hand behind my back and pulls me over and my head drops on to his shoulder. We must look like a loving couple. We are of course, but I'm filled with an empty frustration of hopelessness. I can do nothing to change the situation except, perhaps follow his advice, and pray to God.

The journey is long, bumpy and noisy but I do pray and by the time we are back I feel hopeful. We're not due to return to work until the following day so we spend the rest of the day eating, sleeping and making love at his digs. I've had a wonderful short holiday. I feel elated but still with that nagging fear for my little brother.

Chapter 39

I can't help but tell everything to my best friend Millie. There's a lull in the wards waiting for the next train to arrive. The student and junior nurses are making preparations and we're sitting in our office with our feet up drinking tea.

"So ye see Mills a've given in to pure lust after all this time."

"Good for ye Em, so ye don't mind gettin' pregnant again then."

"Wey aye ah do but ahm tryin' this natural safe period system. Ye know days one to seven an' after twenty one an' all that." I smile wickedly. "That means a've got two more days before ah have to lock myself up."

"So what does Stan think about that?"

"Umm, he says he'll find the key – no chance!"

Millie doesn't laugh and instead looks glum. "Me an' Frank try all the days one to thirty an' ahm exhausted, we both are. It's not fun anymore."

I know they've been trying to start a family ever since they were married nearly two years ago now. They're such a lovely couple. There's no hint of blaming each other they love each other too much, they just keep trying. If that's not enough stress Frank has been called up and he has applied to be classified as a Conscientious Objector. I support him whole-heartedly. He is always kind and considerate and is a man of high moral standards. He will gladly thump someone who in his view is basically evil or to protect someone he loves. But why should he try to kill someone he doesn't know, who is no different to him? Once it's known he will be vilified for his action and called a coward, all for following his heartfelt compassionate views. I have already written my supporting letter to the tribunal and so has Charlotte my friend the school Matron. It's set for next month but I'm not confident. So many have failed, it seems the panel is made up of war supporters and even some women with husbands on the Front. How can this be humane and fair?

I feel guilty talking about babies and our way of avoiding having them. "Sorry Mills, it must be so frustratin' for ye both." We're interrupted by a knock on the door. One of the junior nurses peers around and looks at me. "There's a lady te see ye Staff."

I feel pleased for the diversion. "Alright show her in." A well dressed lady appears and I gasp "Celia!"

"Emily pet, ah hope ye don't mind ah was in town, saw the hospital an' ah just wondered. An' there ye are a Staff Nurse."

"It's so canny to see ye, take your coat off an' I'll get ye a cup o' tea."

She removes her coat to reveal a very pregnant lump. My heart sinks, not for Celia of course but for Millie who almost immediately gets up to leave.

Celia notices and insists that Millie should stay that she won't be long and she didn't want to stop our discussions. I remember Celia's story and also insist that Millie stays.

Celia starts immediately. "Ah wanted to thank ye. Ah followed yor advice like an' ah left me husband. Ye know the one who hurt me." She made arm movements trying to imitate the violence. "Ah hid at me Auntie's house for six months, hardly went out. Her family were very kind, they protected an' looked after me an' guess what? Me husband was sent to prison for violent assault against another woman. She nearly died of her injuries."

All I could say was "Thank goodness fo' that."

"So he's away fo' ten years." She smiles and then adds proudly. "Ah managed to get divorced, married a friend of me Auntie's son would ye believe an' at last after all these years ahm in the family way." She proudly pats her lump.

"Ah remember ye so wanted a family, ye just picked the wrong man." I look at Millie and explain that Celia had more injuries to her body than some of the soldiers in our Ward.

"Mind it took a time, we tried for two years, we thought it would never happen but ah gave up me job, put me feet up at home, just looked after me new hubby an' boom, here ah am."

I feel a tingle, that's just what I wanted to hear. I look over to Millie, her eyes are wide open and her mouth is agape. I can picture her mind cogs whirring around apace.

My ward sister enters and asks for Millie to manage the registration of a new patient into her Ward.

After she leaves I'm so pleased I rise and startle Celia with a big cuddle. "Ye don't understand what you've just done. You've given hope to me best friend. You're a godsend."

"Wey aye that's canny."

Our quick chat extends to almost half an hour of reminiscing. She finally leaves with a promise to meet again and also a promise that I'm to be the baby's God-Mother.

I slump back in to my chair thinking what a beautiful piece of timing that was. I couldn't have stage managed that any better.

After my shift and before I get back to my own digs I call in to see Stan. He's only just back himself and has removed his jacket and helmet and is in the process of filling his kettle for a cup of tea.

"Ah just in time, fancy a cuppa."

"Not half!" I strip of my cloak, loosen my top and slip off my shoes.

We sit each side of the kitchen table mugs of tea in our hands. We tell each other about our day including Celia's visit. He's had an uneventful day and got a bit bored and is apparently ready for action!

I reprimand him. "Down boy, far too early". I try to be serious. "A've been talking to Millie about Frank's tribunal. It seems to me that no-one ever gets registered CO with this lot. They're all pro-war an'

I've been told someone from the army is always there. He's got no chance has he?

He thoughtfully sips his tea before he answers. "There's no hard an' fast rules. Sometimes it's doon to if the panel has had a good breakfast or are feeling a bit poorly. But your right, it's unlikely he won't have to join up like." He pauses thinking back. "Although a've heard that some have been allowed to take non-combative duties. Ye know, cooks, drivers, store-men an' the like"

"Well a've written an' so has Charlotte. We may make a difference."

He laughs. "It may help if ye appear yourselves an' perhaps wiggle ye backside a bit."

I try to look serious. "That's a very sexist remark Stanley." He looks embarrassed but I smile.

"Perhaps ah should go in me nurses uniform with a few buttons undone like this an' show a bit of flesh."

He looks shocked at the idea. "Don't ye dare an' besides they're maybe women on the panel an' that won't impress them."

I smile at his outrage. "But if ah did this to ye, ye may be influenced just a wee bit?" I undo a few more of my buttons and bend forward and wiggle." He looks uncomfortable and I think I've gone too far. But he puts down his cup and comes around my side of the table and in one swoop he lifts me out of the chair and he carries me off to his bedroom.

I can't help laughing. "Stan Stan put me doon."

"We've got two days left an' ahm ganin to make the most of them!"

Lying naked in the bed cuddling after our love making I can't help smiling and thinking, he notices. "Don't ye even dream about it." Then he adds, "But Charlotte, mmm, now that may be interestin'."

At that point he is the subject of pillow violence never before seen.

Chapter 40

Now that has been another victory for women's liberation. Something that shows the power women have over men.

I paid a visit to Charlotte at the school. She has been rejuvenated. No signs of a return of the moustache and she now dresses with elegance and poise. The new manager has brought in many new ideas, with her advice and help, and as soon as you enter the great reception hall the changes are obvious. Brighter colours, exciting paintings contrasting nicely with the oak panelling and it's clean from floor to ceiling. Even the children I saw seem to be livelier, happier.

As soon as I walked in I'm met with a welcome smile and hug.

"Emily it's so nice to see you, let's have a look at you." She pulled my arms away and examined me. I still have my cloak over my nursing uniform. "Wow, you look vibrant and eager, yes those are just the words."

I laughed. "What about ye, that dress is new isn't it, an' so elegant." She did a twirl and acted like a school girl. "Well, you may have noticed I've worn the same two dresses forever but with all the re-decoration I thought why not me as well."

"So the new manager is makin' changes then?"

She beamed immediately. "Mr Charlton is a breath of fresh air. You've seen the re-decoration and that goes all the way through the school and we've had better facilities installed for the children and the food, well, it doesn't compare to the slop you were fed. I'll take you around later if you've the time. I know how busy you nurses are."

I opened my cloak to show off my promotion to staff nurse.

"Oh Emily you've done so well."

"Thanks to ye Charlotte. Now tell me about Mr Charlton." I smiled eyebrows raised.

"Oh you, there's nothing like that, Jackie's just good at his job."

"Jackie?"

Charlotte's blushed furiously. I took her hand. "Sorry but ahm just very pleased fo' ye an' for the school."

She recovered her composure. "I'll get you a cup of tea and biscuits and we can talk about this CO business for young Frank."

Sitting comfortably in the armchairs I related my plans for our presentations to the panel. "We have te be well rehearsed an' be super confident of our positions. We must stress how patriotic Frank is despite his tough upbringin' in the workhouse. How he always acted responsible like an' helpful. How he helped to uncover Proctor's evil habits. Ahm ganin to tell them how he rushed me to hospital after the accident, I won't say it was him that ran me over! An' we must be ready with answers to any possible questions."

"I think I can manage that ok."

"An' one mare thin'. My Stan has discovered that the panel is all men, no women. So..." I smile sweetly, "perhaps we can dress to attract their inner feelings!"

She laughed. "I hope you don't mean we walk in naked? I think that may put them right off – well me anyway."

I laughed goggle eyed. "No, we dress smartly an' elegantly, like ye are now. An' perhaps tighten up arund our curvy bits, nothin' unseemly. Perhaps a wiggle or two as we walk in."

"Do you think that'll work?"

"Why not they're men aren't they?" I had to add, "An' ye didn't wear that canny dress just for your own benefit do ye?"

We tried it out with limited success. Charlotte has a lot to wiggle. "Perhaps take smaller steps so ye vibrate an' tremor." We laughed out loud at our efforts and were caught by surprise by a knock on the door and a smart man in a check suit walked in looking down at some papers he was carrying. When he looked up he realised that perhaps he was interrupting.

"Sorry Charlotte I should have knocked." He has a deep dark voice and looks very embarrassed.

We recovered quickly and smiled at him. "No problem Jackie, this is Emily one of my old school children. She's come back to visit and we were just having a laugh at old times."

He smiled handsomely and approached with an arm outstretched. "Nice to meet you Emily. What do you think of the school?"

I answered in a rush complimenting what I'd seen already.

"Charlotte is the real power behind all this I just arrange the funding." He looked over to her his eyes full of admiration and to my surprise he took her hand and said."We make a good team don't we."

All she could do is nod. The both smiled at each other as if it was the most natural thing in the world. "Anyway I must let you get on with your reminiscing. Please have a look around the rest of the school and let us know what you think." He waved his papers. "I can come back later to talk about this." He turned to go and added. "Come back anytime Emily, bye."

As the door closed I just looked at Charlotte. "He is amazin' an' ahm comin' to the weddin' alright?"

"Maybe after the war's finished."

"No, no, as soon as ye can!"

****

I just about ran all the way back to the hospital to see Millie and tell her the news. I arrived soaking wet from the rain but hot and sweaty from the run. To my dismay I realised that a train had only just disgorged another load of injured soldiers and the two wards were full of new admissions with nurses and orderlies flying in all directions. I saw Millie and gave her a quick wave. I was off duty but I removed my cloak to leave in her office so that I could help where I could. In the office I met the Ward Sister.

"Staff Nurse Mulligan, what are you doing here, you should be off."

"Ah just popped in to see Millie ah didn't realise a train was due, so ah thought ah could help like."

"A train wasn't due, This train was for Glasgow but it was diverted here because of problems further North." She waved me over to a chair. "Sit down Emily. Everything's in control. What I would like you to do is go home and rest. I need all of you in good, healthy condition and that means not working every hour God sends. I can give Staff Nurse Tanner a message if you like."

I've known the Sister for five years now and I can say that we both trust and support each other implicitly. Even in my early militant years with the WSPU, when perhaps I should have been sacked, she kept faith in me.

I explained about Millie's husband's tribunal and my intentions for making a representation.

"And you're going to stand in front of them and give your evidence? Well good for you." She became thoughtful and gave a small smile. "I shouldn't say anything but my husband has been drafted on to the panel. I think I'll have a quiet word."

"Oh Sister if ye could, that would really help."

"Leave it with me. I'll let Millie know what you've done."

****

The tribunal was nerve jangling. Charlotte was strangely calm and collected before she went in and smiling when she'd finished. I was shaking like a leaf but I was determined to give a good impression. I tucked my blouse in, made sure my uniform was perfectly in place and with my head up, chest out I walked in with just a small but noticeable wiggle of my bottom.

The sight before me was daunting, six men behind a long desk but as I looked at each man in turn I could see their expressions were not of hostility but of respect for my uniform and I suppose the job that I do. One surprise I didn't expect was to see Jackie Charlton sitting there.

199

His calm, deep voice brought an extra gravitas to the occasion. I wondered why Charlotte didn't let me know.

I hoped my presentation went well. I tried to smile when they were speaking and answered their questions as carefully as I could. When I left the chairman commented that I had done well. I was so pleased that I forgot to wiggle on my way out!

Charlotte was waiting for me. "I didn't tell you about Jackie, I thought it might affect your appeal."

"But can he affect their decision?"

She just smiled. "We'll see."

****

Before any official notification was received Frank and Millie learnt that although he had to join up his 'Conscientious Objector Registration' application was successful and his duties will therefore be restricted to non-combative duties only, for the duration of the War.

News came of this via the fleetest route of Jackie Charlton-Charlotte Sprote-Emily Mulligan and finally over to Millie Tanner within hours. Smiles abounded with cups of tea all round.

I can't help but consider this as another success for women's liberation. That is: get what you want using any means at your disposal – within the law of course!

Chapter 41

1917

I gaze through the window at the autumn countryside rushing past. England is so beautiful, fields of gold, steeples so tall reaching in to the sky so blue. In this time of war I feel at peace with myself. I've made my choice, it's been difficult. I've waved goodbye to my friends and family and to my lover. Some understand, others think I need treatment. I love them all but I know what I want and this is it. What's happening in France is not right. Why does this Kaiser think he needs to take over the world? I try to believe everyone is equal no matter where they come from. But every time I hear or think of him I tense, my hands roll in to a tight ball and I feel a wave of hatred filling my body. This can't be right. I must see for myself, make my own judgements and make my own decisions. I'm going to make a difference, I hope.

Clouds of steam waft by my window at times completely blocking my view and I recall my last journey south. I was full of hope and determination. The expected week away from home turned in to months, a time that's been engraved deeply into my brain forever. I visualise still shots as if they were yesterday, Celia's mutilated body, the house engulfed in fire and the girl's face in the window, my own cell window. I can still feel the hurt but I was part of a country wide movement and I feel so proud.

Changing trains in London and boarding the Dover train at Charing Cross highlights the change in four years. The majority of the travellers are now in uniform. Most are soldiers, noisy, excited, nervous, play fighting with their mates, trying to chat up women. Kit bags fill the luggage racks, no seats empty, the corridors full to overflowing and the windows open to release the smoke and smell of humanity.

I walk down the platform peering in to each compartment searching in vain for any empty seat. I have to get on or I'll miss the boat to Calais, I assume I'll be standing all the way but I hear above the din a railwayman beside me.

"This way Miss." He leads me to a compartment with windows labelled 'Ladies'. My eyes light up, I'm so pleased, I smile and thank him profusely as he opens the door and helps me on with my bag. He recognises my nursing insignia on my coat, he smiles and wishes me 'Good Luck Dear'.

My compartment luxuriates in having bench seats made for eight with only three other occupants so far. I settle in to a position next to a young lady who is nervously looking all about, her hands tightly clasping a small bag on her lap. She glances out of the window then turns and her eyes flit over me and the other occupants then the sepia paintings of countryside scenes fitted above the seats. There's a sudden commotion in the corridor as a large soldier with a huge tubular kitbag slung over his shoulder, a vision in khaki, suddenly blots out our view through the window. He smiles and waves at us before he moves on but not before my neighbour has averted her eyes down to her lap in horror.

Even before any conversation she shows herself to be completely new to this situation. I would be surprised if this wasn't her very first train journey. I want to relax her and start talking.

"We're lucky to find this compartment aren't we?"

Her eyes widen realising that someone is making conversation. She grapples with her bag and looks over to check if I'm actually talking to her. She doesn't speak.

"Hello ahm Emily, are ye ganin far?"

She coughs and looks away but then gaining some confidence she answers. "France."

I am completely shocked. I realise she's on the same adventure as me. She can only be eighteen at the very most but behind all this uncertainty and nervousness she must have the courage to volunteer for work most probably way beyond her experience.

"So am I. Ahm going to work in a CCS in Flanders. CCS that a Casu..."

"Casualty Clearing Station, I know, so am I."

She now has my full attention. Her voice is quiet but her accent is pure cut glass English. Our conversation is cut short by a railway whistle being blown shrilly and then by our door opening wide and three gasping, panicking young women throwing on their bags then jumping on board themselves all at the same time as the train starts to move. From there on our compartment has changed in an instant from being a quiet oasis of calm to the centre of a raging storm. The ladies, obviously all friends, are all of a chatter. Cases fly up to the luggage racks joined by coats stripped off hurriedly in an attempt to cool down after their heroic entrance.

Pretending to read my book I overhear their conversation. This can easily be heard, despite the rattling of the train and the whooshing through tunnels. I can see my neighbour is doing the same. We both learn that the girls are also going to France as VADs, we exchange glances of understanding.

She whispers. "My name is Gwendolyn but please call me Gwen."

"Nice to meet ye pet." Her eyebrows rise in recognition and then smiles.

"You come from Newcastle don't you? Mother does, she says 'pet' and 'like' and 'divvint'. It's nice. But she says she doesn't want me to speak like her," then adds apologetically, "sorry, I think it's nice."

The ice has been broken and she's off giving me her life story, her schooling, her family and why she's volunteered for work at the Front.

"Mother didn't want me to go but Father encouraged me. Mother eventually gave in so here I am, exciting isn't it?"

I smile and think what a different childhood she's had. I wonder how her Mum met her Dad, I bet he's not a fisherman or a miner. I eventually learn that she was born and raised in a village called Lymm in Cheshire and her father was in shipping, well connected apparently.

I have no time for window gazing on this short trip to Dover. Before long everyone in the compartment has been drawn in and we're all chatting and laughing, even the two elderly ladies sitting together in the corner. They are just going home after their short holiday 'in the smoke'. The 'last minute' VADs are Alice and Ruth Withers and their friend Edith Coleman all from Ealing in West London. All three are outgoing, very friendly and well educated and all bound for the large military hospital in Étaples near Boulogne. Gwen and myself have been ticketed for a CCS near Poperinghe, a charming sounding village name in Flanders.

I'm shocked to hear that none of them have had any proper nursing training, indeed only Edith has ever been in a hospital! I smile when I hear Alice and Ruth trying to justify their presence by exclaiming that they had to look after their mother for several months when she had a bout of pleurisy. Their medical training consisted only of a few sessions with British Red Cross instructors. A good deal better than nothing but I've had seven years of experience and I don't know if I'll cope with the expected horrors of war. In their case ignorance is bliss but reality will be immediate and I wonder if their enthusiasm can be maintained.

I talk proudly of my work in Newcastle and they're suitable impressed. I regale them of my last years of nursing the war wounded and I feel like their mother with her children hanging on to her every word...until.

"My friend and I were nurses in the Boer War."

It was one of the elderly ladies who had been listening quietly in the corner. She stunned everyone in to an awestruck silence.

"Yes, Mildred and I had been Army Service Nurses for some time when the battles started and we were there for nearly three years I think. Is that right Millie?" She looked over to her friend alongside who nodded. Afterwards the Service reorganised themselves in to the

204

QAIMNS but we were getting on a bit by that time and we thought we'd had enough and retired." She looked at me and smiled I was still completely dumbstruck. "I'm so pleased you've joined. You'll find it very different from your highly organised hospital at home but I can see that you'll cope and you'll be a great help to the boys."

I feel so humbled. Here I am thinking I'm being brave and courageous, showing off to the VADs and here are these two ladies who have done it all before on the frontline and for three years. I'm shocked and don't know what to say and have to stop myself from staring at them in awe. I realise at last that they've paid me a compliment and I must answer.

"Thank ye so much. Ah didn't realise...ye know...you've done all this before. That's so amazin'. Can ye talk to us about that time?"

"Oh well, I don't know what to say. I can say it was a time in my life I will never forget. We still talk about those years and strangely, despite the so sad stories of some of our boys, it was, dare I say it, a happy time for us. It was a time when everyone pulled together, made do with what was available and we were appreciated. No matter how old, what rank or the severity of their injuries our boys were kind, helpful even, in some cases, until their last breath." She stops obviously thinking back to her 'happy times'. Her friend Mildred takes over in her place.

"These were mostly young lads as young as eighteen but in every situation when it seemed the 'Angel of Death' was on their shoulders, they would turn to first principles. They would talk, dream, write about their mothers, not their wives, girlfriends, children, always their mothers."

The ladies have the floor completely to themselves while the rest of us listen spell bound. When they stop there was a flood of questions, the VADs wanting to know more but for me the mention of mothers transports my mind back home to Mhairi. I ask myself would she be thinking about me. I doubt it, I doubt she would ever think about me ever again. Uncontrollable tears fill my eyes. I have to wipe my face discreetly with my hanky, a pain has gripped my heart, a pain I feel so often. I so want her back.

****

Our short journey has terminated at Dover and we've bade farewell to our two Boer War nurses. We now have to find our ship for the short jump over the channel to Calais. The salty sea air smells so familiar but the view over the harbour and its approaches are like nothing I've ever seen. Great grey hulks sprouting funnels, masts and guns are everywhere. In between, scuttling about like ants around buckets, are tugs, corvettes and tiny patrol boats. It seems the steam era has relegated the serene, majestic sailing ships to another time. The scene before me is business like, utilitarian. Everything I can see: the ships, the swinging cranes the myriad bustling railway lines are here to do a job and that job is to fight the war, no more, no less. Myself and my new friends are now part of this production line and like everyone else here we have a job to do and we march down to the reception quay for our onward journey.

I'm standing in front of a long desk behind which is a man in uniform scratching his head. I suppose because I'm older and more experienced I have been pushed to the front of our little gang. I'm holding a batch of identity certificates hoping they would open doors on to our next step of the journey.

"It says 'ere that you're not due off until tomorra."

I feel exasperated, I've been travelling since four o'clock this morning, I'm bone weary. I know we have to get over to France tonight as our hostel in Calais is already booked. I try one last time, I put on my best pathetic little girl lost look and look him straight in the eye.

"Please, just fo' us we're expected at the hospital, they're short of staff. We're needed desperately."

He starts off. "I'm afraid you can't.." but then he looks at our faces, me at the front and my four friends just behind. We're all gazing at him longingly, appealingly, beseechingly even.

He visibly relaxes and laughs. "I'm going to look under the desk if I don't see ya, I won't know you're on board." As he turns away he shouts over his shoulder. "And the best o' British to ya."

Our transport ship is surprisingly comfortable and well equipped I think it must have earned its living as a pleasure or holiday cruising ship before the war. Its comforts are completely wasted on our small group. We spend the whole journey on deck in the deepening dusk watching the naval activity all around us and the receding white cliffs of old England. A small but very fast frigate is acting as our escort reminding me of the danger of submarines. I'm aware that many ships have been lost on this short route but I try to bury this thought in to the depths of my mind. I don't worry my young friends with this fact. They may be blissfully unaware of the danger. The little frigate circles and zig-zags around us, we wave but there's no response. I'm pleased, I want them to maintain their look out duties, I don't fancy swimming in the grey, churning waters far below.

Arrival on dry land in Calais coincided with complete darkness. Thanks to my friends' broader education including linguistic abilities we're able to find the hostel without wandering for hours lost. I'm now ready for bed. The dorm is large, bunk beds are a plenty and I flop down on my allocated mattress, a lower bunk thank goodness. The three Londoners are as chirpy as ever, I can see Gwen on the far side making her bed carefully and precisely, plumping up her pillow. She looks happy, I believe her day has gone better than she expected.

My eyes close and I feel a wave of tiredness creep through me. I feel certain I'll be asleep in no time but no luck.

"Come on Emily we're going to sample some French cuisine. Aren't you hungry?"

"No."

"What! You haven't eaten since we met, you must be."

"Well ahm not, ah was but ahm too tired t' move." I try to bury my face in to the pillow. My eyes are closed but I can hear movement nearby and then my bed creaks as someone then another join me.

"I bet you've never tasted French food Emily, it's so tasty so different from the English meat and two veg."

I then have to listen to vivid descriptions of the gastronomic delights of typical French menus they've sampled and to cap it all they go in to ecstasies on puddings or as they call them desserts. Mouth-watering fruity clafoutis, deliciously smooth crème brûlées. It was all too much, my taste buds have come alive and woken my stomach reminding me that it was empty. I sit up.

"Ye realise ye may have to carry me home?"

"Good for you, come on Gwen we're all going for dinner. Come as you are"

Surprisingly Gwen smiles and comes over immediately eager to leave.

I complain. "We're all ganin to oink a bit after our journey."

"Who cares, come on before we die of hunger."

The restaurant is really a cafe and full of khaki but we find a table and the waitress is patient as we attempt ordering en français. I have to admit to a second wind and I'm enjoying myself thoroughly. The food is tasty and the repartee fun. I think we all feel excited and free from worries. This an adventure, none of us really know what's in store but as Gwen keeps repeating 'this is the best'.

The morning finds us all waiting for our train to St Omer. This time there is no 'Ladies' compartment and we are shepherded in to a scruffy carriage along with many others head to toe in khaki. We're able to sit together but our conversation is constricted by the closeness of other bodies and kitbags. The view through the window is of a very green, lush countryside not unlike England but the longer we journey the more

I feel the approach of the battle lines and the horrors lying in wait within.

Gwen and I get out at St Omar, our new friends are staying on board for their onward journey South to Étaples. They step out with us so that we can hug each other. We promise to write.... somehow. It's with a heavy heart that we wave them goodbye as the train pulls away. I wonder if we'll meet again.

Chapter 42

The final leg of our journey is to be by road. I imagined it would be a lorry or perhaps a horse drawn cart. A group of us, all bound for the CCS at Brandhoek near Poperinghe, are waiting at the railway station for its arrival. The afternoon is chilled. The Autumn of 1917 is turning to Winter and we're scattered sitting on our kitbags or just leaning against brick walls. The conversation of course is the war, the obscene number of casualties, gas attacks and America.

The resources of this great country have now come down on our side and their highly trained forces will make the difference to the stalemate and push the Germans back from where they came – apparently. From what I know their armies have been in France since June and are training, all this while our lads have been dying in their thousands! I'm not the only one with doubts. Everyone wants to see results, advances, anything that points to an early end to this war.

But I still hope. You need hope to carry on. I'm determined to be positive and believe that this 'War to end all Wars' will finish and will finish soon.

Our conversation dies and we lean back and concentrate on our own thoughts on what is to come for us, novices in the battle. The town shows evidence of an industrial past. I can see typical coal lifts in the distance or maybe they're for iron ore. The station behind me is a fair size with several platforms and many sidings full of trucks and wagons. It's all strangely quiet, few people about and less traffic on the road. There must be an airfield nearby from the occasional aeroplane landing or taking off. The sun is struggling to raise the temperature but I'm warm in my cloak and in comfort I wrap my arms around myself and listen to birds twittering in a stand of trees opposite still full of leaf. I think I could fall asleep but my reverie is broken by a familiar sound growing louder every second. We all strain our necks around looking down towards the bend in the road. A motor vehicle is approaching and when it appears it shocks all of us, our faces agog in surprise. It pulls up alongside us and there for all to see is a double-decker bus. A Londoner next to me is the first to react.

"Cor blimey it's a London Bus."

Certainly the windows have been boarded up and the whole has been painted dark grey but there's no mistaking where it came from.

"We could have caught this at the ruddy 'Bush' save all this changing abaht."

There is general laughter all round. The driver and conductor are of course in uniform and fail to see the funny side.

"Never mind where this came from just get inside, we can't hang about."

I know we should shelter snugly on the lower deck but I grab Gwen and make for the rounded staircase at the back and to the seats at the front of the open top deck. She looks horrified.

"I've never been on a double-decker before. Is it safe? Are we going to freeze?"

The same Londoner comes up behind us. I've learnt that he is to be an orderly in the CCS.

"Don't worry girls, I'll keep ya warm! I'm Baz by the way that's short for Basil"

He sits himself with another man on the opposite side to us. He gives us a toothy grin and folds up his great coat collar around his ears. I smile back and prepare myself for the journey. I could feel Gwen pressing herself against me for warmth and I guess for protection against marauding men.

With everyone on board we growl away soon leaving St Omer behind us and we venture deep in to the countryside. Our high level seats provide a panoramic view. I don't really know what I expect to see, ruined buildings, stark remains of stately trees, lines of prisoners but there were none of these just a flat green landscape with hills visible ahead but in the distance. After an hour my interest wanes, Gwen is leaning heavily against me, I can sense she's fallen asleep. Baz and his friend talk spasmodically and the bus growls on. Villages pass by with very little happening I wonder if anything does ever happen. For them life is passing peacefully but how can it? The trenches are close, they must see convoys passing through. Perhaps they hide in their farms and houses and pretend that nothing has changed. If you don't look maybe you can believe the war is not happening.

My head droops, I must be dozing but I'm suddenly alert. My eyes flick open. I feel Gwen stir. The bus is swinging in to a side road and squeals to a stop. The noise of our bus is replaced by a much deeper throbbing. I guess there is a convoy of lorries approaching and we have just made a detour out of their way. From my vantage point I can see over much of the vegetation edging the road. A flat wagon top moves in to view. It is emblazoned by a large red painted cross. The noise increases as the full vehicle appears round the bend. It's followed by another and then another, six in all. The first lorry screeches to a halt alongside our bus and the driver jumps out to meet our own driver. I can hear them talking. I can't make out the detail but their tone is sombre. I feel certain it's not good news. Their conversation ends I see the lorry driver walking back to his cab, he shouts over his shoulder.

"Good luck mate, keep yer 'ead down."

The convoy grinds its way past our bus, each driver waving at our own. None of them are smiling. A soldier makes his way up the stairs and speaks to us all.

"No hold ups to worry about but I reckon you're going to be busy. There's been a big push. That convoy is just clearing the way before the casualties appear. I'd better get a move on we've still got another hour to go."

He immediately turns and runs down the stairs before we have a chance to ask questions. The bus starts up, we reverse back to the main road and we set off with a noticeable increase in urgency. We can only look at each other, all of us trying to understand the implications. Baz speaks for us all.

"Ruddy hell, I reckons we've arrived."

By the time we do arrive the light is fading fast. Our first glimpse of the CC Station is of a field of tents and marquees connected by stone tracks or wooden walkways. There's a good deal of activity centred around a large group of lorries and horse drawn carts. Injured soldiers are being helped or carried in to the largest of the marquees, medical staff are walking briskly, gesticulating, trying to bring order to the influx.

This last step of our journey from England has brought us in to the war with a bump. The pastoral scene has vanished replaced with the burgeoning movement of battle preparations. Our road from St Omer met a major road at a junction and there we had to stop and wait to allow convoys of khaki painted vehicles pulling field guns, the last two pulling trailers holding tanks, something I've only ever seen in the newspapers. Next came soldiers clad in khaki walking in pairs, in time, singing music hall songs. Overcome with patriotism we waved frantically and almost to a man they waved back blowing kisses as they passed by. We are in a world painted khaki.

We park away from the hubbub and stiff from in-action and the cold Gwen and myself make our way carefully off the bus and follow directions from the driver.

"That's the reception, wait in there. If you're lucky you'll find some sandwiches but you'll have to make your own tea. Someone will be there to show you to your dormitories."

It seems we aren't lucky. There's no-one here and there's very little of anything else. A hurricane lamp is lit on a small table in the corner throwing flickering shadows on to the canvas sheeting. It seems colder inside than out. The mention of food has woken my stomach. I only just realise I haven't eaten since my sandwiches on the train to St Omer and that was many hours ago. All our little group search around, collars turned up, looking for a means of heat and sustenance. I spot a stove by a pole in the middle with a wonky chimney pointing to a hole in the roof.

"A heater an' look a kettle."

I walk over, lift the lid of the stove and peer down. I smile when I see a glowing ember. One of the orderlies followed me.

"Come on let's get this going."

With new vigour we hunt for some kindling of any sort. Our eyes fall onto an innocent folding wooden chair which, if it could read our thoughts, would have tried to escape but fortune favours the seat. We find a bundle of sticks and branches stacked in the corner and with a bit of help from a scrap of paper and some prodigious blowing we have a fire. Not exactly roaring but comforting beyond belief. With the stove nicely warming and water found for the kettle we continued our search for food and tea. There is a shout. Baz has found and opened the lid of a packing case.

"I've found the grub and look 'ere's some Rosie Lee and a teapot, very posh aren't we, no milk though?"

Within ten minutes we're all sitting on seats or on our kit bags tucking in to some potted meat sandwiches and a warming mug of black tea. I can feel a warming glow both inside and out, bliss. I look at Gwen, she looks longingly in to her mug probably hoping for some milk to magically appear and then nibbles at a sandwich. For all the world she looks like a lost puppy and I wonder if she'll cope with this austerity. But she looks up at me and smiles. I remember again she's had the guts to volunteer and leave her comfortable life at home with her family. Yes she'll manage, privileged upbringing or not, she'll adapt. Our reverie is suddenly broken as the entrance flap is flung open suddenly allowing a cold draught and a nursing sister to make an entrance. She takes in our number, the food and the stove. She speaks with a strong Irish brogue.

"Oh grand you're here, pleased yer found everythin'. Look oi know you've only jist arrived but wud yer give us a hand wi dis convoy and den I'll get someone ter show yer to your tents." She looks in to our mugs still cradled in our hands. "By de way we keep de milk outside in a case between de tents. Ter keep cool, yer see."

We gulp down the last of our sandwiches and empty our mugs and follow her out in to the night. I expect everyone is like me: feeling nervous, anxious and wondering what on earth we can do to help.

Chapter 43

We're taken to tents to dump our kitbags and coats and to wash our hands. Me, Gwen and the other VADs in one, the orderlies, all men, are shunted in to another. There is soap but no hot water but we do what we can. The sister takes me aside.

"Oi assume you are Staff Nurse Mulligan?"

I nod, "Yes sister."

"Grand, tank goodness. We need trained nurses more than anythin'. Why we have so many VADs is beyond me. For the-nite oi want you ter clean an' re-dress wounds, you'll 'av ter find your own way around. De VADs can 'elp yer an' can 'elp de orderlies make tea. Look after dem as best yer can an' um.." she hesitates before continuing in a whisper. "Some of de boys are in a brutal state, luk oyt for de fainters." She turns to speak to the other girls.

"Follow me ter de wards you'll be 'elpin' our boys get a grand noight sleep. Dat means 'elpin' de orderlies with tea and dinner an' 'elpin' de nurses with bandages, takin' temperatures an' de loike. Staff Nurse Mulligan 'ere will 'elp you as will Nurse Wallace, she's already in dere an' me of course. Oh yes, yer can call me Sister Brogan."

She sees we're all ready and we march off out of the dormitory along criss-crossing paths of duckboards to a huge marquee tent. The flaps are tied back to allow the last soldiers in the convoy to be brought in. I look at them. Bandages cover various parts of their anatomy, head, arms, full chest and some with great casts over one of their feet. Most look at us and smile and nod their heads in greeting. This is all familiar but there's one aspect that shocks me: they are all filthy and smelly, mud is everywhere, blood stains have spread through the bandages. Their hair and moustaches are clogged, uniforms are indistinguishable and boots caked. It is obvious the first job is to remove their clothes for incineration, the second is the need for a bath.

Inside there is organised chaos. Soldiers who can are sitting receiving or awaiting attention. Others are still lying on their stretchers. A doctor and nurse partnership is examining each man in turn writing notes and attaching labels. We stand in a group mesmerised by the frenetic activity in front of us.

"Ah, just in time. Follow me, you can help getting our new 'guests' ready for bed." A nurse has joined us businesslike, uniformed stained but she's smiling. She beckons us over to the men already inspected and labelled. "Don't worry, all this looks as if we're rushing around like headless chickens but everyone know what they're doing," then adds, "more or less!" She laughs out loud. I can tell her adrenaline is working overtime. I suspect she's been up since early morning and perhaps dealing with this late, sudden influx is dragging out her last reserves.

"You can see the doctor is examining them in turn, the labels detail what we have to do. We just have to do it, easy. When they come in it's all about removing the uniforms, re-dressing the wounds, baths and bed so they're ready for their tea and dinner. The walking wounded are for us. You can work up to the stretcher cases. We'll pair up. I'll introduce you, VADs with VADs and you nurse with me. Leave your coats somewhere and come with me."

Gwen and the other three VADs in our party are soon helping. I follow the nurse. "Sorry I didn't realise you're a Staff Nurse, my name's Wallace, Jessie Wallace."

I feel pleased that my rank is respected but now worried that I can live up to expectations.

We walk along the ranks of soldiers being treated all the while Nurse Wallace is talking to them answering their questions giving them a bit of cheek, making them laugh. No softly, softly, you poor little sick man dialogue here. She gives back what she gets and makes them relax. We reach a group of men already in their gowns, uniforms gone, steam bath taken, injuries to be properly cleaned up and re-dressed.

She points to a large wooden packing case. "This box is our dressing station. It's got everything we need: bandages, slings, disinfectant, pins all sterilised." She turns to the first soldier staring at a long deep gash in his upper arm and holding his lower arm tightly for support. "Now then what's this little scratch you've got?"

He turns quickly and now stares at us wide eyed. "Is it a Blighty?"

"What, you'll be back in the trenches this afternoon." She waits for some seconds preparing the wound and reaching for some bandages. She looks back at his face now racked with disappointment. "Mind you the doctor may have too many Blighty tickets left and want to get rid of a few."

His faces lightens to reveal a beatific smile, the tension leaves his body and he relaxes in to the chair.

A typical dialogue follows with all the men mostly very young probably in hospital for the first time in their lives. Dressings completed we take them to their beds where a VAD serves up dinner and a mug of tea. The same process is repeated over the next two hours and I'm beginning to flag. I wonder where Nurse Wallace gets her stamina from.

"Come on let's get a cuppa for ourselves, you must be zonked after your journey." The marquee beds have emptied the waiting area and their patients are now either still eating or drinking, chatting to their neighbour or are slumped back down fast asleep.

My hands are curled around one of the very best mugs of tea ever tasted and intermittently munching in to some wonderful pastries apparently made in the local village. Nurse Wallace, I can now call her Jessie out of earshot of the patients, is talking about the convoys, the common injuries inflicted and the condition of the 'boys'.

"When they first come in they're quiet, nervous. I think they imagine visions of nurses and doctors wielding long blooded knives, huge hypodermics and unknown instruments of torture." She laughs. "Mind you it's as well they don't see the saws and grips in the theatre."

She goes quiet before continuing again. "Some of the boys are so young and some of the injuries......shocking, such a waste."

My eyes are drooping, I feel my body collapsing in on itself. It's all I can do to stop myself falling asleep while Jessie is still talking. She's talking about supplies, provisions, shifts, making do with what we have but her voice is receding down a long tunnel getting gradually fainter.

"Sorry Emily I'm keeping you awake. I'll take you to our quarters."

My head clears and my eyes open wide and I realise I've been asleep. "Sorry Jessie ah think ah do need to get to me bed. What time in the morning did ye say?"

"Nine o'clock in the ward. You'll get woken at seven thirty for breakfast."

We get to our quarters someone has put my kitbag on a bed and I start digging out my nightdress but it's cold and I'm so tired I just remove my travelling dress and slip under the covers slapping a spare blanket over the top. I hear a 'goodnight' called from the bed next to mine. I think from Gwen but I must have fallen asleep before my head hits the pillow. The next thing I remember is a shake of my shoulders and a whisper in my ear. "Come on sleepy head let's get some breakfast." My eyes flick open and focus on the face looking at me, it's Gwen. I sit up thinking I'd overslept. I had.

"Eh up it's Rip Van Winkle, got enough beauty sleep then?"

It was a woman shouting over from the other side of the tent. I groan and try to rub sleep from my eyes.

"Don't worry about her. I'll show you where to wash, here's your dressing gown and you'll need a coat and hat. I'll wait for you. We can go to breakfast together."

I see Gwen looking at me, I'm embarrassed. First day and I'm late.

Chapter 44

So starts my first day of my first week of my first month. Coping and making do with stretched resources and crucially making the lives of our boys as comfortable as possible, filled our waking hours from bedtime to bedtime. We are scheduled for a day off every week but this scheduling is a target not a certainty. But when they come and it only comes when there's a promise of no convoys we get away from the Station. Maybe jump on a transport to a local village or more likely a walk in to the countryside around. The little towns have without fail their own bakeries, patisseries, and what feasts they have to thrill our taste buds, éclairs, pain au chocolat, wonderful fruit pies. Our CCS close by has done wonders for their businesses and we enjoy their delights in our canteens but nothing compares to huddling by a rippling stream in a quiet field our feasting disturbed only by grazing, nosy cows and interested birdlife. My village trips are usually made with another nurse or VAD who can handle the language. Gwen has never before been away from Cheshire but can speak French like a native. She teaches me some of the basics. I jot them down determined to learn and show them off when I get home.

When I'm by myself, wherever I am, my mind switches to my family and friends back in England...and Scotland. It's at times like this that the ache of home sickness hits. I wonder how Stan is coping. I hope I haven't hurt him too much by leaving for France. We write but the letters are irregular sometimes coming in twos and threes. I can sense the hurt in his words. I'm sitting on my bunk reading his last letter. It's more cheerful. He tells me he's helping a Mrs Dyer, a woman who has just learned of the death of her husband. I know her or at least seen her a few times. She's a plump, homely sort with two young children I cannot imagine the heartbreak she has. But I'm confused. Inside my feelings aren't right. I should be sad for her imagining her grief for the loss but it's not there. In its place is the selfish, jagged pain of jealousy.

Home leave is booked after three months, a full week away. Knowing my friendship with Gwen Sister has scheduled our leave together. I know the course of the War could change everything. A sudden surge from either side, demands from other CCS's or hospitals and so on may mean a cancellation or at the least a postponement. But I'm eager to go but I will return to complete my term.

Death is commonplace, a daily occurrence. Sometimes the boy lingers much longer than expected and when it comes it's a happy release. Others improve rapidly but, like a shutter dropping, he's snuffed out in a single moment.

So difficult to accept at first, young men, many just teenagers, struck down in their prime. But a wave of acceptance engulfs you unnoticed and your heart is hardened by the inevitable. I'm so grateful that we are just a transitional stop in their journey. There is no time for patient/nurse bonding before he moves on to Blighty, back to the trenches or to his final resting place. This is how it has to be. We do the best for them. They have put their lives on the line for their country, they deserve nothing less.

Their camaraderie, wicked sense of humour and their love for their 'Sister', 'Auntie', 'Hospital Mum', or whatever our pet name happens to be, fills our lives and makes the endless hours worthwhile.

Another convoy arrives. Unexpected as it is we make a mad dash around to complete our daily tasks before we switch our attention to our new patients. Sister Brogan speaks to me over the hubbub.

"Staff Nurse Mulligan. Dees men are to use de spare tent."

My eyes shoot sky high and my mouth opens wide as if to start an opera. "But it's not ready. We've got room in here."

"Just do as oi say."

"Yes sister."

Sixteen men are led or carried to the spare tent. The porters are quiet and grim faced. I wonder what's wrong. A new type of gas attack? Something contagious? I spot the difference in their uniforms and a helmet in amongst and I understand. Our new patients are the enemy, they are all German.

Completely stunned I watch from the sidelines. Some are moaning, all are muddied, bandaged, tunics torn but apart from their uniform and the odd muttered German word they could be any 'Tommy' of ours. I cannot deny my immediate reaction of hatred, of my desire to shout at them, hurt them. My fingers curl into fists, my whole body stiffens. I cannot nurse these men I just ca......

"Staff Nurse Mulligan. Dees are our prisoners, oi know what you're tinkin but they must be treated jist loike any other injured soldier. Dat is your duty. Oi expect yer ter understan' dis an' ter ensure everyone else does. Do yer 'ear me?"

I close my eyes, breath, repeat her words quietly to myself. My hands relax. I breath out long and slow.

"Yes Sister."

Chapter 45

I spot Gwen with another VAD preparing the new intake: making the beds, removing uniforms and grimy bandages as if they are just another Tommy convoy. Their dedication embarrasses me. I wonder how I find it so difficult, they're all someone's son. They'll be worrying like any other parent praying for their safe return probably hating the war and the leaders who made it all happen.

I'm called over by the doctor. "You'll need to come round with me, Sister has been dragged away." So begins my introduction to the Bosch, the first I've met since I arrived in Flanders nearly three months ago.

Early putrification makes for a familiar smell but there is a particular aroma over and above this. It's something I've been told about from our boys. Maybe it's something in their provisions, their food, whatever it is - it is known as the Hun hum.

As the days go by the German patients become more comfortable but instead of being grateful for our care and attention they become loud and arrogant, taunting our British-ness, making fun. I make no apologies for the odd tweak of their injuries. I give as much as I get, maybe more. Neither side understands a word only the meaning behind.

One man is badly injured suffering from gas gangrene of his lower leg. It may have to be amputated. He's also suffering a blast injury to his chest notoriously life threatening. He has to be an officer. His compatriots never include him in their conversations. There is an obvious respect for his seniority. He is expected to die. I cannot deny a certain wish that he should and soon.

Today has started as a beautiful clear day. The air is cold but the temperature soars in direct sunlight. Taking advantage during our tea break we forego our usual seat by the stove and clutching our mugs we search and find a sheltered sunny spot. The air is still, winter birds are singing pleased as we are in having such a wonderful respite from the cold. From our position the war seems miles away, no guns, no convoys of rasping lorries heaving up the incline to the Station. I close my eyes and I feel a tiredness creep in to my bones.

"What's that noise?"

One of the VADs with acute hearing demands our attention. I hear nothing and prolong my slumber.

"It's a plane or maybe two."

I flick my eyes open and notice everyone focused on the sky ahead. I concentrate on the horizon but see nothing but I can hear an undulating rattle typical of the bi-planes that often fly high overhead. Gradually the noise builds but nothing is visible in the air. We are agreeing it must be some sort of vehicle when, like a pair of eagles taking off from the tree tops, two triplanes expose themselves and head directly at us.

Someone asks a question. 'Why are our boys flying so low."

Large black crosses shout at us from the underside of the wings. It suddenly dawns that these are not our boys. We throw ourselves to the ground in terror.

The roar of the engines seem just a few feet above our heads and then we hear the nightmare rattle of their guns. I look up to see the tent sheeting waving madly as bullets rent the air and tear gaping holes in the canvas. They're gone in seconds. We scramble to our feet and race to see the damage inflicted. It is the POW tent. Inside is mayhem. Men are screaming, there is a distinctive smell of cordite. Small fires billowing smoke are taking hold, the butt is spouting a stream of water. We are the first of the staff to enter after the raid. I try to take in the damage and the injuries. It appears one side of one end has borne the brunt. Two patients have been flung out of their beds and are riddled with bullet holes their blood still draining into the ground around. I see protruding a pair of feet, I gasp as I recognise a VAD uniform. I run to her aid but she is dead, a bullet has blasted away half of her face. The shouting has subsided replaced by a commanding voice speaking in

German. I'm completely shocked when I notice its origin stems from the officer. He has lifted himself up on to his arms and speaks to his compatriots in a calm and assured voice. He must be in considerable pain but his control is impressive.

Fires extinguished we check every patient. Two are plainly dead, two more are badly wounded and unlikely to survive. All the others should live. The Doctor and Sister Brogan arrive and quickly assess the situation. Porters are summoned to carry away the dead to the mortuary, the first badly wounded is removed for treatment. He is unconscious. It seems a bullet has pierced his thigh and exited causing blood to flow unchecked. It is clear he will only survive if the artery can be sealed and quickly. The other wounded man is whimpering. A bullet has grazed his skull but internal haemorrhaging is suspected but he'll have to wait his turn. Our poor VAD's head has been wrapped to give the body some respect. It is a sad sight and there are many too upset to help. It is one thing to nurse a wounded man you've never seen before but quite another to pick up the pieces of someone you've been working alongside for months.

The attack has been horrific and deadly. No-one has known this to happen before. It is abhorrent. The pilots must have seen the red crosses and other obvious signs of a CCS yet they pressed forward with their attack. The Bosch have hit a new low. It is ironic in the extreme that they picked out the one marquee with their compatriots inside.

There is no time for wailing and complaining. Within a day the canvass has been repaired, damaged equipment replaced and the surviving patients settled back into their beds. Their arrogance has been replaced with acute embarrassment of the attack and a new respect for our fortitude. The officer has fallen back into silence. His health remains critical his life expectancy short, but he's still with us. The infection in his lower leg is retreating but his blast injuries remain the concern. He stares at me as I change his dressings but says nothing. I talk as I do with all the patients but there is little reaction.

Our team are wary of him. They don't understand his silence. They do the minimum and I find I'm doing most of his nursing. I'm listening to his chest my face close to his.

"Hello Nurse Mulligan." I jump hearing his words, they're in perfect English. I stare at him, shocked. I gather myself.

"Staff Nurse Mulligan."

"Sorry."

I try to appear calm unflustered. "So ye can speak English all this time? You're a dark horse."

He smiles, his face lightens immediately reminding me of my Stan. "No, not a dark horse just a German soldier on the losing side."

"But why?"

"Why are we losing or why am I a German soldier?"

"I know you're losin'."

He smiles again, my legs wobble. "I was at school in Newbury and educated at Oxford. My parents are German; they returned to Bavaria but kept me at school and brought me back when this war started." He shrugged. "That's it."

Is it the smile, his unusual history, his un-assuming manner I don't know but I feel we are drawn to each other, certainly to me like no other before. As the days go by I spend more and more time with him, I see his improvement, his determination to improve his walking. Others notice but I shrug off their comments. I still do my duty to our boys, I'm not shirking but I love how different he is. He is a breath of fresh air and I enjoy being with him.

The day before I'm due to start my leave we go for our usual slow and steady walk around the camp. I know he can walk by himself but I let him clutch my shoulders as a fake support. Our closeness comforts me. I find him so attractive. It's so difficult to keep my distance but I must and I do. We both know this is the last time we'll be together before I leave and I realise he could well have gone before my return.

Our walk returns around the back of the tents. He stops and looks at me.

"Goodbye Emily." He pulls me to him and kisses me fully on my lips. I resist far too feebly before I fall into his arms and join in a lovely, sensuous farewell.

Chapter 46

Gwen and I are paddling along the sea shore near Calais. Our shoes are off and our skirts hitched up. The water is cold, invigorating, the waves are lapping against our ankles with the occasional splash up to our calves. The first part of our journey home is completed. It's been cramped and hot and it's lovely to get away from the crush of bodies and be by ourselves. The sea is busy with boats of all sizes from coble like fishing boats to ferries and Navy destroyers. We know of the dangers unseen below but we push these thoughts to the back of our minds. We cannot stop the submarines so we just hope our crossing tomorrow is unmolested. The majority are, only the unfortunate hit the headlines.

Gwen has been amazing from day one. She's never flinched, never backed away from any injury no matter how horrific and always willing to help over and above her shifts. I think of poor Ellie another VAD. Full of bravado at first but not realising how the sight of blood could turn her stomach and make her run for the exit hand over her mouth. She was distraught and embarrassed, unable to join in with our discussions and chats. It was Gwen that brought her round. She sat and chatted with her, brought her back in to the everyday life of the Station. It was her suggestion that Ellie should be used on non-dressing duties and it worked a treat. There is always blood on show somewhere but avoiding the very worst 'blood' duties she was able to cope and become a vital member of the team.

Another plus was how Sister Brogan's view of VADs changed from her initial frustration to one of respect. It is obvious to me that every member of the CCS from the surgeon to the latrine cleaner plays a crucial part of the smooth running of the camp. The VADs are a vital cog in this machine.

The un-seasonally warm weather means the sea breeze is cool but not freezing and I can unbutton my cloak and feel the smoke laden air from the train dissipate into the endless horizons of my surroundings. We walk together but silently thinking our own thoughts. Mine are focused back to Gunty that is my Oberleutnant Gunther Mueller. Before we arrived back to his ward I had scribbled down my address in Newcastle. He took it carefully and kissed it before folding the paper slip and tucking it in to his pyjama pocket. Nothing further was said then or this morning. As we left on the same London bus as we arrived I saw the flap of his ward tent was closed, tight shut to keep out a sudden shower. I waved at the invisible soldier who had made such a wild impression on me. I felt empty inside, I wonder if we would actually ever meet again. I had closed my eyes as we stopped at the gate check point. I felt a sharp dig in my ribs from Gwen. In response to my sudden irritated queried look she nodded her head towards the window. I followed her gaze and saw him. He was standing as erect as he could, helped by his walking stick and hindered by the buffeting of the wind and the rain. He was standing next to the camp guard who, by his relaxed manner, was obviously unaware he was fraternising with the enemy. Our eyes met, I daren't show too much emotion. To my horror he gave me a wave and one of his beaming smiles.

"Wave back Emily."

Gwen gave me another dig in the ribs. I look at her wide eyed but she just whispers "go on". I turn back as the bus starts away and in panic I give him the widest smile I could venture without looking too enthusiastic followed by a half-hearted wave. I hope he could see from my eyes how much he means to me.

Gwen as diplomatic as ever says nothing just squeezes my hand in support and understanding.

In the digs that night Gwen in the adjacent bunk whispers over. "The Captain seems a nice man."

"Yes he is."

"Do you think he'll be here when we get back?"

"No."

****

I'm now back in Newcastle and it's the early evening. The journey was long but relatively comfortable. I left Gwen in London to make her way back home via Euston. We made tentative arrangements to meet again at Charing Cross in just six days time. All I want to do is collapse in bed and sleep. There's no-one around and I slip the key quietly in to the lock, open the door, throw my kitbag on to the floor, strip off my clothes down to my underwear and slip under the bed covers. Bliss.

"Emy."

I sense a face very close to mine and I smell a familiar aroma of disinfectant. Without opening my eyes I slip my arms around her head and pull her over. "Hello Millie."

"Are ye too tired?

"Yes, ah canna open me eyes but ah want ye to tell me what's happened over the last three months."

"Alright, umm, do ye want a cuppa?"

"Oooh yes please."

Millie disappears to the kitchen and I work on waking up to hear the news. A few minutes later she re-appears with two steaming mugs of tea and a rattling tin.

"Ah bought some biscuits from the bakers."

We sit on the bed side by side and I try to describe the horrors and delights of the CCS. I omit any mention of Gunty. I'm putting up my defences, I need to forget him. If we do meet again by some good fortune then that would be wonderful but the likelihood is remote. I need to put him out of my mind.

She looks dumbstruck. "It sounds horrific, how de ye cope?"

"Ye just have te, it's teamwork. No different to the hospital here but there's more makin' do, an'.....well.....many don't make it but we try to make sure their last few days, hours sometimes, are as comfy as possible. Anyway that's enough about me what's happened here."

There's remarkably little change. No news about my Mhairi, Stan's the same and she's not pregnant, still. She believes Frank's going to be called up for non-combative duties. She's not heard from my family although she believes Con is in France.

I know I must visit Mum and my sisters but before then I have to see Stan. Millie is looking embarrassed when I ask about him.

"He's moved out of his old place, the house has been sold since the Roberts left. He's moved in to rooms above Mrs Dyer ye know the woman. She's got two bairns, her husband was killed in France."

My heart skips a beat the old half-forgotten jealousy pangs suddenly start flowing through my body. I sit up, I decide to pay him a visit, now, this evening.

"Ah best gan an' see him, he should know ahm due home today."

"He may not, ye did say probably temorra. Ah called here on the off-chance. Go temorra morning you'll be starvin', come to me house for your tea."

"Thanks Mills but I'd bettor see him first. If ah were him I'd be upset if ah didn't go. Tell ye what I'll see ye after, alright?"

Millie leaves, I change and try to tidy and freshen myself up for his visit. It's only a short walk and on the way I think back to when we left each other. He was upset, didn't understand why I wanted to put myself in danger. I had called him selfish, only thinking about himself. He never understood why I want to make a difference. We had kissed and cuddled at the station and forgave each other. He wished me luck and said he loved me. But I know deep down I don't really love him. He's been a great friend and lover for many years but I supposed I've used him. I feel guilty but why do I feel jealous?

I knock on his door. I hear a woman's voice shouting for someone to open the door. Slowly the door is pulled back, a little lad's face peers around the side.

"It's a woman."

"Well bring her in then."

He pulls the door fully open and lets me in. I hear a shout from the kitchen. "Sorry I'm feeding the young 'un and Stan's eating his dinner. The door in front is half closed but it swings open fully by the lad who had let me in. A picture of a typical family scene is spread before me. Stan with his back to me is tucking into his dinner alongside is a plate of what looks like apple pie and cream waiting. Facing me on the other side of the table is a plump Mrs Dyer openly feeding a baby both swollen breasts bared in full view.

"Hello, do ah know ye?"

Before I can answer Stan turns and sees me. His face turns a deep shade of pink. He gets up with a sudden scrape of his chair and walks towards me.

"Emily."

"Yes it's me Stan."

Mrs Dyer suddenly understands who I am and pulls her baby off her breast and tries to cover herself with her blouse. The baby, meal interrupted, starts crying immediately.

"Don't let me stop ye but ah want a word wi' Stan if that's alright."

She doesn't reply. Stan ushers me in to their front room.

"I didn't know ye were c..."

"Obviously, a very cosy scene. Maybe we can talk after your tea."

I can only turn on my heels and walk out the door, shutting it firmly behind me. I am shocked, the homely kitchen picture is printed on my brain. I storm back to my flat I'm confused. My mind is in a whirl. How could he?

Chapter 47

I'm walking aimlessly around the streets, my brain is racing. Stan has obviously got his feet under the table. He's being looked after, fed and I suspect his clothes are washed and ironed. I wonder what else is on the menu. It's only been a few months, couldn't he have waited for me?

The streets are busy with revellers. It dawns that this is Saturday night the time to relax with your friends and have fun and enjoy yourself. Of course, I see now, this is what Stan has wanted for years: to be part of a family, children, company, someone to love every day not just when I'm available. It's me that's brought this on, I can't blame him or Sofie Dyer. She's been through a nightmare and now probably can't believe her luck has changed. Stan is a catch and if I were in her position I would grab him with both arms and keep him close. This realisation has also brought a pang of guilt - my intense desire for Gunty. Is there any difference?

I make my way to Millie's house. I'm welcomed there with open arms from both of them. They're such a loving, devoted pair. They have found each other and want for nothing else, excepting a family of course.

After dinner I'm sitting with Millie and I relate the scene with Stan in more detail.

"Ah thought maybe it was more then just an owner/lodger relationship but ah know he still loves ye."

"But Mills, I don't love him. Ah know that an' ah realise ah have to tell him, release him. Ah saw how comfortable he looked. That's what he wants an' he deserves it."

Millie didn't answer, I realise she knows I'm right.

"Ah must get to bed before ah collapse here on yor sofa. Ah want to see Ma temorra I'll stay there for a while. But I'll see ye before ah have to get back. Thanks for me tea."

I stand and we hug each other long and close. Our friendship is forever I couldn't have survived this far without it.

I'm on my way home. Yesterday I managed some Christmas shopping. I found it difficult to be doing something so very different from my last three months in Flanders. My mind is still in the grim reality of war. Hear in Newcastle there are bright lights, shops doing their best to show off their stocks for presents and excited children giving their parents a hard time. There were big smiles and laughter, theatre shows, pubs overflowing. I wonder, have they seen the reality, the pain and horror of the battles, shattered bodies spread eagled in the mud? I understand of course people are well aware but are trying to forget. Many have lost relatives and friends. Others are tormented knowing that their loved ones are still there fighting. I find it difficult to forget, to smile. Gunty, Stan and most of all my Mhairi are taking turns to appear in my mind's eye especially at this time of celebration. I want to start again, have a normal life but then, no, I will always want to make this difference. I'll never be 'normal' whatever that is.

The omnibus growls northwards I gaze unseeing through the window. I jerk myself back to the present I know I must try to be bright and cheerful. I blink and study the familiar landscape. I haven't even noticed that snow is falling. Soft, large flakes lazily slink down covering the land in a blanket slowly but steadily disguising every detail. My thoughts are on the beauty before me but in an instant they turn to concern. Suppose I can't get back? I'm off to a remote village linked only by narrow lanes so easily closed by snowdrifts or ice. My train back leaves in four days, if I miss it, oh my god, they'll think I've deserted. The beauty of the snow is laughing at me or is it protecting me keeping me away from more pain and suffering?

My village is beautiful. I step down off the bus and sink into the white blanket on the footpath. I walk carefully, head down watching for hidden obstructions. I hear a joyous scream and look up just in time to stop a snowball with my face. I see two laughing thirteen year olds a few yards in front.

"Right you two, you're for it."

I scoop up as much snow as possible and start my retaliation. They're no match for me. Despite superiority in numbers my snowballs are bigger and they unerringly hit home. They retreat squealing and attempt an escape through our front door but I catch them both, my arms squeezing them tightly preventing any further close range missiles. We fall into the kitchen, three big smiles in a thunderstorm of flying snowflakes.

"Ahhh, yas makin' the whole place soakin' wet!"

We stop and let the snow mist settle and I see my Ma hands on hips looking cross before a huge smile surfaces stretching from ear to ear.

"Hi Ma, how are ye?"

"Ahm so pleased to see ye." She gives me a big hug then breaks away. "An' so are these two horrors. ah said they should wait 'til you've had a cuppa."

My worries and fears are memories as I take in the wonderful aroma, the whole feeling of a happy contented family. Ma is smiling, fussing, making the tea. My cheeky sisters are searching through my backpack for presents. I notice new pictures on the mantelpiece. One is a group photo in a park somewhere with Ma and Davy, the twins and Con in his army uniform. The other just shows my handsome brother in uniform this time by himself looking serious but proud.

"Wot a bonny brotha ah have. Is he still trainin'?"

Ma's face drops, a worried look is only just under the surface. "No, his regiment left two weeks ago, he's in Flanders. We've got a letter already." She reaches up to the mantelpiece and hands it over. I read it and give it back. He says his regiment is in reserve, waiting. I feel certain he's no longer waiting. I say nothing at first, I can't lie to her. All I can manage is to repeat a hope that the war will end soon especially now that the Americans have joined in.

"Hawa yor tea's ready an' a've done some bakin'." Her smile is back in place and she sets down a plate of cakes in front of us. I force my eyes to light up in delight but behind they are filled with tears straining to flow. My little brother, he's been through so much in his young life and now this.

There was no way I could catch a bus back to Newcastle that day. The snow had stopped all traffic save anything that was horse drawn. I didn't mind in the least, being with my family kept my mind away from my own problems, it was a release for me. But when the roads were still blocked on the next day my anxiety levels started to rise. Blocked in by snow was not going to be an acceptable excuse by the QAIMNS. Davey promised that if by Wednesday there were still no buses he would take a day off from work and take me back to my digs by horse and cart. And so it is. I can understand how he's so loved by Ma and the twins, lucky Ma, lucky us.

I'm sitting alongside Davey. It would have been too much and too far for Bennie so we've borrowed a young energetic filly from a neighbour. We're wrapped up against the elements. Davey is freely talking about our family life and how much he appreciates being accepted in to it. He also completes my picture of his early life before he met Ma.

"A've been married already ye know. In fact ah still am."

My eyes open wide in surprise and wait for more.

"To a lassie called Philomena. She was the love of me life, well ah thought she was. Phil was the daughter of a pal of me father's, a miner, we all were. She was everyone's favourite, not pretty but used te show off what she had. She was thought to be just a teaser ye know lead lads on an' then dump them. Well she wasn't. Ah was goaded by me mates te ask her te dance at the Miners Social. We danced all night, they were mad." He gave a quick laugh. "Ah was so pleased wi' myself, gettin' off wi' her. Well we went too fast an' before long she found herself

236

pregnant of course an' we had to get wed. It seemed so unfair we did it once an' the rest of me life was suddenly fixed, no choice."

We continue along the coast road in silence, then. "Does this shock ye?"

"No Davey it doesn't. Tell me about the bairn."

"Me daughter is called Phyllis, she's eighteen."

"Do ye see her?"

"No. Philomena an' me never really got on. We did try but ah think, like me, she resented havin' to get married an' she blamed me. She ran off with one of me so called mates an' they emigrated to America to start a new life away from all the scandal. Phyllis was just two."

I am intensely interested. "Have ye heard from her?"

He looks over to me. "Yor Ma has told me about yor Mhairi. Painful isn't it?"

I nod.

"Ah got a letter from Phyllis a few months ago, out o' the blue. She's in New York."

"That's marvellous."

Davey nods but hesitates, he looks nervous fidgeting with the reins then takes an obvious deep breath. "Ah would like to take your family out there."

"That sounds great."

He still looks uncertain. "T' stay there, not just for a visit. It's not just to see Phyllis but for a new start ourselves. There's no money in coal minin' here. Before the war started the pit owners were ganin to reduce pay an' increase the hours. The only good thin' about this war is that the pits are now run by the government but when it does end.

He looks over for my reaction. I don't know how to react. He can't assume that I'll go with him but to lose my family, my home.

"What do ye think?"

"Ah don't know what to think. What does Ma say?"

"She's not keen but hasn't said no. She's worried about what you, Con, an' your sisters will think."

We carry on quietly. Is my immediate reaction selfish? I understand how he feels about his daughter. If I knew where Mhairi was living I would go anywhere to find her. But I'm twenty four and living away, I'm not in any position to stop them. I feel as though a large part of my life is slipping away. That is selfish, what about Ma? I can see how much she loves Davey, of course she should go with him.

We arrive in Newcastle. I can see Davey is not used to all the traffic and I take over the reins. We stop behind my digs, wipe down our pony and give her a nosebag. I take him up to my room and we sit with mugs of tea and a plate of biscuits.

"Davey, I'll miss ye all if ye go but ah can't stop ye, that would be totally unfair. If you an' Ma want to emigrate then ye must go. She's had a tough life like, perhaps she deserves an adventure with someone. Ah can see she loves ye very much."

He takes my hands in his. "Thanks Emily that means so much to me. You'll be more than welcome to come with us or join us later, dependin' on what your doin'."

We chat for a while before he rises to leave. I give him a hug and tell him that I'll write soon. I smile and wave until he disappears around the first corner. My smile switches off, I wonder if I'll ever see my family again.

Chapter 48

Wednesday is over half way through and I've got myself ready for the journey back to Flanders tomorrow morning. I've decided to take some books and some food I yearned for last time.

Right I've done the washing, shopped, eaten and, crucially, packed my little pot of Marmite! Oh how I missed it. I've got my dressing gown on, my feet up and hands gripping a steaming mug of tea planning my evening with Millie and Frank. There's a knock on the door. It opens on my invitation to my visitor to come in. It's Stan, he stands on the mat looking pathetic.

"Come in love an' give me a cuddle." I was actually hoping he would come around. I've decided to end our relationship but hopefully not our friendship.

He squeezes me tight, too tight, I can feel he's upset. He breaks away, sits down and looks at me earnestly.

"Emy, it's not what you're thinkin'. Ah like Sofie but it's nothin' compared to how ah love ye." He looks embarrassed and continues. "Ah know what ye must have thought but a've got in to a routine of her feedin' me, it saves me cookin' which as ye know ahm hopeless at."

"Stan, I would never breast feed my baby like that in front of a lodger. Ah can also see how comfortable ye all looked together, it seemed right. You've always wanted to be part of a proper family. It upset me at first but ah realise a've held ye back for years. You've been so patient an' understandin'. Ye don't deserve to put up with my demands. Ah want to stay friends but ah want ye to be with Sofie an' her bairns. She's must have been through hell losin' her husband an' all that. Ah can understand she's attracted to ye - a handsome man with a regular job. Ahm not ganin to stand in her way."

His eyes light up and he reaches out to grab my arm. "No you've got it all wrong. A've never laid me hands on her, never made love to her nor will I. It's you ah want no-one else."

His robust denial surprises me. He obviously doesn't want to end our relationship. I now feel awkward, embarrassed but no matter what - I've decided and I'm not going to change my mind. He recognises my determination.

"Will ye come for a walk, we can call in at that canny boozah ye like, the one that allows women."

"Ah have to finish packing for temorra then ahm going to Millie's house for tea." I stumble through excuses it was only then I realise he's been drinking. He still has a hold of my arm and pulls me so his face is inches away from mine. Waves of alcohol nauseate my senses. I struggle to release his grip.

"Let me go Stan you're hurtin' me."

I could see in his staring eyes and his tightening grip that he isn't going to leave it there. He kisses me roughly, I try to get away but with his other hand he pulls my head back towards him. His face is unshaven and rough, his kissing is hard and uncomfortable, his tongue is searching to find and open my clasped lips. I've never ever seen him like this. I don't remember him drinking alcohol before. He feels so strong, I feel so helpless.

He pushes me back on to the bed and pulls open my dressing gown in one movement. I make an attempt to roll him off me, he is far too heavy. I give up struggling it's getting me nowhere. I hope he would at least treat me gently but he has no control. I lay there semi-naked in front of him. He pulls open his trousers and starts kissing my body in a frenzy. I lay there still, my eyes are closed showing no passion hoping he would understand I wasn't going to take an active part in this intercourse.

He grips my buttocks and drives in to me. I feel intense pain. My eyes are still closed I don't want to see his manic expression. I just want it over with. His jerking slows down, he groans and I feel his climax surging in to me. Finished he collapses on to my breasts and starts whimpering. I roll him off me, get up and pull my dressing gown around me.

"Ah think ye had better gan."

All energy spent he slowly pulls his trousers back up. I can see he's ashamed.

"Oh god ahm so sorry. Ah feel terrible ah shouldn't have drunk those two beers. Can ye forgive me?"

"No Stan, ah canna an' ah want ye to leave, now."

He looks at me red eyed. He sees my determination and walks out the door. There's nothing else to be said. I close the door securely behind him. I can still feel the stinging pain inside and the shock of his aggression. My legs give way and I crumple on to the bed I want to cry but I can't. I see a vision of me Ma busily preparing breakfast for us children despite the visibly growing bruises on her face and the shame of having to give in to drunken, weak minded men. I whisper to no-one. "Oh Ma how could ye put up with all this night after night?"

I slump down but soon the same old drive fills my head and I sit back up. I shout to anyone listening in earshot.

"Well ahm not puttin' up with it. That's the last ah want to see anythin' of you Stanley Symonds." I get up, get dressed and leave for an enjoyable evening with my friends.

Chapter 49

Full of resolution or not my legs feel weak and my insides are churning. I think for goodness sake I've just been raped what do I expect? I arrive at Millie and Frank's front door in a confused turmoil. I knock and stagger forward as the door swings open. I want to forget what has happened, it is past now, I have to move on. But my body won't let me. I fall in to the arms of a surprised Frank. Millie comes running over.

"What's wrong? Come an' sit doon."

I blurt out everything and then try to defend Stan suggesting it was all down to his drinking, something I've never seen him do before. Millie is distraught.

"How dare he, don't give him any excuse, he was completely wrong, evil. Ye should report him"

I snorted. "To the poliss ah suppose? Ah don't think that'll work. No ah just have te forget it but our relationship is dead."

"Good thing too."

Talking to Millie and Frank through the evening has helped me relax. They have their own problems putting my latest escapade in to perspective. I can understand their frustration in not being able to have a family. They want one so much it's so sad hearing their struggle. The thought suddenly flashes through my mind of me falling pregnant again. I set it aside, I can't do anything about it anyway. To cap it all Frank has received his call-up papers albeit in non-combative operations. He's off soon for driving training.

I rise to leave at the end of the evening and, bless them, they insist on walking home with me, my bodyguards. They are such a loving couple it's such a shame that these worries are causing such stress. If she's going to fall pregnant I believe they have to relax, try and remove the worries, accept what can't be changed such as Frank's call up. I try to put this in to words. I remind them of my friend Celia who only fulfilled her dream when her deviant husband got jailed and she married someone she could relax with and not be frightened for her life. They both listen, I hope my message sinks in, I think it has.

I have an early train to catch, I'm all packed, tickets sorted. All I need to do now is sleep. No chance. I'm lying in my bed where just a few hours before I'd been raped. I can still smell the alcohol, his clammy sweat. Now, at some early hour of the morning, I rise still wide awake, I open my window as far as it would go, change the bed covers and turn the mattress. I have to bury myself in the covers to keep out the freezing draughts but I feel more relaxed and hopefully I can get some sleep.

The morning has passed in a fuzzy, sleepy blur. I knew all I had to do was pack my nightdress and washing things in to my kitbag, lock the door, hold my ticket and catch the train. It was as well as I was still only half awake even when I settled in to the corner of my ladies carriage. It is warm and cosy and coupled with the repetitive clicking of the wheels and the swaying of the carriage I was soon fast asleep again. The next thing I'm woken by a hand gently shaking my shoulder. My eyes flick open to see a lady looking straight at me. She has a worried expression that makes me wonder if something is wrong. I straighten up and look around. Three other women are staring at me.

"Are you alright my dear?"

"Yes, sorry, ah just dropped off for a while."

"You've been asleep for a long while. We're nearly in London."

"What." I can't believe it. I must have been out for over four hours.

"It's ok we didn't like to disturb you, you looked so peaceful. The ticket collector wanted to wake you but we saw that you were clutching your ticket in your hand and that was good enough."

I feel embarrassed and smile. I notice they are all elderly and obviously travelling together. I apologise again. "Ah didn't get much sleep last night."

We chat for the rest of our journey in to Kings Cross. The friends are off for a holiday 'in the smoke' and hope to wave at the King on the balcony of Buckingham Palace on New Year's Eve. The time of year had slipped my mind completely and makes me realise that perhaps I should take some presents back with me to the CCS.

"You're a nurse at the Front?"

I nod. All four ladies suddenly seem overwhelmed.

"Oh my dear you should have said. You all do such an amazing job out there. I've read about you in the papers you save so many of our boy's lives. We must give you something."

They all start to rummage in their bags. I have no idea what they are going to come up with and we are already slowing down for the terminus. They get in to a huddle and finally one of them turns to me with some bank notes in her hand.

"We don't know what you need out there so we want to give you some money so you can buy something for yourselves."

She hands me four five pound notes. I've never seen so much money. I'm completely flabbergasted. I start to object but she grips my hand in hers.

"It's our contribution to the war effort, we're not poor and that's what we want to do." The four ladies look at me all beaming from ear to ear, my words are swallowed up. All I can say is thank you. I'm overcome with such generosity from complete strangers.

Our train is now squealing in to the platform and slowing to a halt at the buffers. All goes quiet. We are still looking at each other, stupidly tears fill my eyes. I stand up and give each a big hug.

"A've got some time before me next train. I'll de some shoppin', ah don' know what I'll buy maybe clothes to keep us warmer, gloves an' scarves." I garbled on. "An' maybe some biscuits an' stuff like that which ah canna buy out there. Can ye give me your address? Ah can write an' tell ye all about it."

"Don't you worry about that. We know you'll do the right thing and it makes us feel better."

By the time we get out on to the platform the rest of the passengers are in a huddle at the barrier at the far end.

"Goodbye dear and good luck we'll be thinking about you out there." They give me a final wave as they turn to leave to enjoy their day.

I stare at the notes still grasped firmly in my hands and shake my head in disbelief. I look up again at the group of ladies. They are deep in animated conversation, moving stiffly with a definite waddle to their gait. I smile, I feel so warm inside from such generosity. They have restored my faith that what I'm doing is what I should be doing. I'm a nurse, my job is to look after the needy and our boys are certainly that. Shopping in London, wow, I can't wait.

"You ok dear?" An elderly railway man has asked.

I certainly am. I grab my pack, give him a quick kiss on the cheek and set off down the platform in eager anticipation. I smile to myself thinking I bet that surprised him! This day's full of surprises.

Chapter 50

Shopping loaded down with a weighty kitbag isn't as much fun as it should be. In the end I've just taken in one department store and bought all I need. I'm waiting for a bus for Charing Cross station and just the sight of these open top vehicles takes me back to my first journey to Flanders. Of course when it comes I'm up on the top deck in a flash ready to gaze out at all the famous landmarks, streets and theatres. Piccadilly, Leicester Square, Charing Cross Road, so many. What a wonderful exciting city this is. I wish I had the time just to walk around but the cafe in the station is my rendezvous with Gwen, I hope she's there.

I arrive and look around and spot her at her table with a young man. She smiles and waves then introduces me and we chat generally before her friend takes his leave but not before leaving her a note.

"Is that your boyfriend, he's canny?"

"No I've only just met him in this cafe."

I must look surprised, I am.

"He just started talking to me. His name is Peter and this is his address." She holds and reads the card he left her.

"You're a fast worker." I think back to the shy flower I met on the train just three months back. What a change, she's now confident, assertive and obviously attractive to men. I'd better watch her, no matter how quickly she's changed she won't have had much experience with that breed.

Our train journey to Dover is like our first journey full of personnel going to war. This time we are booked in at a hostel near the harbour. Despite my long sleep on the train I'm pleased to get to bed for our early call to board our floating transport. Gwen on the other hand is wide awake and wants to talk to me about the war, the latest advances, the Americans, any more airborne attacks. I answer in mono-syllables trying my best to let her know that all I want is to sleep. But then she asks me a question that makes my eyes flick open and I wonder.

"Emily, do you think your German soldier will still be there?"

Of course I have thought of him but I've made an effort to assume he'd be gone and that would be the end of it. He was getting much better when I left, he wouldn't be allowed to stay with us if he was fit to travel. No, he'd be in a prison camp somewhere.

I answer. "No."

"I bet he will."

I roll over and look at her, she was smiling. "Why do ye say that?"

Her smile broadens. "I just wanted to see your reaction." She blushes ashamed at her scheming trick.

"Well you're just too bad." I roll back over again but I was hoping she was right."

The rest of our journey passes uneventfully, excepting our London bus, obviously unavailable. We trundle along in the back of a horse drawn wagon. It was freezing. Five of us huddle close together for warmth complaining of the cold, except me. I'm enjoying the slow gait and the clip-clop of our pony reminding me of home.

The camp is quiet when we arrive and the skies are darkening. We make our way to our sleeping quarters tent, swing open the flaps and walk straight in to an ongoing argument. Some VADs, just off duty, are obviously disagreeing loudly on something. They see me and stop, they look awkward, embarrassed.

"Don't mind me ah just want to de-freeze."

"Sorry Staff Nurse."

I look at them baffled. "Ye know ye can call me Emily in here, what's wrong?"

They look uncomfortable. "Sorry Emily, um, how was your leave?"

"Fine thanks but..."

"We're just going for dinner. By the way Sister wants to see you as soon as you get unpacked." They leave quickly heads down.

I look at Gwen. "Oh dear, somethin's wrong but whatever it is she'll have te wait 'til a've turned pink." We both approach the stove, opening our coats swopping the cold air inside for the warmth emanating.

I look at Gwen, even she's looking guilty. "Do ye know what this is all about?"

She fidgets. "I don't know for sure but it could be about your German soldier."

I'm shocked. "He's not 'mine'. Come on Gwen spill the beans."

"Oh Em, it's probably nothing but...."

"Yes?"

"Well, before we left some of the VADS were thinking the Germans soldiers we were looking after had something to do with the raid. They wanted to get rid of them, send them to a prison camp I mean."

I could hardly believe my ears. Do these girls think the soldiers had some sort of radio with them and why should they suggest the camp being shot up when they themselves were actually inside?

"I know it's daft. I think some of the girls have vivid imaginations."

"Ah think you're right I'd better see Sister Brogan see what it's all about. Thanks Gwen. What do you think?"

"It's rubbish of course but one or two of the girls like a good story....."

"And?"

"They can see you were particularly close to them or at least one of them."

"Perhaps I'm a spy! Oh Gwen. Ah think he's a nice man. Ah suppose ah was fond of him. It was nothin' else, how could there be?"

"Look Em, I'll tell you everything I know. One of the girls thought she'd caught you cuddling him or something. The story goes that you two appeared from the back of marquee, after his exercise walk, looking very pink and erm, dishevelled. I don't care if that's true or not and why shouldn't you be fond of him but I know you're not a spy."

"It was a goodbye kiss an' that's all it was. I'd better gan an' see Sister. Thanks for tellin' me anyway."

I change in to my uniform and try to tidy myself after the journey. All the time I'm wondering what I'm in for. Fraternising with any patient is forbidden, I could be sent home in disgrace. I'll just have to act the innocent. No tittle-tattling VAD is going to stop me from helping our boys.

Sister wasn't in her tent, nor in the main ward marquee. I looked very briefly in to the, commonly known, Bosch marquee now completely functional but still showing its wounds. To my surprise she was with the doctor examining the patient in Gunty's old bed. I approached, only when I was alongside I realised it was Gunty they were discussing. She recognised me and took me aside.

"We've nearly done 'ere, go an' wait in me tent. Oi need ter discuss somethin' witcha."

She turned back to the patient. I could see Gunty clearly. He seemed to be asleep. I wanted to stay to ask questions but I turned on my heels and left to wait in her room. Before leaving I noticed the ward was now only half full, I assumed some had been removed to the prison camp.

I waited by her table looking around at the rough and ready decor but my emotions were confused. Pleased that he was still here but wondering why and what's the problem that required the doctor and Sister.

The flap opened and in strode Sister Brogan. "Welcome back Staff Nurse how was your leave?"

"Very enjoyable thank ye Sister." I wasn't going to go into any detail I wanted to know what she wanted.

"You've come back at de right time - for me. Thar's been a big push by de Bosch. They're close an' we may 've ter move. Transport 'as been arranged an' tis standin' by, waitin' for a nod from HQ. Oi need yer ter make sure all the girls are ready packed for an immediate departure. Is dat clear?"

"Yes Sister, I'll gan an' see the day shift before they gan te bed. Anythin' else?"

"Dat's enough isn't it?"

"Yes Sister." I rose to leave.

"Staff Nurse Mulligan. Oi don't take any notice ter blarney. You're an excellent nurse, in every way. Yer understan'? "

"Yes Sister."

I left to plan my arrangements for the camp move. The situation was desperate but I felt strangely elated.

Chapter 51

I've gathered all the girls together in the dorm tent. All the day shift and as many from the night shift as possible. Some I can see are tired ready for their bed but most are inquisitive wondering what I'm going to say. I have all their attention.

"It looks like we're ganin to move base. The Bosch are advancing quickly an' there's a danger we may be overrun. I don't know when but the order can be given at any time, in five minutes, in the middle of the night or in a couple of days time. Hopefully we'll be given some notice but we canna assume that.

Essentials only are to be taken. Medications, dressings, equipment, stores, anythin' that canna be replaced are to be loaded up in to the lorries an' be away. Time is of the essence an' we girls have to do our own bit.

Nurses, ye have to make sure medications are given an' dressings replaced on time, charts completed. Baths are given quickly an' no dilly-dallyin' in the latrines! The patients will have been told but ah suspect they will need remindin' - be ready to move, keep yor belongings in your kit bag an' so on.

VADs ye have to help where it's needed. The orderlies, porters, drivers an' everyone else are bein' given the same information. They will need help: packin', loadin' an' decidin' what is to go an' what can be left. This is where ye come in. Be decisive, our men are canny people but often need help with priorities!"

There is a titter of agreement and some chatter. I smile to re-gain their attention. "Also, there are only a few of us nurses. Most of ye have been here sometime so ye know the routines so please help them when requested.

Personally, keep all your gear in your kitbags so ye can just pick them up an' leave at any time. It may make just the difference between escape an' capture.

Remember, the most important action is to remove our boys an' yourselves from here to our new base safely an' quickly. If ye find yourself holdin' up transport, leave what you were doin' an' jump aboard.

"Any questions like?"

An older VAD shouted out. "What do we do with the Bosch patients?"

I notice some of the other VADs look over to the questioner. "They have to be treated just the same as our own boys. They are in our care. Is that clear?"

There is some dark muttering and a few "yes Staff Nurse" responses.

"Don't under estimate what could happen to us if we're captured. The air raid last month showed what they are capable of. Ah firmly believe this is their last gasp 'big push'. We have to retreat in good formation to be ready when our boys take over the initiative again.

Alright night shift: get back to your wards. Day shift: sort your kitbags an' get some sleep. Rest assured when the time comes we'll get away an' set up shop somewhere else to continue our work."

The girls drift off chatting animatedly. I know they're a decent lot and will give their all when the time comes, if it does. I go and see Gwen. She's getting ready for her bed. She speaks first.

"Any clue how long Em?"

"No, ahm ganin to see Sister now for the latest, ah won't be long."

"She didn't mention your friend then?"

"Not directly but ah know he's still here."

She smiles. "Good."

Sister has no more news but suspects the move will take place but will be in a few days. She's certain it won't be tonight. HQ doesn't take risks. I leave re-assured. I can't help myself heading for Gunty's marquee. I need to know if there's been a complication perhaps his condition has deteriorated.

I slip through the flaps. There are no staff around so I approach Gunty's bed. He hasn't moved since I last saw him, still fast asleep. I read his notes in horror. He hasn't eaten for days and only takes minimal fluids. He refuses to take exercise. He seems to have given up. I look at his face closely. Even in the dim light I can see he looks drawn and pale. I mutter to myself. "Come on Gunty get a grip."

His eyes immediately flick open, his arm suddenly rises from the blanket and pulls me to his face and gently kisses me. I react and pull back completely shocked.

"Sorry Staff Nurse. I've missed you."

I stare at him, I don't understand, I whisper. "Why haven't ye been eatin' or takin' exercise, what's wrong?"

"I've told you. I've missed you."

"But, but..."

"I'm feeling better already, I can eat something now if you want me to."

I'm looking at him still confused. I can't believe he's put all this on because I've been away.

"Ah can give ye somethin' of mine to eat."

"No need there's a full plate on that crate over there."

I look and see the tray, I get up and handover the plate full of un-appetising dried up food. He sits up and starts eating immediately.

"You're a typical man, always wants his own way. You're like a bairn."

He looks up and answers in his perfect English. "Of course but only when what I want is perfect."

I have to smile at such a line. "Look ah have to go, I'll come an' see ye temorra. We'll do some exercise." He smiles and nods. "An' by the way ah missed ye as well but ah canna think why."

I leave smiling broadly to myself. I look back, he salutes me ceremoniously. I shake my head in disbelief thinking men are a different breed altogether.

The next few days are full of tension. Each time I see Sister I expect her to give the signal to prepare to leave but she's been right it wasn't imminent then but now?

We all try to continue normally but ready to crack the whip and set off at a gallop. I'm often with the Bosch patients, the VADs are wary, they feel they are the butt of their jokes. This is not true now. At first they were cocky, arrogant now they are resigned to be prisoners for the rest of the war. My Oberleutnant of course is nothing of the sort. We talk briefly in the ward but to avoid raising suspicion we only converse on our walks - which are for his own good of course. He is proud of his Bavarian ancestry but would prefer to live in Britain. He considers us Brits are more relaxed, less restricted by rules and regulations and we have a sense of humour. We keep our distance, no holding hands and certainly no repeat kissing and cuddling sessions. Our separation is hard. I know we both want to touch but I've learnt there are eyes everywhere so we keep apart.

Today and yesterday there has been a new sound like a far distant thunderstorm. It dominates the everyday noises of the CCS. I've now got used to it and forget it's there until Gunty confirms their origin.

"That's our guns blasting away at the British trenches. It means there will be another attack."

I shudder realising the battle front is close by and It brings home the reason why we have to move our base.

This morning we hear news. It's not for a camp relocation but this day will be the last for the Bosch patients. They are all being moved to a prison camp in France tomorrow. My heart sinks. I know they have to go but it saddens me. He has my address, I can only hope he is able to make contact when all this is finished and we can meet up again. Then it's up to us.

The weather is cold and misty, sometimes this weather will clear but today it's so thick I believe it's in for the day. The 11 o'clock morning health check is to be done. I enter the Bosch tent with Gwen as usual. The normal German banter is missing, we can sense the mood is grim, resigned. They have been told the news. I sit down with Gunty, he keeps repeating that he's not going to any prison.

"I only want to go for walks with you. We'll all get shot."

I insist that he won't. "Don't base your assumptions on what ye lot de. If ye try an' escape ye might be, just behave yourself an' you'll be released at the end o' this war. Everyone says it's ganin to end soon so it won't be long."

"I feel the need for some exercise, now, right now."

I look at him and wonder why I've fallen in love with this man. He can behave like a hero then acts like a spoilt baby. "Alright, but ah need to tell Gwen she'll have to finish the round by herself."

Gwen is as ever understanding and tells me to take my time - just for his recovery of course, our little joke.

We have to dress for the winter conditions. Both donning ankle length great coats we leave for our walk. He limps but this is only for show he can get about with his stick as well as any. Away from the camp we discuss the possibilities: meeting back in England, getting married, family, where we could live but it all seems pie-in-the-sky. Our normal route takes us on well used paths but today he guides me on to another route into the woods on a single track. The trees and the thick mist seem to hide the rest of the world, even the distant cannon thunder is silenced. We walk in silence I'm thinking my own thoughts about the future.

"Emily, I love you."

255

I smile and begin to turn round but I'm caught in his arms from behind. He turns down my coat collar and starts nibbling my ears and then on to my neck. He knows I'm so sensitive there. I should resist but no-one can see us and it's delicious. I angle my head forward and to the side to enjoy his touch the more. His hands open my coat at the front and then caress my body underneath. "You're a beautiful lady."

I laugh "ahm surprised ye can feel anythin' over all my layers."

"I will have to do something about that." He turns me around and starts unbuttoning my coat and then my uniform at the front.

"Wey aye ahm ganin to freeze to death."

But he opens his coat wide and spreads the flaps around me. I pass my arms around his waist and take in his closeness. He is warm and manly. His hands are pulling on my clothes and I can sense they are close to my skin and await their cold touch. I feel him but his hands are warm and gentle. They travel round my waist and then up each side of my spine. I shudder with delight. I can tell his next move as he brings them round and cups my breasts. "These are so gorgeous."

I'm not surprised. He's forever commenting on the figures of the other women. "Not up to VAD Jenny Stanner's bosom ah suppose."

He laughs out loud, too loud. I shush him. "She's like a fat cow that needs milking. We call her Daisy."

"Hawa, enough of your German cheek. Alright she's larger than most but she's good at her job an' she's kind to ye lot."

With his hands still on my breasts he kisses me full on the lips his tongue searching mine. It is a long kiss, maybe our last. This thought arouses a panic inside me and I squeeze his buttocks and pull him closer. I can feel his own arousal it's then I know we are going to make love. He lifts me gently on to the ground soft with spent pine needles and moss. He lifts my skirts and kisses me. I've never made love outside and this feels so fresh, clean and sensuous. We complete our love making in a heavy breathing silence deep in each other's arms.

We whisper and giggle together but a nearby noise alerts us. Someone is running through the woods, then another, then more footsteps. The rustling is interspersed with jolting of kits, leather creaking and then someone trips, falls and swears. My eyes light up in fear, the swearing was not in English. Gunty covers me with his great coat and we lay there undiscovered until.

"Aufstehen, Oder du bits tot."

Chapter 52

Daily Log - Sister Brogan. Brandhoek CCS. 6th January 1918

We were attacked today by a small company of Bosch soldiers. It is only due to the bravery of a small number of army boys in the camp that restricted the death and destruction inflicted on a camp supposedly protected by our Red Cross. I believe this action is as a result of the Bosch being driven back by the Allies and this is their last attempt at showing their strength. It is despicable that our camp, only here to provide help and solace to the boys injured in the conflict no matter what nationality, has been violated by such cowardly action.

Around mid-day under the cover of a heavy mist a force of about twenty soldiers attacked our camp. They were armed with rifles and grenades and showed no mercy on anyone in their way. Our POW marquee suffered the first attack. Every person in the tent whether they be a patient or a member of my medical staff were either killed or very badly injured. Two orderlies and one of my very best VADs died. God bless their souls. By the time the attackers left the carnage our own Tommies were ready and waiting and gave them a good going over. Ten of them laid dead, the remainder turned and fled back in to the woods. Only two grenades were thrown. One blew up a lorry leaving the camp. The driver was killed instantly. The other landed close to the canteen tent, fortunately this was a dud thereby saving the lives of over twenty of our staff inside eating lunch.

Our final death toll is 8 German patients, a VAD, 2 orderlies, and a driver. I also have to assume the sad loss of my Staff Nurse and another German patient who are missing but were last seen on an exercise walk in the vicinity of the entry of the attacking force. The nurse was one the best and cannot be easily replaced.

Today is a very sad day for me and for the rest of our team. We will fight on because that's why we're here but, although I feel ashamed to write this, I cannot wish anything but eternal damnation for the ten German soldiers killed. For those that escaped I dearly hope they are contrite and their consciences give them grief for as long as they live on this earth.

God left us today. I hope and pray for his early return.

Chapter 53

Gunty gets up aggressively at the same time managing to cover my awry clothing with my coat. He shouts fearlessly at the threatening soldier spitting out every word in German.

"How dare you talk to me like that. I am Oberleutnant Günter Mueller from the Second Royal Bavarian Corps. I have just managed to escape the British guards and you shout at me as if I am the enemy. This nurse is my hostage; she will be useful to us."

"Why were you lying on her?"

"I thought you were British you dope. Is our front nearby?

"No, we are an advance party, reconnaissance."

"I want you take me back to your Officer in charge. I have information that is crucial for our advance."

I have no idea what is being said but I can sense this German soldier's attitude has changed from his initial aggression to one of uncertainty. He is twitching, feeling nervous. He's not the only one. Gunty is in command but what's going to happen to me. Am I going to be taken prisoner? I've heard stories of how the Germans shoot prisoners. It doesn't help that I'm half undressed under my coat. If this soldier saw the state I'm in he would realise what we were doing.

Gunty now shouts at me to get up. He frightens me, I hope he's acting. We are escorted away in the opposite direction from the hospital by two soldiers. Their rifles complete with bayonets are slung over their shoulders. They keep glancing at us, they're not convinced of our story.

I hear gun shots behind me, lots of them. It sounds like a battle has started. I hold my breath, it can only be our CCS. I look at Gunty but he marches on staring ahead. I cannot believe what's happening. A squad of German troops are attacking an almost defenceless hospital. They must have had word that we're holding some of their men as prisoners. I feel sick to my stomach and want to retch.

260

Our march becomes a route march. Gunty's bad leg must be giving him hell but he doesn't show any pain. For an hour or more we head roughly north. I assume we must cross the Allied front somewhere and then across no-man's land to the German trenches. We are joined by a group of nine or ten soldiers coming up from behind and the whole group stops to, I assume, discuss tactics. I sit to one side despite this I'm the target of many stares, pointed fingers and muted laughter. They are very much like our British Tommies but in all over grey. They are very young, shy when they're by themselves and full of bravado when in a group like this. However they keep their distance feared of Gunty's seniority in age and rank. He comes over to me and speaks to me with his back to the watchful eyes of the soldiers. He uses an English, heavily accented and threatening tone but what he actually says is re-assuring.

"Don't worry about these creatures, they don't speak a word of English. I have to treat you with little respect to avoid any suspicion, they may think you're my lover or something, lucky me." There's not a flicker of a smile. I drop my head in pretend anguish. "They've pushed through our lines forming a salient. There's a command post nearby I'm taking you there. I'll meet the officer in charge. He'll probably be able to speak in English so don't mind if I call you names, remember I love you and I'll make sure you'll be well treated."

I widen my eyes as though in shock and slap him hard around his face.

"Ahm not your whore, ye can gan an' hang yorself for all ah care." I cross my arms around my chest and turn away. I can act, years of practice managing at school.

Although I was looking in the opposite direction I could hear the reaction. I hope I haven't embarrassed him too much. He talks to them sharply in German, as a result the group rise and we set off again. We soon meet a country lane and our pace speeds up. For the first time I can see the effect of blanket shelling on the countryside. It is a sea of mud criss-crossed by trenches some destroyed, others untouched but all empty. Trees and hedges look as though they've been hit by hurricane winds and then some. Some vehicles are on their sides off the road, abandoned. It is a landscape from Hell.

One of the soldiers points to the remains of a farm building of some sort. Little is left standing but I can see some activity around it. I guess this must be their base. We arrive in just a few minutes. Gunty is escorted to a small enclave established in the corner of two standing walls and go in through a canvas flap entrance. I'm left outside with more than a few interested onlookers. I keep my head down and stare at the ground.

A long ten minutes later Gunty appears outside the covered area and waves me over. I ignore him which makes him march over and grab me roughly by the arm and pulls me.

"Come on you little bitch." He then searches in to his pocket and whispers for my hearing only. "I'll look after you, just do as he says." He comes out with a bit of rag. "And wipe your face, you're a mess."

We go through the flap and in to an office complete with a small table home for two helmets, mugs and sundry items. Rifles with fixed bayonets are leaning against a wall. Opposite is a large packing case supporting maps. There are two soldiers studying one of them. They ignore me. Eventually one of them looks up. I seemed to have surprised him, he smiles but with his mouth only, his grey eyes boring in to me. He speaks in careful English.

"So Günter, this is your nurse?

"Yes Hauptmann, Staff Nurse Mulligan."

"Is she any good."

"She's an excellent nurse, but no patience."

"That's not what I mean." He walks over to me and in one movement he opens my trench coat and examines me. I have managed to adjust my dress on the journey here and he sees my uniform. I hope he would be impressed. He approaches and suddenly grabs both my

262

breasts. I'm totally and completely taken aback. He drops one hand to my crotch, it was the last straw. I slap him hard around his face.

"How dare ye."

His face flares red where I hit him and pink everywhere else. He is livid. I have embarrassed him in front of subordinates. He reacts by punching me hard on the side of my face making me scream and crumple on to the floor holding my stinging face.

He turns to Gunty and speaks in German.

"You should choose your tarts better. This one needs a lesson taught her."

He then orders the other man but looks at me and speaks in careful English.

"Take her away and shoot her, no, use your bayonet. Make sure she regrets hitting an officer before she dies."

Chapter 54

My heart is beating fast, this arrogant man wants to kill me because I didn't give in to his obscene advances. My eyes flare wide staring at the back of his head.

"Who do ye think ye are? A've been told German officers are gentlemen, they know how to behave no matter what the provocation. Am ah wrong? Or are ye all animals that care only fo' yourselves?"

He turns, picks up his rifle and slowly swings it round until it points to my head. His smile is cold, calculating, his words are spat out viciously. "Now tell me, what exactly were you saying?" He is interrupted by a soldier entering. He is panicking, the noise of whistling shells and nearby explosions escalates. Oblivious of what is happening he salutes and shouts a warning.

"Hauptmann, we're under attack."

The officer listens but still stares at me. He shouts at his adjutant.

"Go with him, report back. I'll deal with this noisy English bitch myself."

The two soldiers leave. He clicks back the trigger, I close my eyes. A shot rings out. I feel nothing I must be dead but I can still open my eyes. I see him standing in front of me his rifle pointing to the floor. He looks surprised. He has a neat hole in the middle of his forehead. We stare at each other endlessly until, at last, he crumples to the floor. The back of his head has been blown away. I can't speak. I look at Gunty holding a pistol. My legs give way I stumble towards him, he catches me and holds me tight. I sob uncontrollably.

I hear commotion outside, shouts in German, more explosions, the sound of debris and shrapnel pinging, shrieking through the air, complete mayhem. But I'm in another world apart, safe in his arms.

"We'd better see what we can do. Stay with me."

We release each other, step over the dead officer and throw back the flap. The air is full of smoke, nearby the two soldiers who had left our tent just minutes ago lie on the floor. One of them is clearly dead, the other is moving. One of his arms is holding the other trying to reconnect it at the shoulder. An artery is pumping out his life blood a growing stain spreading in the dust of the floor.

"He is finished." Gunty steps forward, pistol raised and shoots him in the head. The soldier slumps back and lays still. "Come with me we have to get away."

We stagger out of the derelict building. We join others heading towards a group of lorries. I hear engines starting, some already are moving.

Gunty points at a particular lorry, a driver already in the cab. "Get on board that one." I scramble aboard just as it starts to leave, it accelerates quickly Somehow he grabs a handhold and jumps aboard pulling himself inside with his strong arms.

There are five other soldiers with us. Gunty asks them. *"Where are we going to Infanterist?"*

They all look scared their eyes concentrating on the receding view out the back of the lorry. One realises they are being asked a question.

"Retreating to our main base. Who are y...."

A huge explosion diverts his and everyone else's attention. A lorry two behind us has received a direct hit. It swerves out of control and slows. The lorry behind has smashed in to it and is pushing it off the road completely. The two vehicles are locked together, there is another explosion and the whole is engulfed in flame. Above all the noise we all can hear the bellows and screams of pain from the inferno, their last contribution to life.

Other shells are exploding around us. Our Tommies obviously have our range and are blasting away wanting complete annihilation, like a free coconut shy at a fun fare. I see one larger but much slower lorry at the rear of our convoy. It is losing ground, as we climb a hill it is now hardly moving at all. It is a sitting duck but somehow it staggers on, smoke pouring from its exhaust, flashes all around them.

Over the summit and we gain speed, the explosions are behind us, we're getting out of range and we all breathe easier. We watch following vehicles breasting the summit and dash for safety. My heart cheers silently as the others shout out loud as each lorry makes it. I want people to live no matter whose mother's son they are. As if in slow motion the tail-ender staggers in to sight. I ball my hands in to fists and will it on. "Come on, come on." I mutter too loud. The nearest soldiers look at me startled. I take no notice, the firing has slowed to a stop but a last gasp shot found its mark. The lorry topples over but no explosion or fire. Soldiers tumble out the back joined by the driver and another from the cab. They start to run towards us. I look over to Gunty.

"We must stop an' pick them up."

He shakes his head. "It's too late."

I look back. Heartened by their success the Tommies have opened up again. More shells are falling in their midst. Flashes and blown dust clouds hide the scene. When it clears all life has gone replaced by body parts scattered like leaves in the wind. I hold my head in my hands in despair and I cry for the young men. What an obscene waste of life.

We rumble on. I want to lie in my lover's arms but I daren't. So I sit by myself eyes unfocused wondering what is this really all about.

We arrive with the other surviving lorries of the convoy. Gunty jumps down and signals to me to wait where I am. The other soldiers do the same and disperse but not before I'm given questioning looks. They look confused, so am I. What now I wonder, another arrogant officer?

I hear Gunty's voice speaking in German. He is approaching and with him a woman, not in military uniform but wearing a nursing hat.

Gunty speaks in his accented English. 'Come down I want you to meet Fräu Schwimmer she is the Sister of the local Field Hospital.

I swing my legs over the side and slide down to the floor. I look at the woman and she looks at me. She offers her hand and I take it with warm relief. She opens my great coat and looks at me then speaks in broken English.

"I see you are a Staff Nurse." I nod. "I know where you come from but after speaking to the Oberleutnant here I would be so grateful if you would help us at the hospital. Hard work but much better than any prison camp."

I look at Gunty, he is smiling, he is relaxed. I nod. "Of course ah will."

"Fräulein you are a gift from heaven."

Chapter 55

I explain that I have nothing except for what I'm wearing but the Sister smiles.

"I can kit you out with everything you need. What I want from you is your expertise and your understanding of what is required under these conditions."

I also explain that my knowledge of the German language is minimal. Sister shakes her head.

"I just know you'll cope, don't worry. Come on let's get some food and maybe a cup of tea? I'd like to get there before midnight, it's about five miles away, I have a driver ready. So let us leave in about one hour, ok?" She looks over to Gunty. I can sense she understands I am not just his hostage. "Our canteen of sorts is just here." She points to a marquee tent nearby. "Meet me there in a few minutes and we can talk some more." She walks quickly away. I turn to the Oberleutnant standing next to me.

"She seems really nice but all ah want to do is sleep."

It is dark, the only illumination are some paraffin lamps at the tent entrances. There is no-one around. I hold his hand tightly and kiss his cheek.

"Thank ye for savin' me life."

He takes me in his arms and kisses me tenderly then holds my shoulders with his hands and looks earnestly in to my face.

"It's you who should be thanked. You've given me a reason for living. We're going to lose this bloody war but I want to survive it to be with you. I want you to do what you can at the hospital. You'll be safer there than anywhere else." He releases me then adds bitterly. "Unlike some, the British don't attack red crosses."

"Ah know but what do ye do now?"

"I've spoken to the Hauptmann here. He is desperate. He has been landed with a load of kids. I'm to be his second-in-command. I've been promoted to Oberleutnant 1st class, lucky me eh? He tells me there's going to be a big offensive in a few weeks, I suspect that'll become a few months! Sister knows this as well. All this means we gain a few yards and each side lose hundreds of men if not thousands."

I can see he's lost his appetite for war. He looks tired. I'm reminded that this day is his first out of the hospital bed for over two weeks. I feel it's my job to build him up but this is such a dilemma. Do I have to encourage him to kill Tommies? I so wish we could just leave, say we've had enough, but that's impossible.

"Firstly ye need to recuperate after your injuries. Then because you're in command, think of other ways of gaining ground. Don't charge head on, go round, take prisoners." I ramble on as if I know anything at all about battle tactics. He laughs.

"Like you don't meet problems head on, Mrs Suffragette?"

"Ah do but there's always other ways ye can get what ye want. Why bring up the big guns an' blast away for days lettin' everyone know what you're ganin to de next allowing them to be prepared for the attack. Catch them by surprise, be mobile, do somethin' different."

I feel foolish telling an experience soldier to change laid down tactics for a battle. I have no experience whatsoever but he's not condescending, he doesn't tell me to shut up, he listens.

"Maybe you're right but orders for battle come from on-high. I would get shot for disobeying them."

"There's always a way. Look I'd bettor gan an' see Sister Schwimmer." I grab him with both arms. The moment has come for us to go in different directions. The thought makes me squeeze him tighter and tighter until he squeals.

"That's what I'll do: Cuddle your Tommys to submission."

"Brilliant idea, the world'll be a better place for it."

We don't laugh. We both know how true it is.

My journey to the field hospital passes in a flash. By the time we arrive my brain has slowed. A combination of the day's events and leaving Gunty has had its numbing effect. All I want to do is find my bed and sleep. Sister Schwimmer, Brunhilda, understands, she kits me out and directs me to the dorm. I don't think of the day I've had, that's for another time. I'm falling asleep as soon as my head hits the pillow. I wake many hours later to the sound of women's voices speaking in a different language in a different place but with all the same problems.

Chapter 56

I'm still in that half way world of being only partially awake. The harsh tones of German voices are rousing my brain to the present although I keep my eyes shut and body movement limited. My recollections are being jogged. The shocking views of some of the nurses at the British CCS come to mind. At the time I just put it down to them taking in fabricated propaganda. But now I'm here I'll be able to confirm or deny such stories.

I recall one nurse in particular was adamant that German nurses deny proper treatment and kindness to any POW. She told tales of offering refreshments then snatching them away, or even spitting on the plates before handing them over. Ignoring cries of help at the hospital bed and laughing in their faces. This is far away from the Geneva Convention that was drummed in to me during my early training days.

I can remember so well that a nurse, during wartime, must be neutral, without partiality in the care of the wounded. I blush recalling my first feelings when the German POWs were brought in and Sister Brogan's warning words. Acceptance wasn't easy. I was looking for signs that showed the Bosch were a brutal, barbaric race. Many times I thought I saw this in their arrogance before I realised that some of our own Tommys were not perfect. Apart from that I suspect having to surrender as they did was an insult to their male pride and they reacted badly - especially at first. Either way over time they settled in and became no different to any other soldier. One in particular settled in especially well.

A comfortable warmth spreads through me whenever I think of Gunty. He is the first man I have really loved and want to be with at all times. But I'm so scared for him in this war. It's not the fault of the German soldiers, the nurses or anyone else brought in to these battle grounds. If they do seem barbaric it's not of their making, no, it's the leaders, the politicians, the generals. The rich, the powerful and the influential comfortable in their hideaways well away from the action, these are the guilty men. Why can't they be compassionate, reasonable people? I guess it's always been so and this will never change. The bullies always win and why? Because they're bullies.

I feel desperate but I'm going to do my bit to help humanity. I'm now wide awake and ready for action. I sit up and realise I'm by myself. I swing my legs out of bed.

"Good morning Mitarbeiter Krankenschwester?"

I jump and swing round in one movement and see a nurse younger than me looking nervous, hands gripped together in front of her apron.

"Good morning." I extend my hand to shake.

She looks terrified. Her own hands seem to be stuck together and cannot move.

"Ahm Staff Nurse Mulligan, who are you?"

Her eyes widen, I understand she doesn't understand a word I say. I smile and try to work out how to communicate. I sit back down and pat the edge of the bed for her to join me.

I have to repeat the movement before she does sit down and we try a series of hand and body movements. Our laughable antics make her relax. Coupled with some assumptions I realise that Sister Schwimmer has asked her to show me around the building and we set off.

The building used to be a school and seems to be well kitted out and, one big difference, it is warm. The latrines, wash rooms, kitchen and eating areas are clean and there is a sitting room with armchairs. I nod to other nurses and orderlies. There is a recognisable worldwide hospital dress style and here is no exception. But there are some variances distinguishing the German way and I'm going to have learn what these differences mean in terms of rank.

She leads me to the wash room and points to an alcove where uniforms are hanging. I have to choose my own items. Helpfully she points to what I should be wearing. I make my choice. She signals that she'll wait outside for me.

I'm grateful for the privacy. After yesterday I need to freshen up. I still have my own uniform on. The room is luxurious compared to Brandhoek. No draughts, plenty of room and with plenty of hot water. In a short time I'm ready for work properly attired. After breakfast I'm led to the wards. There are curious eyes, questioning, wondering why this foreigner, the enemy, is here. I can only smile and nod and get on with the day. I hope I can show my willingness and my skills to look after the wounded.

I have to go through a slow learning curve to find ways of understanding the staff and the patients. The injuries are obvious and the remedies familiar. Getting the message over to young inexperienced nurses is more difficult, I cannot leave them at first until I'm happy that the correct treatment is given. I am learning some German words and phrases, likewise the others are learning English.

There are three Sisters. I have been fully accepted by Sister Schwimmer, the other two seem wary but just have to put up with me, an English nurse. The acute shortage of experienced staff means there is no alternative.

The German boys, and they're not always German, accept me and proudly produce their photos for my examination. These are fascinating. They show the usual formal family groups, wives, children and parents but the difference is in their attire: children and men often wearing knickerbockers and braced bibs, delightful.

The weeks pass, the weather improves as we move into Spring but I'm lonely. It is the language barrier. The girls are helpful and supportive but my days off are spent by myself. I do a lot of walking and thinking. I have no idea of what's been happening at home. Sending or receiving letters is of course impossible for me. I miss my friends and family and my daughter but that hurt is a permanent ache and never diminishes. In the village I can practice my few words of Flemish learnt from my time at Brandhoek but I'm an oddity. Dressed as a German nurse speaking English, I can see and understand their confusion.

My only companion is Sister Schwimmer. Her English is excellent and on the odd times when our breaks coincide we can converse happily for hours. When I say 'we' I really mean me. Having someone to talk to has the effect of breaching a dam of my unshared thoughts. I talk of my past, my family in Northumberland, women's emancipation, my daughter, everything comes out like a river in flood. She listens. I give her little time to respond but when I do I learn she comes from Munich, she's not married and she has a little boy, Zach. He's not actually little as he's now fourteen, at school living and being brought up by her sister and her family. The father, a Turk, left when he realised she was pregnant. A charming devoted man -Not!

Gunty makes the journey over whenever he can. He always looks tired but I know I can make him relax just by chatting about our hopes and dreams. There is little talk of the progress of the war. He couldn't tell me anyway.

He was particularly tense on his last visit. I guessed this 'Big Push' is about to begin. Thanks to Sister she allows us time together, I believe she has a bit of a thing for him anyway but it gives me the chance to make him relax the best way I know how!

Only a few days later we can hear the guns. It is the low rumble I've heard before, a noise that is ever present no matter where you are, it's the repeat of the continuous rumbling thunderstorm far in the distance. Sister Schwimmer understands the signs. On our shifts together we plan for the inevitable influx. Beds are cleared, the injured sent elsewhere, repatriated or returned to their regiments. Extra provisions are ordered and stored and we sit back and wait. Sister is well aware the war is nearly lost, we both are but we wonder how it'll end. Will we be overrun and taken prisoner, will there be an armistice and we can all go home?

I am told to expect a convoy before midday. Sister, the auxiliary nurses, porters, orderlies, we are all waiting. We are ready for anything.

They arrive, motor lorries, horse drawn trailers, buses. I watch as the grey uniformed soldiers jump out and open doors, let down ramps and drag back tarpaulins. This action releases one by one a line of khaki uniformed, injured soldiers. I do a double take, my eyes widen. All of us stare at the scene unfolding before us.

Our first bunch of British POWs has arrived. They are noisy. Nervous shouts and jokes incomprehensible to the gawping reception committee. I watch their expressions and wonder: now this will test your neutral and impartial nursing treatment!

Chapter 57

For the first few days I keep a watchful eye on the nurses. I so wanted to disprove the rumours of cruelty to the enemy patients. The short time I've been in the field hospital I found the German nurses to be just as efficient and professional as my compatriots the other side of the battle lines. I certainly couldn't understand most of the conversations but I could see the results in the patients' treatment. I know Sister Schwimmer has given similar words of warning as Sister Brogan gave in Brandhoek CCS but I have a nagging doubt. The mess room and the dorms are where the required attitude and proper control can be set aside. In particular the two other sisters repeatedly have heated arguments. Other nurses look away seemingly embarrassed. One of the sisters nod in my direction and I catch her staring at me expressionless. The other raises her voice, she shouts 'Nein, Nein'. I can translate that but little of the previous hurried conversation. Oh I so wish I could speak the language.

A further week goes by some of our Tommies have recovered and been transferred to prison camps, others have died and have been buried and I must add, have been buried with proper honours with records kept of name, regiment, number and date of death. Sister Schwimmer is a hero, she treats all her patients as equal and that of course is how it should be.

Our second batch of Tommies arrive in the afternoon, fortunately enough beds have been vacated. They are quieter than the first batch, always a bad sign. Some are bleeding badly, gaping wounds roughly patched. Others appear undamaged but are gasping for air. It is these that are more likely to perish. Internal wounds are much more difficult to treat. It is these men that shout for their mothers, not their wives or girlfriends. This may seem strange but when you consider their age you realise they've known their parents for so much longer.

Before I go off duty, as always and with a senior nurse coming on duty, I check every patient to make sure she understands what's needed, one by one in each and every room. I approach a bed holding a patient that I've not seen. He is huddled up, facing the far wall and gasping for breath as if it could be his last. The nurse, whom I've got to know well, grabs and checks the notes showing his basic details. Her eyes widen, she reads them again before handing them over now staring full into my eyes. I scan the scribbled writing: Pte Mulligan No. 242017 Northumberland Fusiliers. I want to scream but nothing comes out. My eyes close in silent prayer. I reach over and gently try to turn him over to see his face but there is no need, his profile is enough. There is no doubting. Here in front of me struggling to survive is my youngest and only surviving brother, my lovely Con.

I want to cry and grab him and hold him in my arms and make him better, but I can't. I have to assume he is just another casualty like the hundreds of others we've treated. I always try to make light of their injuries, smile, make them smile, laugh. I feel my eyes moisten, the nurse gently takes my arm, gestures that she will continue with the round by herself and leaves me alone with my brother. I dry my eyes and touch his forehead. He turns and instantly recognises me and between his gasps for breath he gives me his broadest smile.

"Emy?"

I pretend to be cross. "Yes it's me an what do ye think you're doin' here?"

He grabs my hand and takes a while to gather his breath. "Me! You're the one on the wrong side."

"An' you're the one that gets in the way of a shell."

Our conversation continues in the same vein avoiding anything serious. He always acts the 'man of the house', never did show pain, it was a weakness, that was for women! But I know when he's hurting I always did and I know it now. He has been given a sedative, his eyes are closing and his speech becomes slurred.

"OK young Con, you're best get some sleep an I'll be back when ye wake up, alright pet?" He nods and gives me another of his smiles before slumping back onto the pillow his breathing easier. But I don't leave, I stay and keep holding his hand. My mind slips back to our youth: coal gathering, remembering our magic and scary stories we told each other on the beach and in our bat-cave. Then to the Workhouse and the wretched 3 years he spent there at the mercy of the revolting pervert, Proctor. I couldn't help but smirk at his eventual end at the wrong end of Stan's truncheon. I recall how I tried to stop him from volunteering for the army. Oh how I wished he waited for his call-up but he was a big young lad, too young, wanting to join his older friends. "An' now look at ye."

"Are ye his sister or somethin' like nurse?"

I jump. It has gone quiet in the ward and the soldier in the next bed has heard me muttering and has sat up as best he can done up swathed in his dressings. I nodded.

"He's a grand lad, always tries to be cheerful like, no matter what. He's always talkin' about his big sister. Emy did this an' Emy did that, she couldn't do no wrong in his eyes. She was in the papers for some Suffragette goings on. Was that ye?"

I nod again, I try to maintain my control but hearing this is just too much and my tears flood down my cheeks. I bow my head and shamelessly sob.

"Sorry pet, didn't mean to upset ye. He'll be alright won't he? He's just got a bit of a sore chest hasn't he?"

I pull myself together, wipe my face, take a deep breath and answer. "Aye, of course he will an' what are ye doin' tryin' to get out of that bed. Get back before ah tie ye doon, those bones have got te set in a straight line."

He laughs. "Ahm a bit wonky anyways so a few more kinks won't hurt."

I help him to lie back down and I make sure he's as comfortable as possible before I leave. I give Con a last look and walk away giving the nurse a 'good night' and leave for my dorm. I take a long route back, I need some fresh air. I know Con has a blast injury and so many don't survive. Infections can set in or the lungs are too damaged to keep them going for long. My pace quickens my determination swells inside me filling my body. I will do all I can, discuss the prognosis with the Doctor and Sister. If there's anything, anything at all that would benefit him then I'll do it whatever it takes. I have my dinner in the mess and retire to my dorm but sleep evades me for hours and when I do drop off it seems only minutes when someone is shaking me, I assume to start a new day.

I shake my head trying to get myself going but then I see it's still dark outside. I'm shaken again. I focus and recognise the nurse from Con's ward. I'm immediately wide awake.

"What's wrong with him?"

She answers in a whisper. "Nein Con ok but come quick Sister Von Agenhauser."

I'm confused. "Sister ill?"

She shakes her head and repeats "Come snell."

I slip on my coat, slide in to my shoes and rush after the nurse. I'm wondering what on earth it could be. This Sister I know doesn't like me. There's no pretence, she makes her hatred for the British well known and puts up with me only because I'm badly needed.

At the door of the ward the nurse turns and whispers. "Sister doing bad thing." The nurse points to a corner where a hurricane lamp is burning then hurries guiltily back to her desk. I see the back of a large dark figure bending over a patient and I run over unaware of what on earth I would find.

"Sister?"

She hasn't heard my approach and swings round to face me. She recognises me, glares and growls in German. "Das ist alles was du nur verdient hast." She holds a hypodermic needle and syringe in front of my face and goes to push past me. I stand in front to stop her but she's larger and her baulk sends me toppling over the adjacent empty bed. I feel a sharp jab in my side before she makes her escape. The rumpus stirs neighbouring patients and brings the nurse over. I feel my side and to my horror find the hypodermic caught up in my dressing gown. I sit on the bed and examine it It is nearly empty, whatever it was most of it has been injected. My instinct tells me it's a huge dose of morphene. I ask the nurse to wake Sister Schwimmer immediately and bring her over.

The patient unsurprisingly is stirring and I wonder why him? Perhaps his bed in the corner allowed an undisturbed attack. Either way such a dose will over-sedate a patient. In the worse case his lungs won't function and he'll die. I've heard of new drugs that can neutralise the effect but have never needed to use them. Despite the excellent conditions and drug supply in the hospital, I doubt if we have any here.

Within 5 minutes Sister Schwimmer bustles in. My story horrifies her. She examines the syringe and shakes her head grim faced. "If all this has been injected this man is in big trouble. I must call the doctor. You stay here and monitor breathing and heart rate." She repeats the instruction in German before retracing her steps out of the ward.

We start to check the patient but quite suddenly I feel tired. I think it must be the lack of sleep and sit down on the empty bed, my head droops. All I want to do is to collapse down and lie full length. I'm confused this is not just tiredness, it's more than that. I feel my side and remember the pinprick. The penny drops, of course she must have injected me with the same drug. I tell the nurse but I'm losing consciousness. I fight to keep my eyes open but my head swims and I drift away into a deep sleep.

"Good she's coming round."

I can hear a woman's voice in the distance. She's speaking in German. My eyes open and try to focus the blur. No luck I give up, give in to exhaustion and drift back to my floating, sleeping world only to hear more German spoken and feel hands on my shoulders. I reopen my eyes and jump when I see a large face filling my vision, Sister Schwimmer.

"Sister, what's happening?" I look around and recognise where I am. "Why am ah in you're room?"

She smiles broadly and lays a hand on my arm. "You got a jab of morphene from Sister Agenhauser. You been out for a few hours, you will be back to normal soon."

The mention of Agenhauser immediately brings me back to reality and the attempted murder of the soldier. "How's the Tommy?"

"He got a very large dose. His breathing stopped almost but he gets better." She shrugs her shoulders. "Tough soldier."

I smile. "He's a Geordie like me. Ahm pleased he's better." My smile disappears. "But what about Sister Agenhauser?"

Her own smile fades and she turns and stares out of her window "I've sent her home. She works non stop for nearly year then her brother killed. I should have realised. It was too much, it is my fault."

I look at Sister's back. She is a wonderful, compassionate woman. I know by taking me in she saved my life, apart from the countless soldiers benefiting from the treatment from her team of nurses. She cannot blame herself. She cannot be everything to everyone. Each member of her team has to take their own personal responsibility for themselves. I sit up and take hold of her arm. "Brunhilda, ye do a wonderful job here, ye bring order to the confusion an' hope to the dispirited. Ye are a hero an' ah won't take any more of that talk."

"Thank you Emily, you very kind." She turns and stares at me. There is something else I can tell. "Emily, I'm afraid your own brother is very poor."

I tense every muscle, with all that's happened I've completely forgotten about my own kid brother Con. "Ah must see him."

"Come I will help you."

Sister helps me out of her bed and in to my uniform and arm in arm she guides me to the ward. At first my legs are shaking and my brain is still disorientated but by the time I reach his bed I'm walking unassisted and my head has cleared. I have to be prepared and ready to give my brother anything he needs.

I find him sitting up but slumped back on to the pillow. His eyes are closed but he convulses with every rattling breath. As I approach a coughing fit takes hold. I quickly slid my hand around his back and rub his chest with the other. His eyes open and stare into mine.

"Ma?"

My heart jumps, my eyes moisten. "Aye ahm your Ma."

He relaxes in my grip and manages a small smile. "Thanks for comin'. A've missed ye."

I'm not going to cry, no I'm not. It takes me a while. "A've missed ye too, me brave laddie."

Another convulsion shakes his weakened body. I hold him tight waiting for his body to relax. "Ah want to gan hame."

"That's why ahm here pet. Ahm takin' ye back with me."

His face relaxes, his body sinks in to the bed. He says nothing more. I pull my hand out from behind his back and hold both of his with both of mine. I hold them tight, I can feel his grip loosen and I pray and I pray.

I feel a hand on my shoulder. "He has gone."

I know. I bend over and gently kiss his cheek, release his hands and leave the ward. I feel so very sad and so helpless.

Oh God, why do you let this happen?

****

Con is buried in a Flanders field with hundreds of others but he is not an unknown soldier. He has a proper wooden cross scripted with his name, date and regiment. The off duty nurses and some of those on duty, some of his comrades and of course Sister Schwimmer support me at his burial. I so appreciate this show of kindness, it proves what I already know: no matter our nationality we're all just the same under our uniform.

****

In the last few months I've heard very little from Gunty. In particular in the last month I've not heard from or seen him at all. Initially I fear the worst but as always I reject such negative thoughts. It's the only way I can get through the days. On the few occasions we've seen each other I could see and feel his complete exhaustion. We would cuddle and lie in each other's arms and unrealistically plan for our future. Like everyone else he knows the war is lost and his main strategy is now to save as many lives as possible - on both sides. Strategic withdrawals, no 'courageous' last stands or pointless counter attacks. His desire was to get as many men safely back to their families as possible. I am lost in admiration.

News of the surrender came today. I should be joyful but I just feel numb. There are no more long casualty convoys, thank goodness, we're just left with the last of the war injuries. We can concentrate all our efforts in trying to ensure no-one dies after the armistice but of course it doesn't work like that.

The end was expected but my thoughts and feelings are unexpected. Not just mine but talking to others I realise it's not just me. For the last two years in Flanders I have cried, begged for it to end but now it has I still cry, but quietly. I sit with Sister Schwimmer and we recall the horrors, the tragedies to our young men. Now it's over the world can't just forget, we have to learn. The British have named this war as the 'War to end all Wars.' We both fervently hope so, but we both have our doubts.

I woke early this morning, my last day. I'm being picked up by a British officer in his car to be transported to Dunkirk. Of course I'm pleased, I'm going home but I've heard nothing from or about Gunty, good or bad. The rest of the staff have to wait. Repatriation arrangements are apparently complicated! With everything packed I

283

visit Sister in her room. I go to knock when the door opens before I get the chance. A German officer stands there with his back to me still talking to Brunhilda. She sees me, her face immediately brightens with a beaming smile. The German officer turns in unison, sees me, grins and opens his arms wide. I fall in to them shrieking, laughing, completely lost for coherent words.